D0983494

Advertise for Treasure

DAVID WILLIAMS

Advertise for Treasure

A Mark Treasure novel

St. Martin's Press
New York

This one for
John and Jean Wilson

ADVERTISE FOR TREASURE. Copyright © 1984 by David Williams. All
rights reserved. Printed in the United States of America. No part of
this book may be used or reproduced in any manner whatsoever without written permission except in the case of brief quotations embodied
in critical articles or reviews. For information, address St. Martin's
Press, 175 Fifth Avenue, New York, N.Y. 10010.

Library of Congress Cataloging in Publication Data

Williams, David, 1926-
    Advertise for Treasure.

    I. Title.
PR6073.I42583A66   1984   823'.914   84-2078
ISBN 0-312-00724-8

First Published in Great Britain by William Collins Sons & Co. Ltd.

First U.S. Edition

10 9 8 7 6 5 4 3 2 1

CHAPTER 1

Helen Wintly wore her long black hair swept back in a loose bun. Few men who met her could avoid speculating how it looked when she shook it free: fewer still had ever found out.

She was tall, sharply beautiful and elegant — dressed entirely in white. The collar of the crisp blouse was ruffed, like the cuffs. It accentuated the long, slender neck. The pleated skirt swung with a sensuous rhythm as she stepped across the pavement in the sunlight. The cashmere cardigan was draped around her shoulders. Casually she rearranged it while pausing to let Henry Pink, the chauffeur, open the door of the Rolls-Royce.

'Good morning, miss.' He saluted smartly, Navy style.

She nodded back. The smile was more gracious than familiar. Not so many years before she would have returned that greeting with a self-conscious smirk and the comment, 'Look at me going to the office in a Rolls. They'll never believe it back home' — or something like that.

At 27 Helen Wintly had learned a good deal — only some of it from McGill and Columbia Universities and the Harvard Business School. The white leather document case by Gucci nicely reflected the owner's personality richly feminine but uncompromisingly businesslike.

'Good morning.' Now it was Mark Treasure who greeted her as she settled into the seat beside him. The Chief Executive of Grenwood, Phipps, the London merchant bankers — and Miss Wintly's employers — added an approving nod. 'Mmm. Charming. We should do this more often.'

The compliment about her appearance had been especially welcome. Despite her assured demeanour, her ego had taken a knock the night before from which it was unlikely ever to recover. Treasure's second comment registered only as a pleasantry. She was certain *The Times* he had just set aside commended itself to him at this hour more than she did.

As it happened the last speculation was far from accurate. Perhaps Miss Wintly's judgement had been too recently upset to be wholly reliable. In the six months she had been employed at the bank, she and Treasure had seldom been thrown together. This was the first time he had been given the chance for close inspection.

She was certainly very striking — the face, figure and deportment of an up-market model girl. She was highly intelligent, too, by all accounts. He knew her age. There was great solace in the fact. He was not old enough to be her father — by conventional standards: he would need to have been an irresponsible fifteen year-old. Yet these days most of the bank's female employees . . .

'You didn't mind my phoning?' She broke in on the rumination.

'Of course not. Very sensible.'

'It was late.'

He looked at the time. 'And this is very early. I don't imagine you normally leave home at seven-forty-five.'

'Not without this kind of incentive.' She could have meant the handsome car or its equally distinguished-looking owner. In truth she often left earlier than this, but to say so would have sounded like crawling for good-conduct marks. 'It's kind of you to call for me.'

He shrugged 'Dolphin Square from Cheyne Walk isn't a detour.' Nor was it. Both places are on the Thames Embankment, a mile apart with Chelsea Bridge in the middle. 'I'm breakfasting with an Arab at nine. Could hardly put him off. But with Harry Karilian available for eight . . .'

'Lucky to get anyone in August.'

He wrinkled his forehead, glancing up Vauxhall Bridge Road as Pink hurried the car across into Millbank. 'Suppose you're right. We haven't gone the way of all Frogs, of course, putting up the shutters on Bastille Day.

Sorry, I believe you're a strong Francophile. You don't sound French Canadian.'

'I'm not. Well, a quarter maybe. My maternal grandmother. No, I'm just a late, ordinary Canadian convert to the Common Market. Euromarket. Better for everyone that Britain's in, not out.' The 'out' came distinctly from north of the 49th Parallel.

'Very commendable. D'you want to start telling me about Rorch, Timms and Bander?'

'Yes, sir.' She uncrossed her extremely attractive legs, obliterating his view of them with the document case which she pulled on to her lap and snapped open. A new pair of tights in their transparent wrapper fell out from the pocket in the top, slid over her copy of the *Financial Times* and on to the floor. Treasure picked them up with affected diffidence.

'Thanks.'

'Bet none of our male executives carry spare socks,' remarked the banker amiably.

'No,' she answered with just a touch of irritation. 'The company's usually known as RTB. It was founded five years ago. You know that, of course. You kind of did the founding. Right?'

He nodded. 'Advertising agencies were out of fashion, at least as prospects for ultimate public floatation. They've picked up since. This one looked promising, though, as a useful growth investment. I liked the three principals, especially Rorch.'

'Roger. Roger Rorch.'

'Yes. He approached the bank in the first place. For funding. Sorry, really, I lost touch with the thing. I got kicked upstairs into this job just after we got involved. As I remember, the company did well enough in the first two years, then fizzled a bit. Didn't we have to increase the loan capital?'

'That's right.'

After beating the traffic lights in Parliament Square, Pink had done the same in Bridge Street, turning left on to the Victoria Embankment at speed. The momentary and presumably involuntary shifting of Miss Wintly's left knee against Treasure's right the banker found entirely agreeable.

'Anyway, I shed Rorch, Timms and Bander—sorry, RTB—on to Cecil Oakley. Don't suppose it rates very high with him.' Oakley was one of the bank's three Joint Managing Directors.

'He keeps abreast of it.' The knee returned to its proper position.

'But it's your responsibility?'

'Since I joined Corporate Finance. Mr Oakley figured it fitted with my portfolio. I did a second degree in communications. Before my MBA.' No harm in keeping the front office reminded about meaningful inputs.

'So you understand advertising. What makes an agency tick.'

'A little of both. I worked in agencies for a while. In New York. I seem to have gotten along with the RTB management.'

'Do we have you on the board there?' Grenwood, Phipps held a quarter of the ordinary shares in the company and had funded the whole of a financially more significant medium-term loan.

The girl nodded. 'Three months ago. Actually it wasn't the bank's idea. It was the founding directors. I'd been in attendance at the monthly board meetings to represent the bank's interest. They asked if I'd like to join the board formally. Mr Oakley agreed.'

'Good for you. You'd been attending all the meetings?'

'Sure. My predecessor didn't. Figured the fellows in the agency didn't really want him around unless they asked him specially. That was Mr Morris.'

'Mmm. Now retired. Probably didn't fit the image.' It was hard to imagine poor old Morris in tights. 'Sound chap, though,' Treasure continued aloud. 'Perhaps they found him a restricting influence. Touch of the big brother. But when they realized you were . . .'

'You can say it. Something more than passably decorative, then I got pressed to pitch in. So I did.'

'But you didn't hear about this takeover offer from Crabtree at a board meeting?'

'No. Nobody did. The first the agency heard of it was in this hand-delivered letter yesterday afternoon.' She passed him a copy. 'Financial data on Crabtree came with it. I have copies of that too.'

'And Karilian has it all?'

'Plus RTB's current vital statistics. I left them on his desk at seven last night. I'd been in Birmingham. Got back to the office at five. Roger Rorch had been calling since mid-afternoon, on the half-hour. He came round. Later we had dinner. I rang you from the restaurant. The President of Crabtree and the Executive Vice-President should be checking into the Savoy this morning.' She paused. 'With Mr Oakley on vacation . . .'

'Another Euromarketeer. Spends every August in Port Grimaud. They've a house there, and a boat. A motor-boat.' Treasure made a painful grimace while studying the letter. 'Not everyone's idea of heaven. Suits the children, of course,' he added, a touch wistfully. 'Anyway, I'm delighted to stand in for Oakley.'

'Just so I can get your view, Mr Treasure. It looks like they're aiming to railroad the agency. With the bank so involved, I figured . . .'

'You did absolutely the right thing, Miss Wintly . . . er, Helen, isn't it?' Should he ask her to call him by his first name? It was the sort of thing that put other people's noses out of joint, of course. 'My name's Mark,' he compromised, satisfied it was as much a statement as an invitation.

The car swept past the Mansion House, entered Threadneedle Street, then went left into Old Broad Street. The traffic was still light.

It was five to eight when the better-acquainted Treasure and Miss Wintly stepped from the lift on the third floor of Grenwood House. Harry Karilian was waiting for them in Treasure's office.

At 8 o'clock precisely on that same Tuesday, August

11

23rd, Howard John Crabtree the Second, President of Howard J. Crabtree Incorporated of New York City, emerged from the 'Nothing to Declare' green exit of the Customs Hall at London's Heathrow Airport.

He was short, spare and tired. He was wearing a crumpled, three button suit and a furtive look.

Howie Crabtree had not knowingly broken a law since at the age of three he had screamed until his nurse had laced his hot milk with bootlegged gin. That had been fifty years ago, towards the end of Prohibition. The gin had made him sick and the nurse had been dismissed. The lesson had endured. Howie's penchant for law observance had become legend.

Now he could breathe freely again: almost. They could still stop you — even after you had left the airport: he knew that. He would gladly have gone through the Customs' red route, declaring everything in his possession on the chance something was chargeable. He had done as much at several airports. Nothing had ever been elected contraband. Once he had been admonished for wasting the time of officials. There was no pleasing bureaucrats. Still, the thought of being accosted with an overlooked dutiable item or because his tranquillizers had suddenly been exposed as dangerous drugs gave him stomach trembles.

He even carried a note from his doctor about the tranquillizers.

'They didn't arrest you yet, Howie?' called a familiar voice from some way behind.

That did it. Crabtree started nervously, glanced backwards, and overturned the baggage trolley with the faulty front wheel he had been carefully manipulating down the polished ramp.

Porters had been available: using one had seemed a needless expense — and a bad example to the others. So now he was floundering on a foreign slope with an upset trolley, and trying to regain control over his two large bags, a document case, a raincoat, umbrella and several diagnosed neuroses.

12

Hordes of fellow travellers surefootedly navigated around the disaster area. Nobody offered to help. Good Samaritans didn't come off seven-hour night flights. Several porters pushing big trolleys glared at him stonily. Did they spend their time between flights sabotaging little trolleys?

And none of this would have happened except Lee Jackson had this compulsion to utter imbecilities at super-sensitive times.

'Howie, I declare, if you don't have the *darnedest* luck. What-all happened with your little old pusher? Lee, come and help Howie.'

So now, at least, the Jacksons had caught up with him. Lee Jackson with that round, open face, that encouraging smile, that wiseacre mask generating permanent care and consideration for all other members of the human race. Here was 168 pounds, five feet ten inches of all-American dependability, responsibility and — in Howie's private view — over-promoted capacities, forty years maturing and encased in uncrushable seersucker. Joanne Rutledge Jackson, his thirty-five-year-old wife, was a blonde, athletic community and corporate asset with an IQ of 135, a golf handicap of 12, and a commanding, upper-crust Kentuckian accent that in some registers could be distinguished over six city blocks or three longish holes.

And here was Joanne, right in front of her mate — actually, as always metaphorically — ready to open the way for him onwards and upwards. Naturally she had been free to come to London at a day's notice. Two of the children were already at summer camp: the other had gone to doting grandparents.

'I wish you hadn't called like that, Lee.' Howie had meant to sound angry, not just hurt. 'I could have been stopped . . . or something.' He felt his left eye twitching.

'Sorry, Howie. Didn't know you'd turned over.'

'I hadn't till . . .'

'Got a bum steer here, old boy, old boy.' Jackson wasn't listening. He pushed the broken trolley to the side and grasped one of the cases.

Howie fumed inwardly: that's how it always went. So why hadn't Lee got the broken trolley? Why hadn't Howie's wife Rosalind been able to make the trip at no notice? Because she was half way through a summer school in New Haven devoted to 19th-century English poets, and couldn't get away. The time his first wife couldn't get away she wasn't there when he'd got back—left him for a tennis coach. Rosalind didn't play tennis.

'Our chauffeur should be in that group.' The Executive Vice-President of Howard J. Crabtree Inc. had somehow got all Howie's impedimenta on to his own trolley. Effortlessly he guided the thing along, allowing it to propel itself towards the people standing on the concourse at the end of the railed-off enclosure.

'There he is, Lee.' Joanne was stepping out ahead of the others. She was not a pretty woman: taut and lithe though, she looked her best in leotards conducting her neighbourhood aerobics class. 'He's holding a board with Crabtree chalked on it, and he's just too British for words.'

What did she expect? A Hottentot in a grass skirt, Howie mused.

The chauffeur responded to Joanne's wave. He touched his cap with a servile grace, first to her, then to her husband. He had heard her comment. He was a resting actor, used to playing to small audiences.

'Mr Crabtree, sir?'

'No, I'm Mr Crabtree,' Howie uttered from behind. His new analyst had told him to assert himself on every available occasion. 'This is Mr Jackson, my associate.' His eye was twitching again. He pulled at his jacket. The creases were beginning to look permanent.

'And I'm Mrs Rutledge Jackson.'

'That's right,' said Howie confused by the oversight, then feeling foolish since the woman's identity hardly needed confirming when she had established it herself. He had been thrown by the appearance of the chauffeur. It was Jackson who had ordered a big car to stay with

14

them through the visit. Howie would not have authorized the expense. But he had delegated all the arrangements to Jackson. He had to delegate more. His new analyst had said that too: except he had so little to do already, if he off-loaded any more he'd be practically unemployed. He'd spoken to his father about it.

Howard J. Crabtree Senior—known to everyone as HJ—was still Chairman of the advertising agency, still came into the office daily, still effectively controlled the business. He'd been threatening to retire every year for the past decade. This year he'd be seventy-five, and at last he was committed—to retire next year. But it was in writing. This time Howie had it in black and white. On April 1st he became Chairman.

After April 1st Lee Jackson would *have* to report to Howie—not by-pass him by getting Joanne to nobble HJ over every important issue. HJ thought a lot more of Joanne than he did of her husband.

In future, too, there would be no overriding Howie's known intentions on lesser domestic items through the 'democratic' decisions of carefully packed corporate committees.

Take this London business. Howie had not been present when they briefed the hot-shot company broker. It had been the same when they had bought the other foreign agencies. And Howie had yet to agree they were buying the right outfit in Britain. It was too big and too expensive. The other one on the short list—the fallback company—looked a better proposition to Howie. They didn't need a whizz kid like this Roger Rorch. Whizz kids could be difficult to control, and it was Howie who would have to do the controlling in future.

'If you'll follow me, Mr and Mrs Jackson. Mr Crabtree.' The chauffeur took charge of the overloaded trolley— still getting the precedence wrong.

'It was mighty kind of you to ask me along, Howie.' Joanne Jackson had fallen in beside him, taking his arm. 'Smart, too,' she added.

'It was?' Howie looked perplexed. 'I mean . . .'

15

'Two of the agency principals are married. Maybe I can do a job on the wives. I'm sure you figured that, Howie.' She squeezed his arm. 'Shame Rosalind couldn't make it.'

And the other principal—the one that counts—was divorced. So what kind of job did she expect to do on him? It hadn't been Howie's idea to bring Joanne. He had agreed with Jackson the wives should come before he got a turndown from his own wife. So now the party was lopsided: much better if they had brought the company treasurer instead of relying on people from the London branch of their New York accountants. HJ had decreed the opposite. Smarter to leave the financial wrangling to outsiders, HJ had said: made for easier relations in the future. 'And most anybody can do arithmetic,' HJ had repeated. It was something he repeated all the time.

Arithmetic was the only thing Howie was good at.

'Don't know about you folks, but after a shave and shower, guess I'll be ready for the takeover trail.' This was Jackson at his heartiest. Howie felt he could do with a morning in bed.

Joanne smiled approvingly at her husband. 'I'll settle for the little old shower, then you two hunters can drop me at Harrods on your way to the jungle.' She twined her other arm around his. Howie wished Rosalind was as demonstrative.

They had followed the chauffeur into the car park lift. Now they followed him out again on the fourth floor of the multistorey.

'I'll call Mr Z when we get to the hotel. Then the lawyer,' Jackson volunteered.

'HJ said we needn't take the lawyer to all the meetings,' Howie interjected firmly. 'Those fellows charge by the quarter-hour. He's not going to do much. Ziebal is paid for.'

'But Mr Z stays behind the scenes. We don't acknowledge we're using him. Better we don't mention his name, Howie,' Jackson added pointedly, lowering his voice. The chauffeur was scarcely out of hearing. 'The

16

lawyer is fronting for him when we need someone along. Right now, all we need's an update. What reaction there's been from the RTB people.'

'Got to keep things moving, of course,' Howie offered sagely.

'You've said it, Howie.' Jackson shook his head, winking surreptitiously at his wife. 'Nashville moving up the British launch by a whole year.' Now his voice was even lower. 'Could have thrown a whole lot of agencies. Not us, though.'

'You think we'll be ready with a bottler's presentation six weeks from now, honey?'

'Darned right we'll be,' Jackson answered his wife.

'But what if RTB aren't selling, Lee?' asked Howie.

Jackson stopped, so Howie had to do the same. 'At two million pounds, they'll be selling,' he almost whispered.

'But what if they're not?' Howie whispered back.

'Then we keep upping the ante till they are. At three million we're irresistible. But if Mr Z is right, at three million pounds it's still a steal.'

The chauffeur had opened the rear door of the big Jaguar. An expensive smell of leather wafted from the interior. Howie would have settled for something less opulent. He had just converted three million pounds into real money.

CHAPTER 2

'The timing's so fast, it's fishy,' pronounced Grenwood, Phipps's sixty-year-old head of New Issues.

Harry Karilian was a very big man. Only the dark eyes were small, and given to darting decisively under the thick bushy eyebrows. His deep upper lip was hardly adorned by the short thick hairs. They might have been overlooked during shaving, and passed for a moustache only when matched with the grey, close-cropped stubble that covered the immense cranium — and to contrast with the flourishing growth of soft long hairs that sprouted, untended, from each aural orifice.

His voice was deep, resonant and capable of astonishing tonal contrast. He was sometimes given to slow, expansive gesticulation as he spoke, the histrionics aided by the cloak-like, long cut and double-breasted jackets which were his habit—invariably worn un-buttoned.

Standing, Harry Karilian was a formidable figure: seated, as now, he was yet a commanding presence—in a way fearsome even, unless you knew he had begun his career in grand opera, and at least until you experienced the smile.

The smile came after every completed statement. It was a form of punctuation—an effulgence that engaged every fold and crevice of the fleshy countenance, as well as most beholders of it. The smile would have followed even if its owner's solemn duty had been to announce the collapse of the Bank of England—or the disbandment of Tottenham Hotspur Football Club, an institution which Harry held in as much respect, and far greater affection.

'There appears to be a reason,' Treasure offered. He was seated alone on a buttoned leather sofa. Opposite, across a low mahogany table, Helen Wintly and Harry Karilian occupied a similar sofa, in very unequal proportion.

'The reason's the buyer's problem, of course,' Harry observed blankly. He did not smile, so he was not finished. 'Accept his reason and we just make money. We're in business for more than that.' Now he was smiling.

Treasure's forehead wrinkled. 'You mean it behoves us to act as advisers as well as lenders? That's a very commendable attitude, Harry.'

'So characteristically Armenian, wouldn't you say?' The smile had broadened: its owner's family had been naturalized British for three generations. 'I really meant, it could just be we're not making enough money.'

'Technically, we don't control the business.' This was

18

Helen: very down to earth.

The big man turned to her slowly. 'We own 2,500 of the 10,000 issued ordinary one pound shares. That doesn't give us control.' He let a finger drop heavily on to the pile of papers resting on his knee. 'We also provided a five year floating rate loan of £120,000 on the foundation of the company, and another of £60,000 three years later. Both loans to be repaid in stages, together. The interest rates have done us credit—without earning us any.' There was no smile. 'I see the company's in default on the first payment . . .'

'By informal agreement, Mr Karilian.'

Harry didn't seem to hear. 'So, practically, if not technically, we control the company, and we can do so formally at any time by invoking the penalties which informal agreements with loan defaulters do nothing to enfeeble.' A wagging of the head accompanied the smile in Helen's direction.

'But, as you know, Howard J. Crabtree Incorporated, this New York agency, has offered two million pounds for the whole business if the deal can be completed in two weeks.'

This time Harry heard. 'A fancy price for a business with nominal fixed assets, a very short lease, and a five year return on capital which hardly covers the negligible cost of borrowing that capital. Do you suppose Howard J. Crabtree knows something we don't know? You're on the board of the company, Miss Wintly?' The smile was accompanied by an interrogative lift of the Machiavellian eyebrows.'

'RTB has prospects, Mr Karilian. There was a setback in the third year. A bad debt. Existing clients are sound. Mostly blue-chip companies. You can see from the list. The agency's now on target for sound growth.'

'Or else the bank wouldn't have extended the term of the loan,' Harry observed in a tone implying no other explanation was possible. 'In these latest filed accounts, the company had sales of ten million pounds, and a gross income from that of just over a million. About ten per cent.' He glanced up. 'Don't advertising agencies work on fifteen per cent commission?'

'That's the usual commission for space or time bought on behalf of clients from newspapers, TV and radio stations, and the other media. In the case of some big-spending clients, agencies often hand on quite a bit of that to the advertiser. They don't like doing it, or even admitting it,' Helen explained. 'The income they need to keep to be profitable depends on the work load on any account.'

'Account?'

'Means client in advertising parlance, Harry,' Treasure chipped in.

'That's right. Sorry,' Helen went on. 'So, where the agency produces one or two commercials for, say, a chocolate bar account, and they run for ages on TV, over a certain spend the agency will probably agree to keep, say, only ten per cent of the commission. Or even less.'

'Because the agency hasn't done any more work than it would have done for a client spending less,' Harry offered.

'That's the theory, yes.'

'And there's nothing to stop an agency passing on commission to smaller clients too, if it's hard up for business?'

'In theory, no, there isn't, Mr Karilian. But an agency that got careless that way probably wouldn't stay in business for too long. Some accounts are very labour-intensive. Even some big ones. Big retail store accounts, for instance, where the advertising is mostly in the press, and changes every week. With that kind of business probably an agency can't afford to pass up commission. Also there are accounts where even the full commission income is too small for the agency to show a profit. That's when it tries to get the advertiser to pay a fee to supplement commission.'

'That's more common than you'd expect, apparently,' Treasure put in.

Helen nodded. 'On technical accounts, and often on

new consumer products still in their development stage. Good agencies get a lot of fee income.'

Harry Karilian had gone back to studying his papers. 'Profits after tax were £26,000. Around one quarter of one per cent of sales. If that's usual for the industry, perhaps the company chose the wrong industry.' The smile was intended only to greet the appearance of Treasure's secretary, Miss Gaunt, who had entered with a tray containing a white bone china coffee service with gold edging.

'That report runs to last December. You also have figures for the half year.' Helen shuffled the papers in her hand.

'Unaudited.'

'Yes. The projection for the rest of the year is there too. The figures are pretty accurate. Billings, which are what you call sales, they're estimated for the year at fourteen and a half million. Gross income will be just over two million. Profits, after tax, £152,000. That's better than average for the industry,' she ended pointedly.

'And suggests we've been backing a winner, Harry.' As he spoke, Treasure nodded his thanks to Miss Gaunt who with customary efficiency had included some of Harry's favourite chocolate digestive biscuits on the tray. Treasure didn't take biscuits, chocolate or otherwise. Helen Wintly didn't look as though she did. Miss Gaunt left the room as unobtrusively as she had entered it.

'There's better news, yet.' Helen spoke up confidently. 'RTB is making a presentation —' she caught the start of a quizzical look from Harry —'that means producing an advertising campaign, for an important prospective account. It involves a new product range from Carter Cousins Ltd, the toiletry and cosmetic people. It's a very confidential project. The products are still classified. If the client likes the RTB approach, they get the business. Initially the agency will work for a fee. A big one. Later, if the product range is a success and it's marketed nationally, the billing will be around one and a half million pounds a year. There's also a strong chance

Carter's will transfer other existing accounts—other products—to the agency.'

'How confidential is the confidential project?' Harry bit into his second biscuit.

'It's common knowledge in the industry RTB has been briefed. Carter Cousins looked at a number of agencies before inviting us to pitch. Otherwise security is very tight. Even I don't know yet what the product range is. And I wouldn't tell if I did.' She stared disarmingly at the two men.

Harry responded with a frightening convulsion which turned out to be a chuckle rising from the region of his lower stomach. 'When you find out, don't tell me. I have enough responsibilities.'

'We don't believe Crabtree is offering for RTB over anything so speculative,' Treasure interjected.

Harry shrugged. 'I wouldn't think so. It's just I wonder how advertising agencies keep secrets. They make pictures, still pictures, moving pictures. They write scripts. The words for the advertisements. Secretaries have to type things.'

'It's not too difficult when the product range is so new it doesn't even have a name,' said Helen. 'Roger Rorch was briefed by the client and he's working on the project by himself for the time being. It's a basic creative problem—naming the products, packaging them, devising the selling concept. When Rorch believes he has a viable concept he'll bring in an agency team and they'll work very fast.' She paused. 'I've told Mr Treasure, it isn't Carter's that have provoked the takeover bid. It's Dandy.'

'The American soft drink, Harry,' Treasure put in quickly.

'Oh, *that* Dandy. You can buy it here?'

'Not yet, Mr Karilian. In the States it's Crabtree's biggest account. They even have an office in Nashville, Tennessee, that's the Dandy Corporation's home town. That's mostly for show, of course. The important advertising work is handled in New York.'

'And Crabtree is coming to London because of Dandy?'

'That's what Helen thinks.'

'I'm sure of it. In the US, Dandy is a licensee operation. Different bottlers in different parts of the country. Dandy Inc. produce the syrup, the concentrate the drink is made from. They ship that to the bottlers, who do the rest. Dandy pay for and control the advertising and merchandising. Also the pricing, quality, and, of course, the consistency.'

'It's a fairly successful operation, Harry. I gather Dandy isn't up to the volume of Coca-Cola, or Pepsi-Cola. In fact it's not in the first five most popular soft drinks in the USA . . .'

'But getting there,' Helen interrupted. 'Same thing in Canada and Brazil. The product's less than twenty years old. The international operation is still pretty new. Hasn't crossed the Atlantic yet.'

'But it's about to?' Karilian poured himself more coffee.

'They've been talking about it for some time. There's been no public announcement. When they opened the other non-US markets, Crabtree bought good, youngish local advertising agencies in the territories. That was ahead of Dandy appointing licensees to bottle and distribute the product . . .'

'They bought the advertising agencies outright?' This was Treasure.

The girl nodded. 'And there's a reason why Crabtree have to be ahead of the game. The licensees, who are usually brewers, have to be kind of sold on the privilege. That's where the agency first comes in.'

'To recruit licensees?'

'Yes, Mr Karilian. To help, anyway—with presentations on how the licensee agreement works. There's a lot of money to be made by the licensees eventually, but they have to go along with the Dandy Corporation on a three-year investment programme at the start. Dandy claim to make the biggest contribution with the advertising and promotion.'

'And after three years?' Harry bit on his third biscuit.

'Dandy allocate a fixed percentage of the previous year's gross for publicity. That figure doesn't plateau if sales rise. There's also a minimum spend if sales fall.'

'But the licensees have to make a commitment too, presumably, in plant and a distribution set-up. How many licensees will there be?'

'I'd guess only one in a market as compact as Britain. But you never know with Dandy. They don't always do things by the book.' The girl paused. 'Relatively, I'd say the biggest commitment is actually the one made by the advertising agency. But Crabtree's have got rich on it. I guess they're willing to give it a whirl in another market.'

'And their commitment is so big because they have to buy new offices wherever Dandy go?' asked Harry.

'That's become part of it. But that bit's self-protection. They wouldn't want any other agency picking up Dandy business anywhere in the world. Especially an office of one of the big international agencies. That's why Crabtree buy foreign offices.'

'Why they don't open their own?' Treasure interjected.

'They need on-going businesses for a lot of reasons. The obvious one is it saves trouble. The big reason isn't so obvious. They have to operate without commission or fees for the first year. They get to keep five per cent of the commission in the second year, another five per cent in the third. They're on a full fifteen per cent in the fourth year, and ever after.'

'You mean they have to work at cost for twelve months?'

Helen nodded in answer to Treasure. Both men looked surprised. 'It's kind of the opposite to the usual arrangement on a growth account.'

'But a great incentive. It'd concentrate the mind to do well.' Karilian evidently approved.

'It's the way Crabtree started with the Dandy Corporation twenty years ago. Now the account is worth eighty million dollars in the States alone. Produces an income there for Crabtree of twelve million, not counting what they make on residuals like producing TV

24

commercials, merchandising material, that kind of thing. Oh, they also handle public relations for Dandy.' She leant back on the sofa, clasping her hands in front of her knees. 'But in that first year everything was charged net to the client. Then there was a three-year build to full agency remuneration. It's a pretty well-known case history. Used in most of the business schools.'

'But the system hasn't caught on. Hasn't become general practice.' Karilian beamed knowingly, although he was guessing.

'That's right. Very few agencies could afford the risk, or even the basic cost of running a major account with no income for a year, and not much in the second.'

'For instance, RTB wouldn't try it on their own?' asked Treasure.

'Unlikely, but if Crabtree took them over they'd have their existing income . . .'

'And enough profit to cover the loss on Dandy?'

'I guess not. The Dandy spend in the first year would probably be around three million. The agency commission on that . . .'

'Which they'd pass back to Dandy?' This was Karilian.

'Mmm, and it would be more than RTB's projected pre-tax profit for this year — and next, even if they get the Carter business.'

'But in three or four years . . .'

'The Dandy account could be billing six or seven million, with agency commission income running at fifteen per cent of that.'

Harry was shuffling his papers again. 'There's no doubt in your mind, Miss Wintly, why Crabtree want to buy RTB?'

'None.'

'And the very first interest Crabtree ever disclosed is this solicitor's letter with the offer to buy?'

'Right. I believe Crabtree have used a company broker who sorted through the possible available agencies,' said the girl. 'Roger Rorch agrees RTB would look like the best candidate at this time.'

'And you learned about the Dandy operating method at business school?'

'How they started in the States, yes. Actually, the product was quite an old one. Used to be called dandelion soda. It was part of a range of soft drinks made by what's now the Dandy Corporation.'

'Is it really made of dandelions?' This was Treasure.

'I don't believe so. It's a secret formula, or so they say. Apparently the company suddenly woke up to the realization it was outselling most everything else in Tennessee without promotion. So they gave it a brand name. Got a special bottle made. Ran some advertising. The rest's history. The story's in a lot of the communications industry textbooks.'

'Mark, you have a pressing date.' Harry regarded the remaining chocolate biscuit, decided to resist it, and turned his whole attention to Helen. 'Two more questions. What happens if Dandy is a failure, in a new market, inside the first three years?'

'It's never happened. If it did, if a distributor's sales fell dismally below budgeted volumes, consistently . . .' She hesitated. 'I guess Dandy would have the option to pull out. Yes, I think they'd cut their losses. It's a risk for the agency, especially since Dandy don't hold with test marketing. That is, they won't try out the product on a small section of a new market before going national. They can't, or won't, change their product to suit a market, so they figure it's all or nothing.'

'Hmm. Second question. Rorch, Timms and Bander own three-quarters of the company's ordinary shares, in equal proportions. How do you rate them?'

'Rorch is brilliant at his job. Innovative. Outstanding. George Timms is a slogger. Runs the engine-room. He'd never have made it on his own, but he's indispensable. Peter Bander is very close to the agency's biggest client, the OPD Company . . .'

'Which used to stand for the Orthodox Pharmaceutical & Drug Company before they diversified or went ecumenical,' joked Treasure. 'You know they're old customers of the bank, Helen?'

She nodded. 'Peter Bander's brother-in-law is Marketing Director of the Food Division.'

'Is reliance on nepotism his only commendation?' This was Treasure again.

'He's nowhere near the calibre of the others. Not any more, anyway. I think he's developing an alcohol problem,' she finished quietly.

'Thank you, Miss Wintly. So, you both want my opinion on the offer, even though at this stage it's probably worthless, even dangerous.'

'We'll risk that.' Treasure volunteered.

There were perhaps three others in the City of London whose special capacities compared to Harry Karilian's: none could better them. You could call it a knack, a sixth sense, or astonishing good luck over a long period. It was probably all those things combined with an outstanding intellect and a massive experience. The fact remained when it came to company floatations, fixing the size of rights issues, going in with a takeover bid, or other situations involving the absolute necessity of accurately deciding what price a market would bear, Harry was next to infallible: close to God, and a long way above Mammon.

'Just your gut feeling, Harry,' Treasure pressed. 'We can confuse ourselves with the facts later. It's small beer, of course, but since we're being rushed . . .'

'Small beer? No.' Karilian paused, frowning. 'We backed these three men five years ago. With employed capital of £190,000 they're projecting taxed profits this year of £154,000. The further expectations are good. After five years the managers should know their strengths and weaknesses. So one of them has a problem? He should take the cure. Two of the three are good. Nowadays that's above average for managers. One, Miss Wintly says, is outstanding. He has flair.'

'Creative flair. Produces very accountable advertising,' Helen interjected.

'Not sure I know what that means, but I expect the

customers appreciate it. Advertising's a flashy business . . .'

The girl made as if to protest, caught a sign from Treasure, and remained silent.

'And these three men will favour selling out, at the right price?'

'Rorch is uncertain, Harry. I gather the other two would sell.'

'Thank you, Mark. So these Crabtree people, or their scouts, they know a good thing when they see it. How they know enough to make a firm offer we can only guess at. Also it's only an opening shot. The two weeks they're giving us can obviously be stretched to four. If they can't, that's a Crabtree problem. They'll have to pay us to go their pace. And they'll have to pay a little more for an agency that suits them for Dandy, and makes an attractive buy in its own right. Perhaps they have other clients in America who'd use their London office if they had one.'

'They have. One in particular . . .' Helen let her comment tail away. Karilian was happy with the approbation but his expression indicated he could do without the details.

'So, since these people like round numbers, I think three million is better than two, plus the discharge of the Grenwood, Phipps loans. The three principals should have a good lawyer to protect their future interests. There'll be three lean years to come.' He shrugged. 'For the bank, we're passing up a possible public floatation in letting this fledgling creation quit the nest so early. In another five years who knows what our quarter interest might fetch?' There followed a slow, considered shaking of the head. 'Then again, it's a volatile industry. Let's take a premium now, and believe it discounts the future.'

Then came the uncertain silence. 'Ten times post-tax profits plus assets. That's been the child's guide to valuing an average agency of this age and size. You're proposing about double that,' said Helen bravely.

Karilian nodded sagely. 'But who cares for the average?

Grenwood, Phipps doesn't back average enterprises. Go for three million, Miss Wintly. Don't settle for a penny less.' The big man paused. 'Not a penny less than two and three-quarter million.'

The girl grinned. 'That's the figure Mr Treasure suggested on the way over.'

'So who needs Karilian?' came before the expansive, punctuating beam, and as Harry leant forward to reach for the last biscuit.

CHAPTER 3

'Crabtree is just an extension of Dandy. Not much better than a house agency. Bottle-washers, that's what they are, and that's what we'd be. Once removed.'

Roger Rorch moved across his office, and stood for a moment looking down at the garden in the centre of Red Lion Square, Bloomsbury.

The RTB offices were in two adjoining, late Georgian terrace houses. The four-storey units had been fashioned into one behind the preserved stark but dignified façade on the south side of the square.

Rorch watched a black Labrador liberally anoint the base of the 'Dogs Must Be Leashed' notice before it entered the gardens unaccompanied. Then he turned about, impelling reaction from his two partners seated in the high-ceilinged, first-floor room. The impatient eyes were, as always, the key to the thrusting character and the stress that lay within. The speech was sharp but not clipped, the phrasing usually pedantic, the body movements suggested boundless energy expended with diffidence.

He was tall, with the concave stoop common in lean men of six foot three or so. At thirty-five there was no thickening. The strong bone structure of the face was accentuated by the unfleshy hollowness. The forehead was high, the nose well chiselled, the chin obtrusively square. Only the wide, sensitive, thin-lipped mouth diminished the boldness in the handsome visage: it evidenced more of faded aristocracy.

He pushed back the regularly errant strand of lank blond hair before returning both hands to their characteristic delve in the side pockets of the long grey jacket. Silhouetted now against the full-length sash window, he was the re-embodiment of a lanky Spy caricature.

'Crabtree bill two hundred and fifty million dollars, Roger. May not be American top twenty, but they're a hell of a lot better than a house agency. They're Jebbit, Fowler's major agency for a start.'

George Timms, who had spoken, was two years older than Rorch. Short, earnest, bespectacled and balding prematurely, he was seated on the least comfortable chair in the room — the one he always chose. He had left his jacket in his own office. His sleeves were rolled back, and although it was only 8.45, and still cool in the north-facing room, he was sweating at the temples.

Timms, the Joint Managing Director, never cared to oppose Rorch, the Chairman of RTB. This had nothing to do with their allotted ranks. Financially they were equal partners, along with Peter Bander, the other Managing Director. Simply, Timms deferred to Rorch because he respected the other's judgement more than he did his own — while despising himself for the fact. Bander had no compunction in deferring to both of them — for the unconsidered reason he enjoyed the quiet life.

'In America they say if Jebbit, Fowler weren't so big they'd be bankrupt,' commented Rorch.

'I don't think that's quite true,' answered Timms. 'They've diversified a lot there in the last few years. And everything's gone right for them. Well, mostly.'

'Wouldn't be seen dead in their green lipsticks. Nor would the rest of our rugger team,' Peter Bander joked from the depths of a swivel armchair — one of four at a round table set at the other end of the three-windowed office from Rorch's desk.

30

Bander talked fast and breathily, with marked pauses between sentences. At forty-one, he was the oldest of the three, although he looked younger than Timms. An agreeable light-weight — mentally and physically — he had drifted into advertising after a short and unpromising attempt at a stage career. He was tallish, good-looking in an undynamic sort of way, with brown wavy hair worn over an almost permanent, eager grin. Popular with staff and clients, he was enjoyed for his humour and optimism by everyone save his wife — who didn't understand the first and could never credit the second.

'It's quite true JF have lost market share here in cosmetics, and that's still the backbone of the business outside the States.' Rorch was agreeing with the point underlying Bander's quip.

Jebbit, Fowler Consolidated, an American multinational, had its commercial origins in cosmetics. The recent spreading of interests had involved the purchase of established companies in markets very different from those JF were used to — as well as different from each other. A fast food chain of restaurants, a sports equipment manufacturer, a men's clothing group and a cable TV company were now included in what was increasingly beginning to shape as an old-fashioned conglomerate. The diversifying had not yet spread to JF's subsidiary companies overseas.

'Still a million pound advertising spend in this country,' said Timms.

'Split between two execrable brands covering both ends of the market. Cheap and nasty and expensive and nasty. All with Fentley Advertising.' Rorch looked at Timms for confirmation. He got it in a nod before continuing. 'Then it's Stuart Fentley's biggest account.'

There was a momentary embarrassed silence.

'He probably pays JF to stay with the agency.' It was Bander who broke in, facetiously. 'Been with them since Stuart's late revered father started the outfit.'

'It would hurt Stuart if he lost it,' put in Timms carefully. He was watching Rorch's face as he spoke. 'It's

31

the sort of account that may lose money on paper but still pays the overheads. There's the prospect it'll get bigger, too. When the diversification gets to Europe.'

'Well, as far as I'm concerned, Stuart Fentley can keep the lot.' Rorch was firm.

'He won't if Crabtree buy into London. Buy us.' Timms hesitated, expecting a verbal reaction from Rorch. There was none. 'JF would be almost certain to switch. They've gone to Crabtree in Canada and Brazil already. Remember there was talk some time back of their using an international agency? Crabtree's expanding the way they have seems to have scotched that.'

'You mean if they bought us we could be saddled with massive losses on Dandy for three years, no certainty the drink would catch on here anyway, *and* the probability we'd have JF thrown at us, all with terms dictated from somewhere on Sixth Avenue, New York. Not on.' Rorch continued shaking his head as he moved to the chair behind his desk.

'We'd also have half a million each to soften the blow. I'm all for that bit,' said Bander cheerfully.

'And JF are deep into Carter Cousins markets, too.' Rorch had dropped into the chair, ignoring Bander's point. 'With their traditional stuff, I mean. Carter's have more sense than to plunge into beefburger chains and cable TV.'

'They're just a European operation, of course,' offered Timms carefully.

'Wrong. They're in Australia, New Zealand, the posh parts of Africa, and growing. Look, George, Carter Cousins could be the making of this agency. Competitively we're clean for them. Not just the new products. Everything they make and advertise. We could have the lot. But if we took JF they wouldn't want to know us.'

'Aren't we straying a bit from that lovely half a million each, chaps? Personally, I like that figure. It has . . . it has a fine feel to it. Tangible.' Bander tried again, looking from one partner to the other with staccato neck movements, his head thrust out, forehead furrowed.

'Our independence is a lot more tangible, Peter.' This was Rorch: the tone was tolerant. 'You might also figure what the agency could be worth two or three years from now.'

'If we get Carter Cousins, if we don't lose anything we've got now, if the rest of the new business programme produces anything, and if you don't think two million is a very good price for the business today.' Timms had spoken flatly, his gaze fixed on the carpet.

'George, you don't have enough faith.' Rorch rocked back in his chair, clasping his hands behind his neck.

Timms sighed. 'Two weeks ago, before Carter Cousins came along, you were depressed as hell. Worried the momentum had gone. Worried we'd sunk in as a worthy agency with no special allure. That's what you said.' It was a brave statement.

'That's right, Rog,' put in Bander. 'You said it in front of the lovely Helen Wintly, too, the Lord keep her magnificent mind and body. Just so I have first option on the body. You were positively suicidal, as I remember.' The speaker's boldness was spurred by what Timms had said.

There was a snort from Rorch as he straightened his chair, pushing his arms and hands flat out before him on the desk. 'Well, I'm not suicidal now, so listen carefully to this. We're going to get the Carter business. I'm ready to bet both of you your lousy half-million we're going to get it. I've got the idea. What we name the product. How we sell it. It's going to be a knock-out.' He pulled a red felt pen from the china mug on the desk, and started doodling on the drawing-pad before him.

'Good on you, Rog.' Bander put more enthusiasm into the expression than he actually felt. Still, it was heartening to know something would come out of the wreckage if good old Rog fouled up the Crabtree deal for them.

'Solo still, or ready for the collective?' asked Timms, smiling, and glad to be on something uncontroversial and positive.

It was accepted among them that if Rorch took sole responsibility for producing an advertising concept, he exposed it to the others only after he had carefully refined it. When he deemed it meet for collective action, it meant it was ready for execution without the need for 'paddling in the shallows of the group think'—which is how he described his least favourite activity.

'I need two more days. Maybe three if we're going to waste time on these Crabtree predators.' The arms went up in mock surrender when Rorch saw the worried expression return to Timms's face. 'OK, we'll see them. Listen to them. Listen to the bank. Then make a democratic decision.' He was all too conscious he had spread enough discomfort among the others: still, it had been in a good cause.

'If Crabtree do take us over—I mean, if we decide that's the right thing—I was just wondering, how will it affect Victor Grimalt?' This was Bander, on a sensitive topic.

Grimalt was the Marketing Director of OPD Foods Division—the agency's biggest client. He and Peter Bander were brothers-in-law.

'Hardly at all,' said Timms firmly.

'If it came to Crabtree finding out there's a client kick-back, they'd probably ask why it's so small. They're from New York, not Neasden,' Rorch put in cynically.

Twice a year RTB paid £20,000 to RDE Counsel AG—reputedly a commercial and technical research organization in Zürich. What the agency received for its £40,000 retainer were monthly slim volumes of typed data. The documentation was arranged to look impressive to the inquiring layman. In fact, it contained nothing but extracts from technical journals serving the food industry in all parts of the developed world. If the RTB auditors ever required proof—and they never had—that the agency received value for the expenditure, the data was there. The research, development and exploitation material they obtained in this way provided a valuable input towards their work for a very important client. That it could have been obtained at one hundredth of the price they paid was neither here nor there,

Once a year, Victor Grimalt journeyed to Switzerland to arrange the disposition of the equivalent in Swiss francs of the £36,000 credited to him by a sister company of RDE Counsel AG.

'Roger's right,' Timms confirmed. 'If it comes to it, the Americans will think it's cheap at the price. It underwrites a five million pound account on which we're taking nearly full commission.'

'The bank's never queried it.'

'Or noticed it, Peter.' Timms frowned as he spoke. 'Helen figured it out. That there was more to it. I told her there was. An arrangement with the client. She didn't press for details. Sensible attitude. That was months ago. I'm sure I told you both.'

'You did,' put in Rorch.

'Victor does a lot for the agency.' Bander paused. 'I mean, he works very hard in our interests.'

The voice trailed off. All three were uncomfortable about the deal with Grimalt. None was prepared to say so outright. None wanted to own that keeping their largest and most profitable account involved a clandestine payment to its Marketing Director.

One of the telephones on Rorch's desk began to ring, breaking the silence.

'Good morning, Helen.' Rorch glanced at the others. 'I see . . . So you got down to it pretty early.' After the preliminary exchanges, he listened for the best part of a minute before asking, 'Can I tell George and Peter? They're both with me.' He lowered the phone. 'Helen wants to come over straight away to tell us what Mark Treasure and the experts feel about the offer. Then we're invited to lunch at the bank with the two Americans. That's if Helen can reach them. OK?'

The others nodded. 'Treasure doesn't think it's too early for a meeting with the Crabtree people?' asked Timms.

'It'll be entirely noncommittal. Helen's talked to our solicitors. Our partner there, Sebastian what's-his-name, he approves so long as the other side's lawyer isn't invited. He also issued the usual warnings about everything being without prejudice.' Rorch shrugged. 'Simply a chance to size up the . . . the other people, on our ground.' He had decided not to call them 'the enemy'.

'And for them to do the same. Good idea. All for it.' Bander was especially enthusiastic.

'Right, Helen,' said Rorch into the telephone. 'Everybody's on. See you here.'

When Helen Wintly walked into Rorch's office twenty minutes later, he was alone. The others had gone to their own offices to deal with their mail.

She displayed an initial awkwardness. He rose to meet her, then, without hesitation, held her by the shoulders and kissed her on the cheek.

He sighed. 'I'm in disgrace, of course. Sorry about last night.'

She had not responded to the formal embrace. 'For teaching a girl not to be so eager? Or should I say easy? Anyway, you shouldn't be sorry.' She turned and sat in the chair Bander had been using.

'You know I tried to catch you? You left so fast.'

'What should I have done? To leave seemed the most ladylike action.' She shook her head. 'Now I'm sorry. I behaved stupidly. It was just I felt so . . . cheap, for some reason.' She looked up. 'She was your wife? Your ex-wife?'

'Actually someone else's. I hadn't expected her.'

'That was pretty obvious, except to the lady.'

'Well, there'd been a vague arrangement. It slipped my mind. I was very preoccupied.' He shrugged. 'What can I say?'

'Preoccupied, and otherwise engaged. Please forget it. Still feel the same way about the offer?' She changed the subject abruptly, then smiled. 'The American one.'

'You're very understanding. I don't imagine . . .'

'I'm usually so available? Or perhaps you were

presuming too much. We'll never know, shall we? Now, shouldn't you be sending for the others?'

'As you wish.' He walked over to his desk. 'You and Mark and this Karilian character, you all think we should sell?'

'On the information we have.'

'Which is damned slim.'

'All right. What we have, plus intelligent speculation, suggests we go for a higher price. But yes, it all points to a good deal for all the shareholders.'

'Meaning Grenwood, Phipps doesn't believe we'll ever get a better one.'

'Meaning nothing of the sort. But five years . . .'

'Is long enough to prove we're not high flyers on the record so far . . .'

'I was going to say, is a pretty short time to be in business and be offered a fancy price for what you've put together. It's very high.'

'Two million?'

'We think they'll go higher. Two and a half. Maybe two and three-quarters. We'll start at three.'

'Indeed?' He stood beside the desk, staring at the telephones. 'Mark thinks that's as high as we can aim?'

'As things are. Obviously, everything's relative. If you go to twice the profit in the next, say, three years, and if there's a buyer about then . . .'

'If there is, he may not have such a pressing need, or a Dandy at stake.'

'That's about it. You might get a good offer then, whereas now, with a little coaxing, we can get a fabulous one.'

'And any idea of eventually going public instead of selling out to another company?'

'Is a long way off. The company's successful, but it's too small. It would mean waiting another five, maybe ten years.'

'The original intention. Only Crabtree have come along to upset it.' He paused. 'That and the fact we're way behind target for the first five years.'

She shrugged. 'Certainly it's difficult to predict for the next decade. This is an upsy-downsy kind of industry. Not as much as outsiders believe, but at the size RTB is now, you're still vulnerable. If you lost OPD Foods, for instance . . .'

'Or if we got this piece of Carter Cousins I'm sweating over.'

'How's the idea shaping?'

'Very well.'

'Can I peek?'

'Nothing on paper to peek at. In any case . . .'

'I understand.' She respected his working principles. 'Any chance of a decision from Carter within two weeks?'

'None. If we decide to go with my idea, I need to make some video-tape commercials. Fairly polished ones.' He sat on the side of the desk. 'We could probably be ready in a week. The presentation date isn't till September 14th.'

'More than two weeks away. They wouldn't move it up?'

'Possibly. If we asked. It wouldn't mean we'd necessarily get a decision any earlier. They have their own timetable for assessment meetings. It's tied in with a research schedule. Going in early would increase our costs. Or something might get spoiled in the rush. I need a fancy location for the commercials. Maybe two.'

'Here or abroad?'

Rorch shook his head. 'Not telling. To be honest, I haven't decided. I'm checking them out now. One thing I'll guarantee. The campaign will get us the business.'

'You're very confident. You know, Mark Treasure wouldn't be in favour of the Crabtree deal if you opposed it. You don't have to sell. You don't even have to think about going public. So far as the bank is concerned, you can go on indefinitely as an independent company.'

'You mean the bank wouldn't vote for the Crabtree deal if I didn't? That would mean a fifty-fifty split. George Timms and Peter Bander want to sell.'

She touched the bun at the back of her head, tapered

fingers spread. 'It wouldn't come to that, of course. I think you know it. If it came to the crunch, they'd change their minds.'

'One of them might,' he mused, but doubtfully. He picked up the internal telephone. 'I'd better get them in or they'll get the idea this is a private affair.' He looked across the room at her: she avoided his gaze. 'What happens about lunch?' he asked.

'I'll get a call here if Crabtree and the other man, Jackson, can come. They're playing hard to get for some reason.'

CHAPTER 4

Lee Jackson finished his telephone call with Joe Ziebal. He was comfortably seated in a chintz-covered armchair—jacketless and tieless. Howie Crabtree had his feet up on the matching sofa. They were in the living-room of their two-bedroomed, riverview suite at the Savoy Hotel. It was 11 a.m. Joanne Jackson had already gone shopping.

'We should definitely take up the offer for lunch,' said Jackson.

'What else?' Howie inquired, trying to sound alert. He had already taken an hour's nap in his room, but still felt he hadn't been to bed for two days.

'He says the bank and two of the agency's founder directors are for the deal. His insider says they'll go for three million, but maybe settle for two and three-quarters.'

Howie pondered for a moment. 'Ziebal won't be at the lunch?'

'Of course not.' There was disappointment in the voice. 'In this deal, Ziebal is the phantom fixer. We agreed we never mention he's advising us. Not to anyone.'

'Sure, I remember. It's just that with the Brazilian deal . . .'

'He didn't have anyone on the inside of the agency he picked out for us. This time he does. Either way he helps us to get the lowest price.'

'Tell me how that works again?' Howie looked pained as well as sleepy.

This time Jackson swallowed the sigh. 'It's very simple. Joe picks the agency that's right for us. Not a short list. One agency . . .'

'Plus one in reserve?'

'Right. Just one. A fallback candidate. I'd forgotten.'

'We want to be accurate, Lee. There's a lot involved.' Howie produced the pipe he had recently acquired, and started filling it with tobacco. A pipe, he found, gave him confidence. He wished he'd adopted one earlier. It would have helped, also, if he enjoyed smoking.

Jackson chose to ignore the stricture. 'If Joe doesn't have anyone in management to help swing the deal from the inside, then it's everything in the open. It's Joe Ziebal working for the Crabtree organization. So Joe makes the approach, comes to all the meetings, does the haggling. Like he did in Brazil.'

'So everyone's alerted?'

'Right. Everybody knows if Ziebal fingers a company for a client, it's going to be the right company. The owners know they're *the* choice.'

'So they ask the earth, Lee.'

'But don't get it. Joe fixes his main fee in advance. He pitches it against what he thinks the company's worth.'

'And we have to take his word for that?' Howie was still forcing tobacco into the pipe.

'Because he's always on the button. But he gets an extra percentage if he brings off the deal at lower than the agreed top price. Only the buyer — that's us — knows Joe's valuation, of course. And he's a red hot negotiator. The guys in Rio thought we were paying our highest price when we shook hands on that deal. You should have been there.' Jackson said it before remembering it would have been more tactful not to.

'I could have been there, except HJ had me locked into

40

a Dandy Distributors meeting in LA the whole of that week,' Howie came in with spirit. 'Missed the second lot of meetings in Toronto, too. I was in on the first negotiations. With the agency we didn't get. I mean, that proves Ziebal isn't all that perfect. In Canada we had to go round twice. We bought second choice.'

And Jackson needed no reminding it was Howie who had fumbled things with the first agency. He was still surprised HJ was letting his son loose in London, especially — as with the Canadian deal — Ziebal would not be overtly party to the negotiations. Clearly, the Chairman was putting his whole faith in the capacities of Lee Jackson — Jackson persuaded himself.

'Pity about Toronto, sure. But Rio went like clock-work,' he offered.

'HJ says we got the company for half a million dollars less than we expected.'

'Half a million less than we're now sure it was worth. Great little agency, Howie. You should spend more time there. Hottest receptionist in the business. That Miss Lomas. The one who makes the play for you, Howie, old boy, old boy.'

'Oh, I think that's your imagination, Lee.' Howie reddened, and not just because no amount of sucking would get his pipe alight.

'Anyway, this time around in London, Joe has an insider. Someone who's given him the whole financial lowdown. Someone he's planned the strategy with — who's keeping him informed every step.'

'Who?' asked Howie ingenuously while digging at the pipe bowl with the end of a handy pencil.

Jackson didn't trouble disguising his irritation. 'Joe keeps that as classified information. You know that. Remember the terms of the deal.'

'Sure.' Howie had laid aside the pipe and was contemplating his stockinged feet on the end of the sofa. 'I suppose there really is someone?'

'Meaning?'

'Meaning it could be a con. The whole thing. Ziebal

spots an agency for us, as you say. That can't be so
difficult. Can't be that many qualified. Right billing
bracket. Free to be bought. Not American-owned
already. No account conflicts. I mean, for instance, we
couldn't buy the London office of J. Walter Thompson,
or the agencies that handle Coca-Cola or Pepsi.'

'Howie, you're absolutely right. Not forgetting
Thompson is a public corporation,' answered Jackson,
wide-eyed.

'So, you get my point?' The sarcasm hadn't registered:
it rarely did. 'Ziebal puts us with the likeliest, qualifying
agency. Sends us the financial data. Anyone can get that
from public records. He adds some industrial intelligence, so-called. Mixture of trade press reports and
scuttlebutt. Then he names a highest and lowest figure,
and collects a fat fee while we do all the work.'

'And quite a big fee up front even if there isn't a deal.'
Jackson shook his head, implying a comity he didn't in the
least feel—except, was there a possibility . . . ?

'Exactly. *And* he has a fallback candidate if the first
agency doesn't bite.'

'Oh, come on, Howie.' Jackson pulled himself together
mentally. He jumped up and stomped over to the coffee
tray. He had humoured Howie enough. 'How long d'you
think the guy would stay in business if he worked that
way?' That had to be the answer: Howie had had him
doubting there for a moment.

'So you can prove it? So who's the insider?' Howie's eyes
had narrowed. He knew he had the other man rattled. It
didn't happen often, and he wasn't letting go.

'He's the one who provided Ziebal with RTB's
confidential unpublished half-year figures. You've got
them with your papers.'

'Could have been stolen.'

'But they weren't, Howie,' Jackson replied loudly to
make up for what the statement lacked in cogency. 'He's
also the one who reported this morning we've got the
bank and two other principal shareholders ready to deal.'

'Except I could have told you that. The opening price is

too high. We're obviously ready to go higher. So the shareholders are falling over themselves to deal. Ziebal could figure everybody's attitude. He doesn't need an insider.'

'Except everybody isn't ready to deal. Joe says one of the principals is undecided.'

'Which one?'

'He couldn't say. Figured we'd find out at lunch, that's if the man hasn't been talked round by then.'

'Ha! So by lunch everybody's selling at three million, but right now Ziebal's fed us some more phoney intelligence to make things more dramatic.'

Jackson frowned. 'You want to call the deal off, Howie? You want to call HJ? You want to tell your father you think Joe Ziebal's crooked?' He picked up the white telephone from the table beside him, and offered the whole instrument to Howie. His suggestion ignored the fact it would be six o'clock in the morning, New York time.

'Now hold on there, Lee. I didn't say Ziebal was crooked. That'd be libellous.' Howie was backing off. Symbolically, he bent his legs and drew them into his chest. He was responding in just the way Jackson knew he would to any suggestion that HJ should be involved.

'So what do you want to do?'

Howie got up from the sofa, started to pace, returned to the sofa, put on his elevated shoes, then began pacing in earnest. 'I just think we ought to demand the name of the insider for a start. At least then we'll know he exists.'

'Howie, it's better we don't know. That's Ziebal's philosophy. If we don't know we can't give the man away. A slip of the tongue. A knowing look. It can happen.' Jackson shuddered inwardly as he spoke. With Howie it was almost bound to happen. 'It could wreck the deal,' he went on. 'If an insider is identified to his partners, they're going to resent him. Change their attitude, for sure. Figure he's on a better deal than they are.'

'But everyone will guess somebody's working for us . . . Won't they?' Howie was back to his old, uncertain self. He took up the pipe. 'I mean, we used Ziebal in other countries. In Brazil he handled the whole deal openly. People will know . . .'

'No, sir. People won't *know* anything.' Jackson had settled himself back in the armchair with his coffee. 'They can make uninformed guesses, sure. They can't *know*. Not like we know things.'

Howie stopped pacing and stood in the centre of the room. He fixed Jackson with the calculating stare that everyone knew he'd been practising since someone saw him at it in the washroom mirror. 'You mean we know the insider must be one of the three founding partners. Rorch, Timms or Bander.' He used the stem of the pipe like a baton, beating out the names as he said them.

Jackson shook his head. 'Could be it isn't any of them. Could be it's the company treasurer, or one of the other directors. There are three others. Maybe it's someone in this merchant bank.'

'That's like an investment bank,' said Howie slowly, as though the point had special significance.

'That's right. It could even be their legal counsellor.'

'But whoever it is gets a piece of the half-million we pay Ziebal if the deal goes through.'

'If it goes through at three million. If it goes through at less, Joe gets ten per cent of the saving. The more we pay for RTB, the less he takes.'

'At two million he'd get £600,000. You think the insider gets the biggest piece of the fee over half a million, Lee?' Howie didn't wait for an answer before adding, 'Could be that's all he gets. You don't know how Ziebal splits the fee?'

'I'd guess the insider does pretty well.'

'Blood money, you could call it,' Howie commented, darkly. He decided he didn't care for someone who influenced his friends for his own gain and conceivably their loss.

Jackson had already worked out what was bothering Howie. He also knew Howie had always been rich enough to enjoy exercising a high-toned moral attitude in such matters.

44

Howie regarded the other sternly, put the pipe in his mouth and blew through it sharply—showering himself with bits of tobacco.

Joe Ziebal intended to enjoy exercising high-toned moral attitudes as soon as he had the time—and enough money.

He was five feet two inches tall, carried too much weight, and jogged for twenty minutes every morning in Regent's Park. The jogging did nothing for the weight except help to keep it steady. His wife, Elly, warned it would also kill him: she'd read in a book somewhere that jogging killed men of forty-five. Joe had just had his forty-sixth birthday. He'd enjoyed beating that book.

Beating the book was what Joe's life was all about. The time he spent jogging—and when he might easily have been considering moral attitudes—he mostly devoted to calculating odds. Joe didn't back horses: just people and companies. Getting the odds right in those contexts kept Joe in business, Elly in mink, and three boys at Eton.

Joe described himself as head of a very exclusive and restricted executive placement organization. This was true so far as it went. More accurately, he was an international company broker—in a specialized field. Executive placement was a useful front for the second and more lucrative of his activities, as well as the source of its especial strength.

He was American by birth. His wife was British. His operating base was London where he had a staff of three. He had other offices in New York and Zürich: total employees six. In addition he had approximately fifty 'stringers'—company directors and top executives in the major cities of the free world. These kept him up to date on the state of the communications industry—advertising, public relations and the media—in which they were all employed. The cost of this discreet intelligence network was small: it took the form of covert retainers in one form or another. The quality of it was unrivalled: the informants were well placed because Joe himself had placed all of them in their jobs.

Joe operated only in a limited field. His start-up fee for finding you the right company to buy, or the right buyer for your company, was £100,000, in advance and not returnable. He tended to treat with a very serious clientele. His ultimate remuneration for a successful completion was by individual arrangement.

'So it's still three against one in Crabtree's favour, you say? Stop relaxing. That's not so much in their favour. It's the quality that matters. You want to tell me who's against?' Joe chuckled into the telephone.

He had both elbows on his desk as he talked. One hand supported his head, the fingers of the other grasped his ear, the earpiece of the instrument enfolded in the podgy palm.

It was a huge, old-style partners' desk. The worn leather swivel chair swivelled only one way, and the mechanism for changing the height of the seat had locked in the lowest position a long time ago.

As always, Joe looked not so much as if he was sitting at the desk as peeking over it. And everything he needed he had to keep close — like the telephones, the well-fingered address book, the cigarette box, and the remote control for the air-conditioning. Reaching anything else involved leaping — the kind that dolphins do before falling back into the water. Joe simply fell back into his too-low chair which it would have cost relatively little to have mended — or even to replace, except Joe liked it the way it was.

Now he scooped the whole telephone into his lap, and swivelled the chair 180 degrees anti-clockwise, which was the only way it would go, and as far as it would go. This gave him a view down upon the narrow private garden in front of Chester Terrace, and beyond that Regent's Park. He was looking through the centre of the three oblong windows that lit the first-floor room in the John Nash terrace. It was for this room and view that he had bought the house as a home and work-place.

The sun would soon begin to flood the place, enhancing its fine proportions and — apart from Joe's chair—its elegant furnishings. There were some good late Georgian and early Victorian pieces, including three leather winged chairs he especially admired. Joe admired style—in things and other people. Chester Terrace had style: in his view it was the best building in Regent's Park. He saw nothing incongruous in his own appearance rarely equating with elegance. For weddings, funerals, bar mitzvahs and Eton Founder's Day he went formal. For the rest he aimed at comfort. Today he was in a short-sleeved check shirt, blue slacks and loafers.

He had listened intently to what had been said over the telephone since his last comment. 'Of course it'll be a sale,' he suddenly interjected. 'And the price will go higher the longer it takes . . . OK, we agreed. I could still have used a blitzkrieg. No more money but good for the image.' He chuckled. 'So we still do it your way, kid. So keep it moving.' He listened a little more, then broke in again. 'There's a few things I want to do. They won't hurry matters any. Just add to the credibility . . . No, I'm not going to tell you. Better you don't know, then everybody's surprised.' There was some protesting from the other end. 'I said surprised, not shocked. Leave it to me, kid. Now I have to go. Ciao.'

He swung the chair around again, put the telephone back on the desk, and adjusted the room temperature downwards. He pulled off his heavily framed glasses, blinked, and wiped his forehead with his handkerchief. Involuntarily, he felt for his hairline—bushy but receding—to see if it had receded any more.

The glasses went back on the end of his nose before he flipped over the pages of the address book. He tapped out the number he had found, grabbed a cigarette and lit it. 'It's me, kid.' He never announced his name. This wasn't arrogance, merely a precaution. Most of Joe's 'phone calls were confidential—beginning with the fact Joe was calling. He never used switchboard operators. If whoever he wanted didn't have a direct line at the office, Joe would wait until he could reach the person at home.

'Well, hello. Thanks again for the hospitality yesterday.'

The man who had answered was Sales Director at a major TV company. He had stopped for drinks at Chester Terrace on his way home the previous evening. He was an important man, so secure in his job that he had no misgivings about being seen at the home-cum-office of a top executive recruiter.

'My pleasure. Come again. You gave my love to your bride? Good.' Joe never stopped for acknowledgement of the niceties: he still left people feeling he truly felt the sentiments expressed. 'Tell you what. I need you to do someone a favour. Some information for the press. Can you arrange?'

'Always glad to mislead the gentlemen of the press, Joe.'

'It's a lady. But it's kosher. Cross my heart. What's the time?' He glanced at his watch as he turned to another page of the address book. 'Just after eleven.' He answered his own question. 'She can catch the second city edition with a juicy titbit. Got a pencil? Here's the personal number you'll want . . .'

The lady the man called two minutes later was totally satisfied about the impeccable source of the information. Even so, being a very good journalist, she called elsewhere for confirmation.

CHAPTER 5

'You'll take coffee . . . Howard?' Mark Treasure inquired of Crabtree whom he had seated on his right. He smiled an apology at Rorch whom he had interrupted, and who was on his other side.

The banker had earlier acceded to Jackson's request that everybody should be on first name terms: except he had an aversion to diminutives—and Howie Crabtree was fairly diminutive to begin with.

'Sanka, thank you, Mark.'

The Grenwood, Phipps butler produced the required powder and hot water with the air of a conjuror from behind the silver coffee-pot on the silver tray.

'So what you do, Roger—' Treasure turned again to Rorch—'is switch to half the time difference between London and the country you're visiting, the day before you go. And that eliminates jet-lag?'

'Sovereign remedy,' Rorch affirmed expansively.

They were six at the oblong table in the smallest of the bank's several formal dining-rooms. Timms was next to Howie, with Jackson opposite next to Rorch. Helen was playing hostess at the other end of the table.

The conversation had been general, and not especially pertinent to advertising. At first Rorch had said little. It seemed he was applying a tolerant, almost amused indifference towards the Americans. Gradually, though, he had warmed to Howie. It was an attraction of opposites.

'Two and a half hours makes for an awkward schedule,' said Howie earnestly. It had been he who had complained about adjusting to British time. 'I mean, that's half the difference between New York and London.'

'So take it out of your working day.' Rorch ran a calculating glance round the table. 'Two and a half hours is perfect. Exactly the time you'd spend in a week managing an advertising agency. Pretend you've done it. Knock off at lunch-time. Play hookey in the morning. Depends which direction you're travelling. You'll benefit. The agency will benefit from less management.'

Howie blinked his near comprehension.

It was Jackson who took up what was evidently meant to be a provocative aside. 'You don't hold with too much management, Roger?'

'In an ad agency? Non-job. The good ones run themselves.'

'You mean they're not like factories,' put in Helen, noting Jackson's frown.

'Closer to merchant banks, perhaps,' was Treasure's

contribution. 'It's true we're in business to help run other people's.'

'You still need management skills,' said Timms.

'And how,' agreed Jackson with vigour. He spent several hours in every day on what he deemed essential management activities, involving a small army of other well-paid executives in the same processes.

'But not to run the agency,' Rorch insisted. 'Navel-gazing management exercises don't produce campaigns. Nor new business. And they don't get the agency talked about. It's creative flair that makes the noise.' He looked at Treasure. 'And that's what we provide for our clients. As you say, it's like you with lovely money.'

'Well, hold on there, Rog.' It was Jackson again, treading warily because he suspected traps. 'Our new business programme at Crabtree takes a lot of corporate management time. We have a schedule of integrated mail shots covering over a thousand advertisers. The data bank we've built up on that over the last few years, that takes regular assessing . . .'

'Never got us any new business, Lee . . .'

'Oh, come on, Howie, that's not entirely . . .'

'And I've always said we spend too much time evaluating our management-by-objectives programme.' Howie seemed to have recovered from his jet-lag, was ignoring Jackson, and addressing himself to Rorch. 'Never really understood management by objectives. Not on the evaluating committee.' He shot a glance at Jackson before continuing, 'Roger, do you have a committee on budgetary control? We do. Meets every week.'

'Not unless George constitutes a committee.'

'It's a pretty essential activity.' This was Helen.

'Still not a committee job. Not in an advertising agency,' Rorch insisted. He had begun doodling on the back of the menu card. 'Job for someone in top management with a flair for imaginative arithmetic. What he decides should be law. The time he takes deciding it will be minimal if his electronic slaves are feeding him right. Internal committees are boring. The

50

meetings should be held standing up. Cuts down the time enormously.' He glanced at Jackson. 'We try to keep our people servicing the clients.'

'Peter Bander's in charge of client services,' said Helen. 'Pity he had to drop out of lunch.'

'Because a client needed service at short notice,' Treasure put in with understanding. 'It happens.'

'And the creative responsibility is yours, Roger.' This was Howie, fresh from savouring the comment about arithmetic.

'I'm not the Creative Director,' Rorch corrected. 'We have one. A lady. She's very good. I help sometimes with ideas. Once a copywriter always a copywriter.'

'Roger's our new business programme.' Timms's tone was serious. 'All by himself.'

'Saves more valuable people from chasing prospects. That's not what the clients pay for, after all,' Rorch offered modestly. 'We don't use mail shots for cold canvassing. We run ads about ourselves. In the trade press. When we have something worth saying.'

'With general rather than specific objectives?' Treasure helped himself to some grapes and a crumb of cheese from the big dish in front of him.

'Keeps our name in front of the right people. Difficult to say what part our house ads play in fetching prospective clients actually to our door.' Rorch frowned at his doodling. 'In any case, that's not why we run them.'

'It's why we do our mail shots. They cost more. They reach fewer people, and they don't work.' Howie looked firmly at Jackson as he spoke.

'America's a big country. We tried ads. Too impersonal. A personalized letter with a brochure works better.' The other American sounded riled.

'Excepting neither works at all,' Howie came back fast.

'Most of our prospective clients seem to approach us, these days,' said Rorch, aware, like everyone else present, that the relationship between Crabtree and Jackson was a good deal less amicable than might have been assumed. 'We just seem to get on more short-lists when advertisers are switching agencies.'

'Result of Roger working to get us better known,' Timms came in loyally. 'He gets such a lot of exposure.'

'Dreary round of after-dinner speeches and conference platforms,' Rorch put in dismissively.

'And articles. And airtime. Especially TV discussion programmes. Not in the least dreary, and very good for the agency,' insisted Helen.

'That's where we miss out. Since my father got too old for barn-storming.' It was another of Howie's admonitions directed at Jackson.

'It's not too difficult to get on to the late talk shows as a so-called expert on something. When most sensible people have gone to bed.' Rorch smiled as he spoke. 'It's why most of our new clients are insomniacs. Anyway, what Helen and George are talking about is dressage. When the chips are down, it's the creative work that makes or breaks an agency. Keeps accounts. Attracts new ones. Creativity is all.'

'Sounds as if you have to have God working for you, or Michael Angelo at least,' Treasure observed.

'You're quite right, Mark,' answered Rorch promptly. 'The trade jargon is impossibly pompous. Fact is, an original advertising concept can make a huge difference to sales—even if it looks pretty banal to an uninvolved layman. It's quite as important as the product, and—to be a fraction cynical—nearly as important as the amount of money spent on the advertising.'

Howie nodded enthusiastically. 'I read once that the best advertising for a given product is probably only one per cent better than the worst. And that's all it has to be, whichever way you calculate the commercial benefit.'

'That might be quite profound,' said Treasure. 'Assuming you accept advertising does motivate people.'

'Other people,' Helen put in with a laugh. 'People always believe advertising manipulates other people. Never themselves.'

'Manipulates is a very emotive word.' Jackson nodded.

'But perfectly accurate,' Rorch came in seriously.

'Advertising manipulates products, not people. It's quite good at it.' He went back to his doodling.

'You believe in our business, Roger?' Howie was serious too.

'I believe it's a business, not a crusade. Even so, it's a good deal more ethical than a lot of people credit. We don't tell lies for our clients. We tell the truth. But we tell it well.'

'Roger, you and HJ, that's my father, you have the exact same views. Isn't that so, Lee?' Howie looked across the table for confirmation. 'You've got to be straight with the consumer. That's what HJ's been preaching a long time before it was the in thing.' His eyes narrowed. 'You ever worked in the States, Roger?'

'No.'

Involuntarily, Timms and Jackson had each looked across at the other to check the reaction to the question, not the answer.

A moment earlier, the butler had left the room on a nod from Treasure. He had placed the silver coffee tray in front of Helen.

'We shan't be disturbed, now,' said the banker pointedly; then, since the remark seemed to have induced total silence, he continued, 'I wonder whether you'd like to enlarge on your unexpected offer, Howard?'

'You want us to increase it?' Howie, taken by surprise, had misunderstood. There was an undisguised glare of exasperation from Jackson.

'Not exactly, but you can if you like,' chuckled Treasure. 'I meant expand on what you've written to RTB. We'd certainly be interested to know how you arrived at the offer you have made.'

Jackson cleared his throat noisily. 'We supplied you with our financial picture, Mark. We collected the same kind of data on RTB. The offer is subject to total disclosure on both sides. I believe our lawyer made that clear. We think our data on RTB is pretty accurate. And we like what we know about the agency.'

Rorch put down his pen and faced the speaker. 'How

do you know our financial situation hasn't altered a good deal since last year's figures? For the worse, perhaps?'

'Let's say we've guessed they've improved.'

'You mean you know they have?'

'We've had a lot of inquiries made about your company. And a whole lot of other companies. You come out pretty high.'

'Head and shoulders above the rest,' chipped in Howie with great conviction—a lot more than his colleague had evinced.

'Did Joe Ziebal do the inquiring?' asked Timms.

Howie reddened. 'Mr Ziebal . . .'

'A number of organizations worked on the project,' Jackson interrupted loudly. 'I don't believe it would help any to say which ones. Not at this point in time.'

'Not now?'

'That's right, Roger.' Jackson nodded, missing the quip. 'We'll tell you about them if we do a deal. And what they said.'

'When it's safe for it to go to our heads.' Smiling, Rorch went back to drawing on the menu.

'Let's say what we've got to date we think justifies the offer. We estimate profits in the current year will run between two and three times what they were last year. Your billings are well up. Discreet inquiries show the clients are happy. You're shot of the hang-over from that bad debt. You have one very hot prospect we know about. Carter Cousins. That was reported in your trade press. Maybe there are other pieces of new business pending. Anyhow, it all makes good news.' He paused. 'We have to move fast for a very simple reason. Our client, the Dandy Corporation, needs a presence in London, and he needs it in a hurry.'

'Two weeks is still very optimistic.'

'I agree, Mark, but it's possible, with good will and openness on both sides. If we've been fed any wrong intelligence; if there's anything important we've missed, good or bad, we rely on you to tell us. From what we've learned about you—RTB and the bank—we figure you'll

54

tell us. Meantime, our offer stands. And it's exclusive. We have information on other agencies, but we're not approaching any of them.'

It had been a credible exposition.

'Thank you for including Grenwood, Phipps in the compliment.' Treasure touched the edge of his mouth with his napkin. 'If we decide to treat with your offer, then naturally you can have access to all reasonable information.' He hesitated, played with his coffee cup for a moment, then went on, glancing at Rorch. 'Of course, it's not just a matter of money.'

'Compatibility, you mean? Can we live together?' Jackson had come back quickly. He extended both arms in the direction of the other American. 'Howie and I are the worst you'll have to put up with. Howard Senior, that's HJ, is a great gentleman. If you like us, you'll love HJ. Unfortunately, he's retiring shortly.' The speaker paused to accentuate the gravity. 'Howie, here, is Chairman designate.' There was another pause while Jackson quite evidently waited for Howie to say something.

'And presumably, you are President designate?' It was Helen who spoke.

'I guess that's for others to assume, not for me. Let's say I don't believe there's a queue of alternative candidates.' He was still staring hard at Howie.

The Crabtree Chairman designate coughed. 'We're not the biggest agency in the United States,' he said unexpectedly. 'Profitable, though.'

'The billing of your two foreign offices you report as fourteen million dollars. Brazil's showing a loss, and Canada's just breaking even. Is that because of Dandy?' asked Timms bluntly.

'Yes,' answered Jackson. 'The Dandy operation does tend to keep profits down for the first three years.'

'I gather it wipes them out,' murmured Rorch.

'You could say that, but only on a temporary basis. The way we work with Dandy is pretty common knowledge. It's a fine company, with fine products.'

55

'It's a company with one product which may or may not catch on in Britain.' This was Rorch again. 'I hear it's touch and go still in Brazil. What happens if Dandy pulls out of Brazil, Lee? What happens to your agency there?'

'Why, we'd stand by our investment.' It was Howie who answered. 'The Rio office was doing well before we bought in. With or without Dandy, it'll go on growing. We've talked Jebbit, Fowler into putting business with us there this year. We have the Toronto office working for JF already.'

'You could say it's an obligation for Crabtree offices to take JF business,' observed Rorch, without looking up.

'Well, it's another fine company. There's no hardship involved,' said Howie innocently.

'There could be in our case. If it meant turning away a competitor.'

'You mean Carter Cousins? You don't have that in the bag yet, Roger,' commented Jackson. 'Or so I understand.'

'This rule that agencies don't handle competing advertisers. It's rigorously observed?' Treasure inquired.

'It's not a rule so much as an understood practice,' Helen put in. 'It's pretty logical when you think about it.'

'Carter Cousins wouldn't live with a London agency that handled JF business,' Rorch insisted.

'I think that's true,' added Timms from the other side of the table. 'It's one of the problems.'

'Maybe we can get around it,' Jackson speculated. 'We don't know the nature of the Carter products. Could be they're not in head-on competition with anything JF makes.'

Rorch grinned. 'Then again, it could be they are.'

Jackson shrugged. 'So, as we say in our letter, the management of the agency in London would stay autonomous if we bought the company. If you decided against taking business we could introduce, that'd be it. There'd be no compulsion.'

'Except for Dandy?'

'That's understood, of course,' replied the American.

Jackson took up the point. 'Dandy on no commission for a year, rising by five per cent annually till the fourth year. That's the only imposed condition?'

'In a nutshell.'

'The creative work on Dandy. We'd have to use the American campaign?' It was Timms who asked the question, staring at Rorch as he did so.

'It'd be stupid not to. If it researched all right,' Rorch put in unexpectedly, ahead of anything the Americans might have said. ' "Thirsty?—that's Dandy." ' He affected collapse and recovery, matching the question and answer. 'It's a good line. Should work here, with the jingle you're using. We'd need to remake the commercials, using British sports, British players. Cricket not baseball. Tennis is OK, of course.'

'You know the campaign?' Howie sounded pleased.

'We try to keep in touch.' As Rorch spoke he looked at the time, frowned, then nodded at Treasure.

George Timms made a similar gesture after a glance from the banker.

'Well, gentlemen. Howard. Lee,' Treasure began. 'It seems the shareholders of RTB would be ready to take your approach further, but on a confidential and uncommitted basis. We more or less decided this before you arrived. Peter Bander agreed to go along on those terms . . .'

'Provided we didn't drink from the fingerbowls, Mark?' Jackson interrupted.

'The criteria involved subtler things than that.' Treasure smiled. 'Obviously you'll need to see financial data on RTB that compares in detail and accuracy with what you've supplied on Crabtree. The books will be open to you, also the doors in Red Lion Square. If you wish, George will take you over to the offices from here. I'd guess you look sufficiently like affluent, prospective clients not to start takeover rumours. Ask any questions you like. We'll feel free to do the same. We appreciate the need for speed. That the Dandy Corporation is really doing the impelling. We don't like the rush, but so long as you're restricting your approach to RTB, it's only courteous to try to resolve matters quickly—while you still have time to look elsewhere.'

The banker paused, looking from Rorch to Timms. 'Despite this, you ought to know at the outset the RTB shareholders are some way from unanimity over whether to accept or reject any firm offer you may make. That's on the principle of the thing. We can tell you now the shareholders are totally agreed on one point. It's that two million pounds won't buy you RTB. It's only fair you should understand that.'

It was Jackson who broke the silence. 'We understand what you say, Mark? Don't we, Howie?' He didn't wait for confirmation. 'We'll go along on that basis. We'd like to take in the agency later today, and set up meetings with the accountants for tomorrow morning.' He hesitated. 'Tell me one thing. If two million won't buy us the agency, do you want to give us an indication of the kind of sum that might?'

'Mmm. I think we have to say that any new figure has to come from you,' Treasure replied smoothly. 'Once you're totally familiar with the company's situation and likely future, we feel you'll be in a better position to put a value on it.'

'Fair enough, Mark. But if it isn't simply a matter of money . . . ?'

'Mark says we don't have unanimity on the principle involved at the moment.' It was Rorch who broke in. 'If there was a majority against we wouldn't be proceeding.'

'What Roger means is the shareholders believe in democratic decisions.' Since she wasn't a shareholder this expression from Helen surprised Treasure a little: Howie thought it enlightening in a context only he and Jackson knew about.

'You mean they'd move on a majority. I guess that's OK by us,' said Jackson.

As the American had been speaking, Miss Gaunt had entered the room. She was holding a copy of the *Standard*.

'I'm sorry to interrupt, Mr Treasure. Mr Rorch's car for the airport is waiting. He doesn't have much time, and his secretary asks if he could ring her urgently. Also, I thought you ought to see this.' She put the copy of the early afternoon newspaper in front of her employer. It was open, and folded to one of the editorial pages.

'Thanks,' said Treasure. 'You'd better run, Roger.' He was scanning the paragraph marked with red ink. Miss Gaunt remained.

Rorch pushed back his chair. 'If you'll all excuse . . .'

'Hold on. I think you'd better hear this before you go. It's the column on advertising they run on Tuesdays. By Margaret Patrick. The headline says "RTB Takeover." Then it goes on: "There are unconfirmed reports that Howard J. Crabtree, the New York agency, is making a bid for Rorch, Timms & Bander of London. A move into the UK by Crabtree (US billing $260m) has been expected following the recent announcement that major client the Dandy Corporation will shortly start marketing in Europe. Last year RTB billed £10m, but claims a projected current year uplift to £14m and rising. As first reported in this column last week, RTB has been hired by Carter Cousins for development work on an important new product. If the agency sold to Crabtree there could be competitive problems. Crabtree has a big piece of the Jebbit, Fowler cosmetic business in the US and Canada which it may be aiming to pick up in London. The account, billing £1.2m to year June, is with Fentley Advertising. When asked to confirm the bid for RTB, Howard J. Crabtree Jnr, President of Crabtree, said in London today he had no comment to make at this time. None of the three principals of RTB has so far been available." '

'Because one's in Reading and the other two living it up in the City. Blast!' This was Rorch who was standing behind Treasure's chair. 'That's the second edition. I saw the first before I came out. There was nothing about us. My temporary secretary obviously doesn't think calls from newspapers worth passing on.'

'She's asked you to call her,' remarked Treasure.

'Now it's too late.'

'Howie. When did the newspaper call you?' Jackson had his elbows on the table, and his head between his hands. There was a forced tolerance in the tone—as though he was addressing a wayward but certified idiot.

'Around eleven-thirty. Maybe a little later. You were taking a shower. That's it. That's why I forgot to mention it.' He nodded and frowned, lips pursed.

Jackson managed a smile, but not much of one. 'You did say "no comment at this time"?' he inquired.

'I believe so. I mean . . . it was the only thing I could have said.'

The other American looked pained.

'You could have denied the rumour, of course,' Timms offered.

Howie showed genuine bewilderment. 'No, I couldn't,' he protested. 'How could I have denied it? It's true. We are here to make a bid for RTB.'

There was a momentary silence.

'So you are. So you are,' agreed Treasure affably.

CHAPTER 6

'But you could have rung me last night? I'll have another gin.'

Victor Grimalt, the speaker, was a stiff-necked, thin, sallow-faced man with piercing dark eyes. His black hair was parted in the centre, brushed flat and clipped short, army style. The narrow moustache put a leer into his smile—but he smiled less often than most people.

He was shortish, the spare build accentuated by tight-fitting clothes. Invariably, for business he wore two-buttoned, double-breasted jackets with both buttons done up. He had a disarming habit of shooting his cuffs, something he had picked up as a child from watching James Cagney in old gangster films. Suddenly both arms would be thrust out in what looked like an offensive gesture—then he brought them back slowly, elbows bent, solid gold cuff-links showing. He collected solid gold cuff-links—as presents from his commercial suppliers at Christmas: every Christmas.

He had another habit of looking sharply from side to side for no evident reason and often to the alarm of anyone close by of a nervous disposition. This was Grimalt's way of physically demonstrating his mental alertness at all times.

Grimalt looked older than fifty-one. He said this was because he had come up through the ranks, working all the hours God gave to compensate for his underprivileged beginnings. In truth, he had wasted an excellent grammar school education, failed university entrance at eighteen, and joined OPD as a junior management trainee through the influence of a remote relative who was on the board. From then onwards, he had applied himself with great vigour and more guile.

As Marketing Director of the OPD Foods Division he consistently produced impressive sales figures, and while cordially disliked by all his colleagues, it was generally accepted the Division could hardly do without him. It was his dedication that impressed. OPD breakfast foods, biscuits and dry snacks, he insisted, came first with Victor Grimalt. In fact, they came second to the protection and improvement of Victor Grimalt's personal fortune, but he believed strongly in advertising.

'Another gin, please, waiter. A double. No, just the one. I'm all right for the moment.' Peter Bander ran a finger between neck and collar. He could have done with a proper drink himself. So far he had managed on a plain tonic water ordered before Victor had arrived. He had to keep his head.

They had met for lunch at the White Hart in Sonning, the pretty Thames-side village four miles from Reading on the London side. The OPD Food plant was the same distance on the other side of the town. They were not

61

likely to meet anyone else from the company here—not at lunch-time.

They had a corner table in the nearly empty hotel bar. Most people were sitting in the garden by the river, in the sunshine. Grimalt didn't care for sunshine.

'It was late when I got the news myself, Victor.' Bander had waited until the bar waiter had moved away. 'And I had to talk it over with Rog and George again this morning. Bolt from the blue. Last thing we expected. Nobody outside knows. You're the only client we've told. Rog is against selling.'

'Then he's smarter than the rest of you. And that includes Grenwood, Phipps.' The arms shot out and back in the familiar gesture, the clenched fists remaining for a moment at the hover position.

What Grimalt really meant was he saw the impending takeover as bad for Grimalt.

Bander breathed in loud and deep, through his mouth. 'It means half a million,' he said quickly, then let out the breath. 'That's each,' he added.

'Peanuts. Rorch is looking beyond the end of next week. You should do the same. He's looking ten years from now.' So was Grimalt—to the time of his retirement. By then the nest-egg building in Switzerland would be something over a million pounds, including interest.

'You mean the original idea? That we'd eventually go public?'

'That, or a better price when you're that much bigger. From some other American agency.' He ignored the reference to going public. In his opinion that option for RTB had always been remote, otherwise . . .

'It's just that the bank thinks the Crabtree offer is as good as anything we'll ever get.'

'That's got to be nonsense. How do they know . . .'

'Well, relatively better. It's just, one has to think in the long term.'

'Long term?' Grimalt looked quickly from side to side. The bar waiter noticed and did the same, apprehensively.

'But you're only forty-one. Rorch and Timms are still in their thirties.'

'But an advertising agency, if it isn't a public company, and if it doesn't join a multinational, well, some day the owners get to retiring age. Then they have to sell their shares to somebody. But who?' He slurped back the dregs of the melted ice in his glass.

'So why are you tied up with a merchant bank if it isn't so there's someone around to buy your shares when you want?'

Bander cleared his throat. 'That's true, up to a point. The fact is . . .'

'Grenwood, Phipps backed you so they could turn a penny in the medium term, but so far the outlook's unpromising.'

'Only because we had that bad debt.'

'The bankrupt airline. The one you couldn't get covered for credit insurance. The one I said you shouldn't have taken on.'

'Yes, Victor. Well, actually that was after . . . I mean, it was before all airlines were bad news. Anyway—' Bander looked earnest as well as strained—'we recouped the loss. Today we have a list of only nine clients, all big, highly respectable. None of them bills less than half a million. Most are well into seven figures—including OPD Foods, of course.'

'Which we'll come back to.' The remark was especially ominous. 'I'll have cold asparagus, then grilled Dover sole, fresh peas, no potatoes. They have a three-year-old Sancerre that'll go well with that.' Grimalt hadn't looked at the menu handed to him earlier. He believed in demonstrating his decisive nature in small as well as large matters. It was one of the secrets of his success, he said.

'Er . . . same for me. And . . . er . . . could you tell the wine waiter about the Sancerre?'

'Certainly, Mr Bander.' The restaurant manager gathered up the menus and the wine list. 'About ten minutes, sir?'

'That'll be fine. Perhaps we'd better have two more gin

and tonics.' He had capitulated. 'Large ones.'

The manager retreated smiling, and signalled to the bar waiter.

'Fact remains, the bank wants you to take the offer.' Grimalt picked up the thread of the discourse exactly where he had dropped it. 'They'd be even keener if they thought you were going to lose my account.'

Bander knew the colour was draining from his face. 'Victor, you wouldn't? There's no reason.'

'Not if things stay as they are. But if you're selling out, there's every reason. Roger knows it, by the sound of it.'

'But Rog said this morning it wouldn't make any difference to you either way.'

Grimalt frowned. 'Then he's less clued up than I thought he was.' He pulled up his chair and leaned across the table, lowering his voice. 'Right now we have a nice neat arrangement. The agency does sound advertising for OPD. My divisional board is satisfied. The main OPD board is satisfied. Any complaints about agency performance from marketing managers, sales managers, product managers and anyone else get sorted out between you and me. The account's safe. Right?'

'Right, Victor.'

'And what are we billing? Just over five million.'

'Yes, Victor.'

'And what's projected for next year?'

'Five and a half, Victor. If the budgets go through.'

'They'll go through.' Grimalt paused. 'And is the account profitable to the agency?'

'Oh yes, Victor.'

'No squabbles about commission? No bickering over production costs? Peter, no agency ever had it so good. And why?'

Bander looked thoughtful. 'Because we deliver. I mean, you really get service from RTB, Victor.'

'Which I could also get from a dozen other agencies. All right. The agency does a satisfactory job. But it's not perfect. But deep down, you know and I know there's a small insurance policy you keep up. The one that sees I'm

64

always on hand to smooth out your imperfections.'

'Oh, absolutely, Victor. If it weren't for you . . .'

'And for such a small consideration, too.' Grimalt shook his head. 'Unchanged since the start, since you got the account five years ago. Then it was two per cent of the OPD annual billing. And have I ever asked for the premium to be increased?'

'Certainly not, Victor. You've been absolutely good as your word on that.'

As it happened, Grimalt had often considered breaking that word. Each time, though, after counselling with himself, he had decided to let the sum stay at £40,000. People tended not to query costs that recurred each year unchanged—especially auditors. He had seen to it the agency increased what he considered to be only fringe benefits—the provision of airline tickets, cases of wine, theatre seats, that sort of thing. They were marginal but they still helped to improve the pleasures and reduce the costs of the Grimalt style of living.

He tasted his third gin and tonic. 'Yes, I've played straight with the agency all right,' he said, really believing his own words.

'No reason why anything should change if we did sell to the Americans either,' offered Bander with more hope than certainty.

'You don't think so?' The head turned to both sides, then centred. 'Well let me tell you. There'll be an examining audit for a start.'

'But we have auditors in every year. It's the law.'

'Examining auditors do a different job. They look for the unusual. They'll want chapter and verse on a £40,000 a year retainer paid to a Swiss consultant. It won't be the mixture as before to them. They'll want to know what it buys. If it's bought for a client, why the cost isn't passed on.'

Bander took one of his deep breaths. 'But we have all the answers on that. The reports are there, and they're used to improve the advertising.'

'And maybe you get away with it. So let's say you do.

Let's say Crabtree buy you. Then, of course, the real trouble starts.'

'How d'you mean?' Bander's mouth remained open for a moment. 'Roger says Crabtree won't find anything wrong with the er . . . the arrangement. I mean, they say a lot of American agencies have er . . .'

'Well, that's where you and Roger are wrong, or out of date, or ignorant about American practice. So, RTB becomes a consolidated subsidiary of an American corporation, right? So, your books will be examined more carefully by the US Internal Revenue than the books of the corporation that bought you.'

'I don't follow, Victor.'

'Well, you can take my word for it. The American tax people take the view it's easier to do a corporate tax fiddle outside the country than inside it. And they're right. They look for financial dodges through overseas subsidiaries because that's where the dodging's done. Ask anyone who works for an American multinational.' The dark eyes regarded Bander closely. 'On second thoughts, don't.'

'But why should they find our retainer to RDE Counsel any more of a fiddle than our auditors have ever done?'

'That's not the question. They'll know the retainer's tax deductible in the UK. So they'll know it cuts into consolidated profits and taxes in America. It's substantial, so you know what the US Revenue could do? They could write to everyone involved. To RTB, to RDE Counsel, and, last but not least, to OPD Foods. And they ask OPD Foods about the value of this research. And no one at OPD Foods ever heard of this research. So our own R&D people ask to see these marvellous reports. They may even be asked to evaluate them.'

'Hum,' was the only immediate response from the other side of the little table.

Grimalt picked up his nearly empty glass. 'Which is how I could come to lose my job.' This time he had to stem an onrush of righteous protest from his companion. 'Except I'm not going to.' And almost anyone who knew

Grimalt could have guessed that much. 'Because before then I'll have shifted the account to another agency. A British one, more like yours when I gave you the business. I've got one in mind.' He gestured hard with the glass. A small piece of ice shot on to the table, slithered across, and dropped between Bander's feet.

'You think it's as serious as that? If we sell?'

'Sure of it. And you'd better think the same if you want to keep the account.'

Bander took some peanuts from the small dish, put them in the palm of his hand, and regarded them solemnly. 'You don't think we could be exaggerating the problem. Like at the start. I mean, five years ago, we thought you and I being married to sisters, being related . . . remember . . . ?'

'People would say that's why you got the business? Well, I saw to it then they didn't think that. That everyone respected the decision as objective. Nobody on the OPD selection team voted for any of the other agencies. I saw to that too.'

The last claim wasn't true. Nobody had voted for any of the other agencies competing for the business because the RTB presentation had been incomparably the best. RTB had won the account entirely on merit — and kept it ever since for the same reason. Grimalt preferred his brother-in-law to think otherwise. Bander wouldn't have been running so scared now if he hadn't thought Grimalt meant the threats he was making — and that he was entirely able to implement them.

In fact, Grimalt had no wish to change agencies. Apart from the private financial arrangement, he got most of his good ideas from RTB. It was no exaggeration to say that Grimalt's success was due to the agency. What he was wondering now was whether Bander would pass up half a million to keep the OPD account. On balance he thought probably not. But if Rorch was against the sale, that was different: he was supposed to be the brain. The others wouldn't be so stupid as to go ahead with the deal if

Rorch wasn't part of it. And if they had any sense, neither would Crabtree.

'If Roger's against selling, you only have half a deal. And if selling costs you OPD Foods . . .' Grimalt shrugged. He was satisfied his firm-sounding intention would be quickly transmitted to Rorch. Not that he personally cared for Rorch, who made him feel inferior—uncomfortable. Timms was a better marketing man—in Grimalt's opinion, and Laura Cray, the Creative Director of RTB, was just as good as Rorch.

'You don't think Rog will go along with the majority? In the end?' Bander was asking. He was almost pleading. It was a good sign.

'I wouldn't think so.'

'But can he really do anything else?'

'He could wait to get his half million and *then* leave, I suppose. Perhaps he'll take my account with him, not to mention a few others. Make it pretty lonely for you and George.'

The restaurant manager had reappeared. 'Your table's ready, Mr Bander.'

'What? Oh! Thank you. We'll be right in.' He was still holding the nuts in his sweating palm.

Grimalt got up immediately and made for the beamed restaurant, shooting his cuffs at intervals. He was going to enjoy his lunch after all. He should have concentrated on the Rorch situation from the beginning. In the last few minutes he had decided it would be too complicated to try moving the account—whatever happened. He just had to keep Bander fearing the worst—which meant giving Rorch ammunition to fight the others: make them pass up the deal. Rorch could do it.

Without Rorch there would never have been an offer: the others weren't so dim they couldn't see that. The bank would know it too.

Just so long as Rorch didn't change his mind. That was the danger. If it happened Grimalt would have to do something more than threaten. He nodded at the waiter who was holding his chair for him. As he lowered himself into it, he darted glances to left and right. A woman at the next table anxiously did the same, a piece of melon halted on a spoon half way to her gaping mouth.

Grimalt flexed his shoulders and frowned at the slim silver vase of carnations on the table. Rorch must not be part of the deal because without Rorch there could be no deal. 'Q.E.D.,' he said, aloud.

'I'm sorry, Victor?' Bander was apologizing again.

CHAPTER 7

'The way they all baled out, you'd have thought the bank was on fire,' Mark Treasure remarked as he strode back into the dining-room. He had been seeing the Americans out. 'Did I leave a gold pencil? Yes, I did.'

Helen Wintly had returned a moment earlier to collect the papers she had had with her at lunch. She had been down to the street with Rorch and Timms, after they had spent some minutes in her office. 'Roger was furious about the piece in the *Standard*,' she said.

'Don't blame him. Not over-pleased myself.' The banker stepped on the electric foot-bell near where he had been seated. The butler appeared from beyond the green baize door. 'Thank you, Mr Bullmore. We're all done. Nice lunch.' As he pocketed his pencil he noticed the menu card abandoned near Rorch's place. He picked up the card and briefly examined the drawings on the back.

'George Timms is sure the leak came from the Americans in the first place,' offered Helen.

'But not from poor Howie.' Treasure chuckled. 'I must admit, I found his bland honesty totally refreshing.'

'If not exactly helpful when he's dealing with bright newspaper columnists.'

'Ah, but that's just what I mean. His alternative was to lie. And Howard doesn't tell lies. Don't you find that a wholesome trait in this wicked world, Miss Wintly?'

'Of course, Mr Treasure.' They smiled at each other as he motioned her through the door into the corridor.

'Well, I can tell you Mr Lee Jackson doesn't.' He was still holding the menu card which, after a further glance, he slipped into a side pocket. 'He didn't say a word to Howard Junior all the way down in the lift. Mrs Jackson was waiting with their chauffeur. A Southern belle with piercing intonation. Mrs Jackson, I mean, not the chauffeur.' He pulled a face. 'I assume she hadn't been sitting in our garage all through lunch. Didn't like to ask.'

'Of course, George had to cancel their seeing the agency this afternoon. He rang his secretary from my office to set up a staff meeting for five o'clock. Roger wants to talk to everybody. He's cancelled his flight.'

'Where was he going?'

'Not sure. Except it was a domestic shuttle.'

They walked down the wide, thickly carpeted corridor. Treasure held open the swing door on to the quietly opulent, square fourth-floor reception area.

'Got another minute?' he asked.

'Surely.' Her office was on the floor below.

This time, the security guard, who had got up from his desk in the corner, was already holding open the door to the corridor serving the Grenwood, Phipps management suite.

She sat, legs crossed, on the same sofa she had used at their early morning meeting.

Treasure stood behind his desk for a moment thumbing through some papers Miss Gaunt had put there during lunch. 'Before the newspaper revelation, I got the feeling Rorch was coming round to the takeover.'

'Me too,' said the girl. 'And I think he'll come back to it when he's cooled down.'

'Seemed to take to Howard.' He shook his head. 'Odd.' He walked across the room and sat opposite her. 'They came together over their views on agency management.'

She opened her eyes very wide. He noticed she usually registered agreement by doing simply that—and at the same time drawing attention to one of her best features.

70

'In Roger's case the beliefs are better than theoretical,' she said.

'Meaning poor Howard's aren't. One got that impression. The Carter Cousins versus Jebbit, Fowler bout seemed to get postponed.'

'Will Crabtree agree to let Carter take precedence, d'you think?'

'My guess is they'll make noises in that direction till after the deal. Once they own RTB they can do whatever they like over that one.'

'Not if Jackson meant what he said about management autonomy here in London.' Helen spoke seriously.

Treasure grunted. 'In my experience, management autonomy, independence, is a product of satisfactory performance.'

'You mean good profits?'

'No sensible parent company argues with the business strategy of a subsidiary that's making money.'

'But the converse . . .'

'Is bound to apply in this case when RTB profits slump,' Treasure interrupted. 'And, of course, they're bound to next year because of Dandy.'

'There'll be no profits. But that won't be RTB's fault.'

The other shrugged. 'If the London agency's running at a loss, and Crabtree can offer a substantial account available for the asking . . .' He paused. 'Well, to refuse would be crass obstinacy—and profligate.'

'It may not be available for the asking.'

'But Jackson talked as though JF were married to Crabtree.'

'In the States, maybe. The JF management in the UK may have strong loyalties to its present agents here.'

'Hmm. It's well known that JF management in the UK is in trouble. Very unprofitable operation.'

'So we're back to the price of independence?'

'Afraid so. If Jebbit, Fowler here are told to switch their advertising to RTB by their parent company, my guess is they'll have to comply. Of course, by that time Carter Cousins may be established clients of RTB . . .'

71

'And growth clients at that.'

'If they come up to Rorch's expectations. There may be growth in JF too. Depends what view one takes of their diversification antics. How soon they're applied in this country. Objectively, I must say I'd opt for Carter.'

'May I say you'd favour Crabtree announcing they have no expectations of picking up the JF account here?'

He looked quizzical in reply. 'Say? To whom?'

'Howie and Jackson. I'll be seeing them tomorrow at the agency. It'd please Roger to have your backing.'

Treasure made a series of puffing noises with his lips. 'I don't see why not. Except it might be more appropriate for Crabtree corporately to say they warmly support the RTB bid to land the Carter business. Would seem less potentially embarrassing for them at home, while achieving the same object.'

'Terrific. Thank you.'

'You said Bander's in favour of selling. Pity he had to cut lunch. Urgent summons to OPD. D'you suppose they'd heard about the bid?'

'If they hadn't, they will have by now.' She hesitated before going on. 'Mr Karilian said the Chairman of OPD is a close friend of yours. A change of agency ownership sometimes upsets clients. You wouldn't consider commending the Crabtree offer to him?'

'To make sure the Food Division doesn't fire RTB?' He frowned. 'Don't think so. That kind of special pleading usually backfires.' Then he broke into a smile. 'Level of approach too high. A word to the chairman — any chairman — can often be the kiss of death. But don't worry. If necessary we'll find a way of getting the message across lower down in the organization. But isn't there a familiar connection already?'

She nodded. 'Peter Bander's brother-in-law is Marketing Director. I'm afraid he could be the problem. Peter has the feeling he may be against using an American-owned advertising agency.'

'Curiously chauvinist.' Treasure shook his head. 'Well, perhaps he has good reason. If the account is, as it were, in his gift. If it's RTB's biggest . . .'

'It is,' Helen put in.

'Then perhaps his view should carry weight. Don't be wholly determined by what Harry Karilian said. He cautioned you not to be. I must say, I'm not wildly impressed with Jackson.'

'Nor me.'

'But you're still keen for the deal to go through?'

'On balance, I still think it's right for the agency. And for the bank.'

'George Timms obviously agrees. Strange chap. Less demonstrative . . . less assertive than I remember. Very much playing second fiddle today. Didn't want to ruffle Rorch. Didn't put his point of view nearly as forcefully as one felt he wanted to.'

'He was very upset at the end.'

'Defensive. Worried Rorch might think he'd tipped off the press. D'you think he did?'

'Out of character, but just possible,' she answered with some reluctance. 'It's something that's going to move things along faster. Roger's tactic is to delay.'

'Mmm. Wonder if Timms would have risked it? I imagine Rorch gives him a very hard time if he misbehaves.'

'If it came from our side, we should have been warned,' said Howie, petulantly. He was seated beside Joanne Jackson in the rear of the Jaguar. Lee Jackson was directly in front of him beside the driver. It was not a disposition that made for easy communication between the two men. The presence of the chauffeur was an added complication.

'We were warned. At least, you were,' Jackson replied, staring stonily at a chain-store advertisement on the rear of a bus stopped a few inches ahead of the Jaguar's bonnet. 'Currys — the Electrical People' read the message: Jackson refused to be sparked.

'But I said "no comment". They didn't get a thing from me.' Still obdurate, Howie concentrated his regard on the

Bank of England which they had been fitfully creeping past for several minutes.

'Would you boys rather I sat in front? We could switch. We're not moving.' The chauffeur coughed nervously at Joanne's suggestion. Playing musical chairs through at least two doors of a large car in the middle of a post-lunch City traffic-jam was not going to endear him to the several policemen coping with the chaos. One set of traffic lights was out of action. He edged the Jaguar a fraction closer to the bus.

Joanne knew she should have taken the front seat when they came down from lunch. At the time it had seemed wrong for her to be cosied up in a garage with a handsome chauffeur.

'It's not far,' said Jackson. 'We're moving now.'

They had broken through the bottleneck and were pushing across into Queen Victoria Street.

'The drive we took before we met you, it was just dilly. Julian here is the greatest guide,' Joanne offered with more than usual gusto. 'Traffic wasn't as heavy as now, wouldn't you say, Julian?

'Yes, madam.'

'We took in the Law Courts, Smithfield Market, the Old Bailey—that's where they have the criminal trials. Do you know the Fleet River runs right under Farringdon Street? Underground? It crosses Fleet Street at Ludgate Circus and runs into the Thames at . . . er . . . ?'

'Blackfriars Bridge, madam.'

'Isn't that the truth? Say, can we go back on Ludgate Hill, Julian? I'd like these men to see St Bride's Church. That's the Wren Church in Fleet Street with the tiered steeple.'

'A lot of them have tiered steeples, honey.' Jackson had been to London before.

'This one's special. It was used as the basic design for *all* wedding cakes. Imagine that? Our very own wedding cake was tiered because St Bride's . . . Say, do you-all have the time to take in St Paul's Cathedral right now? We've got to go right past it. It has to be *the* most . . .'

74

'No, but I'll tell you what, honey,' her husband interrupted. 'Howie and I'll get out there, and walk back to the Savoy. You can take in St Paul's, and Julian here can wait for you. That all right with you, Howie?'

'Sure,' agreed Howie, glad to be escaping from the travelogue.

A minute later, the two men were walking down Ludgate Hill with the cathedral behind them. The freeze between them was beginning to thaw. Howie was feeling a fraction more repentant and culpable. Jackson was steeling himself to remember his companion was also his boss—that Howie could afford to forget about 'phone calls from newspapers if he chose.

'I'll call Joe Ziebal from the suite. He may have arranged the leak. He does things like that sometimes— without warning. May have figured it would speed things along.'

'You don't know it was Ziebal?' Howie, sounding suspicious, had to hurry to keep up with Jackson as they crossed Ludgate Circus into Fleet Street.

'Certainly not. Could be it was his insider working on his own initiative. What's the matter?'

Howie's expression was pained. 'Stepped in something.'

'They don't kerb dogs in this country.' He watched Howie attempt without a great deal of success to clean his shoe on the kerbstone. 'You can be darned sure it wasn't Rorch who told the newspaper,' he went on as the other fell in beside him with a bow-legged gait.

'Rorch is good. Very good. D'you think he'll come over?'

'He was moving in that direction.'

'Up to the time Mark's secretary brought in the paper.' Howie was standing on one foot studying the instep of the offending shoe.

Jackson waited for him to catch up before replying. 'He doesn't want to pass up this Carter outfit.' He glowered across the road at the shiny black Express Newspapers building. Lettering on the fascia acknowledged the *Standard* belonged to the group.

'Could be a big gain for the agency.' Howie was now dragging one foot along the kerb as he walked. A hurrying messenger boy stumbled over it. The boy mouthed an obscenity at the hapless American who now had a wounded ankle as well as an anti-social shoe.

'Or it could be a burnish for Rorch's oversized ego,' grumbled Jackson, looking ahead and largely oblivious of Howie's mounting discomforts. 'The guy's got a fixation about Carter Cousins. RTB is only being offered one lousy development assignment.'

'Well, he seemed to me to be a fine, talented young man.' Howie limped along stoutly.

'Well, I'd say that agency owes more to George Timms than the so-called hot-shot Roger Rorch.'

'But it's Roger who gets the new business.'

'What new business? Most of their accounts they've had since the start. OPD is the biggest. It was brought in by Bander, the one we haven't met. Regal Sun, the insurance company, and the mail order company, Post Emporium, they both came from the agency Rorch and Timms were with before they started RTB. I tell you, it'd be interesting to know which of their eight prime accounts were actually fished by Roger Rorch.'

'The airline was one. Excuse me.'

Jackson turned to see Howie deep in negotiation with the owner of a side-street hot-dog cart. A coin changed hands, leaving Howie in possession of a sheaf of thick paper napkins.

'The airline went bankrupt,' said Jackson, supporting Howie while he stood on one leg again, removed and cleaned his shoe with the napkins, replaced the shoe after first thrusting the bunched napkins on to his companion, then set off again briskly. 'Howie,' Jackson went on, looking for a trash can, 'I believe Rorch *needs* that Carter business to justify his image. He needs it maybe more than he needs half a million pounds.'

'I can't believe that.'

'You'd have to believe it if we bought RTB and because of a piddling piece of Carter Cousins business they tried to turn down JF.' He thrust the napkins into a street bin. 'Howie, if we buy an agency here it has to handle JF. We're committed. The JF board have agreed our figures on the commission rebate. Hell, you worked them out. Means a big saving for JF internationally as we buy more offices. It's why they held up going to an international agency last year.'

'I thought that was because no one would accept the cut rates they were demanding?' answered Howie, frowning.

'Well, that was partly it. Anyhow, they've agreed a co-ordinated volume discount with us in all countries we move into. So we have two ready-made international accounts. JF and Dandy. Except if we can't deliver for JF in England, we could now lose the account in America — and Canada, and Brazil.'

'Well, I think we have to explain the JF situation more clearly to Roger. I'm sure he'll understand.' Howie nodded firmly. 'Say, I think my father will go for Roger. In fact, I think HJ will want him on the board in the States. Maybe it'd be a good thing if we had him work in New York for a while. To acclimatize on the Dandy account. You said yourself George Timms could run RTB here.'

Lee Jackson kept walking, but mentally Howie's suggestion had stopped him in his tracks. He knew how the man's mind was working.

The seed had been sown before they left New York. HJ had gone a bundle on buying RTB — as much on the report Ziebal had filed on Rorch as on the record of the agency. The old man hadn't said so — but Joanne had, and she was usually right about the old man.

Jackson was a realist. Deep down he knew HJ had delayed his retirement all those years not just because he didn't see his son as a worthy successor: he didn't see Jackson as the perfect President either. But HJ hadn't found anyone who would do better than Jackson — not in America at least.

The old man had set up some clandestine executive

searching: Jackson knew it but couldn't prove it. He even suspected Ziebal had been involved at one time: he couldn't prove that either — and he couldn't ask Ziebal without losing face. In any case, nobody new had appeared. HJ hadn't suddenly recruited anyone into the top echelons of Howard J. Crabtree Inc. who could figure as a challenger to Jackson for the Presidency. Maybe no one HJ considered good enough for the job had wanted the job.

Only now did Jackson realize he might have come to London as the instrument arranging his own downfall. What if they bought RTB, and what if HJ took as big a shine to Rorch as Howie had done? What if Rorch went to work for the agency in New York, agreed to stay there, and got promoted to be President?

He pulled Howie back from being mown down by a hurtling 171 bus — and almost too late.

'Want to watch it. It's a filter. Ever so dangerous. You all right, love?' asked the middle-aged woman standing beside them. 'Good thing this gentleman was quick.'

It was then Jackson made up his mind: then, while he and the shaken Howie and the middle-aged woman waited till it was safe to cross Lancaster Place into the Strand. It would be better all round if Crabtree bought RTB without Rorch. Howie had been right in the first place. They didn't need a high flyer: just a sound agency.

And RTB would come cheaper without Rorch. He'd make that point to Howie in a minute. Howie had to be stopped from pushing Rorch's stock so high that the man sounded indispensable.

'Looks safer now,' said Howie. They stepped into the road.

Jackson decided he wouldn't feel safe till Rorch was out of the picture.

CHAPTER 8

'So we're having talks, that's all. You could almost say we're just having talks about having talks. It's got no further than that. I'm sorry you all got the news from the paper. I repeat, the thing's premature. We don't know who leaked the story, but up to now there really is no story. If the talks get serious, we'll tell you. If we did sell we'd make sure everybody benefited. So that's it, boys and girls. If you have questions I'll try to answer them, but honestly you know about as much as I do already.'

Rorch pushed the lank hair back from his forehead. It had been a jerky, nervous talk—not his usual relaxed style: everyone knew that, including himself. He stayed standing in front of the cinema screen in the big RTB presentation room in the basement of the Red Lion Square offices. He was in shirtsleeves, cuffs rolled back to just below the elbows, hands on hips.

There had been enough chairs for everyone—twenty expensively upholstered ones that lived in the room, and another thirty orange-coloured stacking chairs stored outside in the projection room. The sectional tables had been collapsed and put to one side.

It was close in the low-ceilinged room, even though the air-conditioning was working at full throttle.

Fifty-three out of the sixty-strong staff members were there. They were most of them young, like the company. To the uninitiated, appearances would have been a misleading guide as to the income, standing or—at first glance—even the sex of some present.

Some of the better paid favoured bleached and sometimes tattered denim—the prevailing gear for comforming individualists in 'creative' jobs in advertising.

Male members of the executive staff—and there weren't many female ones—although in the main lower earners, affected a more affluent and civilized appearance. Some even sported waistcoats with their blue or grey suits: none wore brown. At weekends they donned the colourful clothing their neighbours in the executive-style housing estates of St Albans, Weybridge and Great Missenden expected of people in advertising.

At weekends the 'creative' people went on wearing exactly what they wore in the week—and let their neighbours go on thinking they were unemployed.

Employees in the media buying and production departments tended towards a middle course—never tatty like the writers and visualizers, which would have confused visiting clients, but not so well turned out as to give management the impression they were being paid too much.

The accountants dressed like accountants.

There was total silence following Rorch's invitation to questioners.

The five chairs that constituted the front row were unoccupied. The people seated immediately behind these were carefully studying the mottled green carpet—except for a seventeen-year-old copy-typist with dyed blonde hair, a gold crucifix around her neck, and a sexy, off-the-shoulder blouse. She was studying all visible parts of Rorch, making estimates on the invisible, and wishing her current boyfriend talked a bit posher. She hadn't been interested in the purpose of the meeting.

People further back looked generally solemn, and less afraid that a glance at the speaker would be taken as indicating a burning desire to ask a question.

The three male executives standing near the door all felt evidently more conspicuous now anyone on his feet might be expected to utter.

It was George Timms who eventually broke the silence.

'If we should merge with Crabtree, and as Roger says, we're a long way from deciding that one way or the other, but if we should merge with Crabtree, of course there'd be no redundancies. They have no London office. We'd probably have to take on more staff to handle the extra business.'

80

Timms had stood up to speak. He had been seated at the side of the room, near the back. His comments produced a murmur of approval, but not a very loud one.

'Would we get the Jebbit, Fowler account as well as Dandy? I worked on it at Fentley's. It's a sod.'

The young woman who spoke had short, spiky-cut red hair, wore a lot of make-up, a pair of huge dark glasses pushed up over her hair, and a faded green open-necked shirt over whitish jeans. She was a talented copywriter who earned five times as much as her father—a disillusioned Norfolk vicar.

'Then it doesn't sound like our kind of account, Jenny,' Rorch had answered swiftly. 'And we're pitching for a competitor right now, as you all know. OK?'

The girl nodded. Timms had looked uncomfortable at the reply.

'If we take on Dandy with no commission,' began a voice from the back, 'I mean, they say you have to work for Dandy for three years for nothing . . . er . . . if that meant no profits for three years . . . er . . . would that mean no staff profit share . . . Roger?'

The halting question came from one of the fresh-faced account executives near the door. He was twenty-five, an economics graduate, and just about to get married. He worked on OPD Foods and the Regal Sun Assurance accounts—both big profit-earners for the company, and he knew it.

Rorch clasped his hands behind his head, smiled languidly and let his gaze drift from face to face. The blonde copy-typist gave an involuntary quiver. 'If we sell to Crabtree—and it's a big if,' he began, looking purposely at Timms because he had avoided using the other's euphemism about merging, 'then as I said, the whole staff will benefit.' He folded his arms in front of him, and began pacing the width of the room. 'That's in the short term as well as the long. On the profit-sharing, we'd find a formula to compensate if . . . if we handled Dandy without commission or fee.'

There were approving nods from people who had been

with the company over a year—the time required to qualify for a profit share. The question had caused a discernible stir. The chief accountant, for one, hadn't liked the answer. For him, what Rorch had promised spelled complications.

Again there was silence.

A staff communication had been made--belatedly, and in a way under duress, as everybody knew. The management believed in staff participation—except the staff wouldn't be participating in the decision to sell or not to sell: everybody knew that too. So there had been very little point in the meeting except to make the management feel self-righteous and enlightened—to make up for being caught out at not communicating.

Rorch stopped pacing, and looked at his watch. 'So. If there are no more questions, everybody take the rest of the day off—if you've got no work to do.'

It was 5.20. There were some sycophantic smiles at the loaded invitation, and some desultory conversation as the people filed out.

'Well, that was a happy little gathering,' said Rorch bitterly a few minutes later. He and Timms were in Timms's office on the first floor.

Laura Cray and Barny Smith were with them. They were both on the board of the company but not shareholders.

Laura was Creative Director. She was thirty—a big, jolly woman with a weight problem, a five-year-old daughter, and a skinny husband who was a legal executive with a law firm in North London.

Barny Smith was Media Director, twenty-seven, single, and lived with his widowed mother in Chislehurst. He was below medium height, dark and bearded. His head, a fraction too large for his slight, tapering body, was generally bent to one side. This, allied to a characteristically dour expression, built up to the impression he was always on the verge of saying something profound.

He dressed well—if conspicuously—in hand-tailored

clothes meant to presage trends in male fashion, but which rarely caught on.

He had been with the agency less than a year—'head-hunted' at the time RTB had decided it was time to set up an internal space- and time-buying department. Up to that time the agency had worked through specialist buying companies, a common practice by the smaller agencies.

Smith had been lured from one of the best time-buying companies. A directorship had been part of the transfer fee. He had also wanted, but failed as yet to obtain, an option on shares in the company. This failure had bothered him. It upset the ingredients of his planned career pattern. Even so, Joe Ziebal had strongly advised him to accept the job.

'Isn't Peter back from OPD?' Rorch walked towards a window.

It was a smaller office than Rorch's, and at the rear of the building. It got the sun in the afternoon, but the view was on to the backs of some municipal flats.

'Poor Peter. Victor Grimalt's been pressuring him lately anyway.' Laura took a cigarette from the pack of 555 Extra Long she kept in the pocket of her loose-fitting Laura Ashley smock. She dropped into a handy armchair, lighting the cigarette from the red disposable lighter hanging on a leather cord around her neck.

'Grimalt should worry. We're delivering on average twelve per cent better rating points per TV exposure . . .'

'Oh, shut up about rating points, Barny, there's a love,' Laura interrupted. 'We all know you're good.' She smiled in a motherly way at the Media Director who was squatting on the ledge of the second window. 'We don't need you to remind us at unscientific times of the day.' She made a kissing motion at him with her big, generous lips. She was the only member of the agency who could talk to him that way and get away with it. 'Slimline tonic with gin and ice, please, George,' she added pleadingly to Timms. He nodded, smiled, and went to unlock his drinks cupboard. His secretary had already brought in some ice.

'All I meant was, with Dandy and probably JF we'll have even more buying clout as an agency. Good for all the clients,' said Smith.

'Well, good for you, love.'

'But meaning we don't have enough clout now?' Timms paused, bottle in hand.

'We could do with more. To justify my being here. And my department.' It was better he said what other people were thinking. It had cost the agency a lot less to buy its TV advertising time through outside intermediaries, the way it had done before he was recruited. Probably the clients were no better nor no worse off. So in terms of professional efficiency there was nothing in it—only a net loss on the profits to RTB. 'A big increase in billing would work wonders with my department costs,' he added.

'Profitable billing, of course,' offered Rorch quietly.

'You mean there won't be any proper lolly from Dandy for a bit.' Laura drew in deeply on her cigarette.

Timms raised a questioning eyebrow at Barny, who pointed towards a can of Coca-Cola.

'Well, you're all a damned sight too early with your prognostications about what'll happen after the takeover.' Rorch sauntered over to the drinks cupboard and helped himself to a large gin and a little tonic. 'If you take the tone of that meeting, the kiddies aren't a bit keen about being sold to the Indians.' He grabbed a handful of ice cubes and dropped them into his glass.

'Nothing like a touch of democratic fervour. Jacks up the honesty of conviction no end.' Laura was as outspoken with the Chairman as she was with everyone else. 'Come on, Roger love. When did you last take the pleas of the peasantry into account?'

Rorch turned to her slowly. He was smiling. 'More recently than the rest of you, probably. Why d'you think people like working here? The way we are now, I mean. If we'd always been the London branch of Crabtree, half of them wouldn't have joined in the first place.'

'With enormous respect, bullshit,' countered the Creative Director. 'The slaves like your style, specially your Peter O'Toole sang-froid. They respect your methods, also the size of their salaries. They even forgive you for exercising seignorial rights.' She pulled a face. 'Like the Creative Director doesn't get a smell of the Carter project till you've planned the whole bloody campaign.' She poked her tongue out at Rorch.

'Oh, come on, Laura, I'm only saving everybody . . .'

'Time they need for other things. I know, darling, and I understand. And I don't mind. Well, I do mind, but I strive for the greater good. And deep down I probably *want* you to rape me.'

'Laura's right, Roger,' put in Barny. 'People work here because you—that is, we—pay well. You can forget the rest. The employee benefits. The *esprit de corps* and all that jazz. It's the same everywhere. Given more money, most people will shift or stay, as the case may be.' He was nearly describing his own attitude. He certainly felt no sense of guilt because he had an interview arranged for another job at the end of the week—one that included an equity stake. The RTB profit-sharing scheme was fine, but it didn't make you a fortune at takeover time. On balance, he'd probably stay with the agency if the Crabtree deal went through. Being head of media-buying at Crabtree's second biggest office introduced a new dimension.

'So nobody rates company loyalty. What we stand for? Where we've said we're heading?' Rorch's tone was tempered, inquiring—not abrasive. He stood looking into his glass. Only Timms believed he might be very angry—or desperately sad.

'Those things obviously mean a lot to you, love. I wasn't meaning to knock them. You and George and Peter will have to pass up a packet if you turn down the offer. Kind of makes your point. Can you say how much they're offering?'

The size of the bid hadn't yet been disclosed to Laura or to Smith: she was fishing with her question.

'It's not relevant yet. Better it's not disclosed unless it has to be. Puts a price on the agency that sticks, otherwise,' said Rorch. 'Says what we think our independence was worth,' he added with coolness.

'I think you're over-dramatizing, Roger,' put in Timms. 'At lunch . . .'

'You and I were being conned by people who'd had the arrogance to tell the *Standard* about *their* plans. That was on the assumption they could railroad us that much quicker into accepting them as our plans too.' Rorch stepped over to the cupboard and poured himself another drink. 'All right. Just so long as Laura and Barny have the picture. They're directors. They should know what we may be letting ourselves in for.'

'You said the Americans are coming for talks in the morning, that they'd have been here this afternoon if it hadn't been . . .'

'They're invited because the bank and at least one other shareholder thinks we should honour a promise.' Rorch had cut in on Smith. 'Sure they're coming. But I shan't be seeing them.'

'How d'you mean, Roger?' Timms asked in surprise.

'Because I have work to do. I won't be here. There's a deadline on Carter Cousins, remember? I've got a peach of a concept that's very nearly ready. I need tomorrow . . .' He paused, looking at the time. 'Hell, I need tonight to work on it.' He looked at Laura. 'Don't worry, the decencies will be observed. You'll all be here. Peter too. Lined up for inspection. Frank Moss is bringing the figures up to date.' Moss was the chief accountant and company secretary.

There was a ring from one of the telephones on Timms's desk. He answered it. 'It's for you Roger. Carter Cousins.'

'At last. And I hope it's not to say goodbye. Been trying to reach them all afternoon. Take it in my office.' Rorch hurried out.

Laura heaved herself up from her chair. 'Got some work to approve. Should be ready. Thanks for the drink,

George.' She left too, fumbling in her pocket for her cigarettes.

'The rumour is you'll be getting half a million each.' Barny sipped his Coca-Cola.

Timms shrugged. 'You heard what Roger said.'

'I understand. But whatever it is, it'll be quite something to pass up.'

'Except if Roger's not selling . . .'

'Roger may not want to sell, but he'll have to in the end. That's if the rest of you outvote him.'

'It's not quite as simple as that. We'd get the money, sure. But Roger might leave.'

Smith looked puzzled. 'Crabtree aren't making the offer dependent on all three of you signing long-term contracts?'

'Lee Jackson told me they don't believe in contracts.'

'So they're not expecting to have any hold on any of you? Not after they buy the agency? They must be crazy.'

The other shrugged. 'Jackson insists they're buying the company, not a group of indispensable individuals. They don't hold with the personality cult.'

'It's a point of view,' commented Smith, but there was doubt in his tone. 'So if Roger's outvoted and leaves with the money . . . ?'

'So we're left without . . . well . . .'

'So we're left with you as Chairman,' Smith put in firmly. 'Also with fifty per cent more billing, one less fat director's salary and expenses, Laura running creative, and share options in Crabtree Inc. for everyone with sense enough to take them up.'

Timms had been polishing his glasses. Now he put them on again, studying Barny Smith more carefully than ever he had done before—even on the day he had hired him. From the start, he had seen Smith as sound management succession material.

'You're still fixed on holding shares. I don't blame you. If we ever went public, of course . . .'

'There'd be options for all. Big deal. This agency will never go public, but Crabtree is owned by its employees.'

'Most American agencies are.'

'I've taken the trouble to get the details on this one. The family have a big holding, but out of five hundred and ten employees, a hundred and sixteen are shareholders. The share price has increased on average ten per cent compound every year for the last decade. And they're valued strictly against real assets. Now that's the kind of democracy I subscribe to.'

'You have to find the money to buy the shares in the first place, Barny.'

The Media Director shook his head. 'Can be done on a loan scheme. They lend you the money to buy the shares. The dividend is used to cancel out the interest. Plenty of American companies do that. The employee still owns the shares. Gets the capital gain when he leaves, or retires. I tell you, it's a legitimate way of printing money.' He paused. 'It'd be a good way of investing some of your loot.'

'Except, as I keep telling you, without Roger . . .'

'We'd save money.' He calculated whether this was the moment to dangle the fattest carrot: he decided it was. 'And who knows? You could end up running Crabtree's New York office.'

'How d'you mean?'

'The source of my information about the shares says there's an acute shortage of top management at Crabtree. They're always looking for people. Never get any. Not in the States.'

'But Roger could . . .'

'I don't believe Roger would fit. Not his kind of agency. Remember you said they don't hold with personality cult stuff? Roger's much too autocratic. They like sound company men.' He nearly added 'collectivists': instead he went on, 'You'd fit, George. Like a glove, from what I've been told.'

'Who told you?'

'A friend. He's with an American agency in London. Knows Crabtree's well.'

'Not Ziebal?'

'Certainly not.'

The Media Director was quietly checking Timm's every reaction. Barny's thinking was several jumps ahead of the scenario he was propounding. It was no daydream to imagine Roger Rorch out of the picture, not the way things were going. It was even possible Timms could be shipped to New York—though he had sewn that seed more to feed the other man's ego than for any other reason. Either way, there could soon be a lot more room at the top for competent Barny Smith. He was sure he would shortly be facing the opportunity of a lifetime—all through the passing of Roger Rorch.

'I wouldn't vote for the merger if Roger didn't.'

Smith was brought back to earth with a bump by Timms's flat pronouncement.

'You can't mean that?'

'I do, you know.'

The other man was silent. He had to decide whether Timms was telling the truth. Timms had to make the same decision about himself—which was an even harder thing to do.

CHAPTER 9

At the time Roger Rorch had begun addressing the RTB staff meeting—and two hundred miles north of Red Lion Square—Karen Gradely stepped off the double-decker bus in St Peter's Square, Manchester. She immediately moved towards her ultimate destination which was directly in front of her—the Corinthian portico of the Central Library.

She was a pretty, well-built twenty-two-year-old. Her long, straight, flaxen hair was well brushed and caught in a pony-tail. Her skin was a rich bronze—including most of the bits not on display. Since leaving Warwick University in June, she had spent the summer working as a sailboard instructor in Majorca. In two weeks' time she was starting work as a trainee copywriter with RTB. The job had been confirmed in writing that morning. She had returned to England for the final interview on the previous Friday.

It would have been fun to go back to the Mediterranean for those two weeks, but someone else had taken her place at the sailing school. In any case she owed it to her parents to spend a little time with them before leaving again. She had already arranged to share a flat with two girlfriends in London. The parental home was in Sale, near Manchester. That was why Mr Rorch had called her: he had remembered—said one of the reasons she'd got the job was because she came from north of Watford. Most of the other candidates were Home Counties, apparently. They'd joked at the time about the need for some northern leavening in London-produced advertising. Mrs Cray had said something similar: Karen had been interviewed by her first, then Mr Rorch.

It was an odd kind of assignment he'd given her on the telephone an hour before. Important though, he'd explained, and very urgent. At worst people might think her dotty—but at least she wouldn't be arrested. She'd been warned you could get involved doing crazy things in advertising.

Her appearance was neat and conservative—a pale yellow frock, white sandals and a matching shoulder-bag. This was a technical experiment, after all, not a demonstration—it had only sounded like a demo when he first told her what to do. She only wished Mr Rorch had told her the end purpose of the exercise.

Once inside the library she made for the huge, circular reading-room under the big dome. She knew the place well enough. She had come here sometimes to work during the vacations—though she preferred the John Rylands Library in Deansgate which, in a way, was quieter.

Feeling increasingly less confident with every step, she moved down one of the walk-ways that radiated like spokes from the centre between the circles of reading desks. Although it was late, the library was still fairly full. This helped her purpose though it increased her nervousness.

Naturally she remembered the curious acoustics. Most big libraries—churches too—tended to shut off noise from the outside, almost daring you to make any inside. But this particular library had been designed in the 'thirties as something extra special—in all kinds of ways: in one way it was extra noiseless.

Outside, Manchester bustled and teemed: the second biggest, busiest city in Britain. A few steps inside and you entered a sound vacuum, a pall of silence that was almost tactile—created without obtrusive or obstructive technical equipage. All exterior noise was eliminated, but, in contrast, the sounds made by those inside the building were acknowledged, even acclaimed, by massive, perverse amplification. And everyone who uses the building knows of this curious property. Karen knew it: Mr Rorch knew of it.

Only a very insensitive person tears off the crackling wrappings of a chocolate bar in the reading-room of the Manchester Central Library—because the effect resembles the scraping of jagged metal against concrete. To drop a book is to create an indoor thunderclap: to drop several is like letting off an artillery barrage: normal human speech resounds like enthusiastic public oratory.

Karen stopped as near to the centre of the great room as she could get. She turned about, her back touching the main inquiry desk. She removed the paperback copy of *Romeo and Juliet* from her bag, opened it at the appointed place, cleared her throat, swallowed, then began to read exactly in the way she had been directed.

'I gave the chap fifteen minutes because my secretary described him as desperate. I think she was right,' said Mark Treasure over the telephone to George Timms.

'But he just barged in on you. I'm sorry if . . .'

'Nothing to be sorry about. He got here around three-thirty. Announced himself as Stuart Fentley, Chairman of Fentley Advertising, and a friend of yours.'

'That's what I mean. I've known him for years, of course. So has Roger . . . well, not so long . . . Peter Bander too.'

'So he said.'

'But we're none of us that close to him. To use my name so he could . . .'

'Shows it's a good name to drop,' Treasure observed tactfully. 'Miss Gaunt said I was tied up for at least an hour. He said he'd wait on the off-chance of seeing me. Couldn't disclose his business, except to say he was controlling shareholder in Fentley, and that he needed to see me about the Crabtree report. She offered to try Helen Wintly for him, but he wasn't buying. More fool him. She knows a hell of a lot more about advertising than I do. Better-looking, too.'

'He could have come to me first.'

'He may do now. What's the time? Good lord, it's gone six. Time to go home. He left here over an hour ago. Probably brooding on what I said.'

'And he wanted the bank to buy his company?'

'Not sure he really knew what he wanted. He'd read the news. Jumped to the conclusion he'd lost the JF account. I gather it's the backbone of his business. So, on impulse he comes round to beg us to take on Fentley Advertising. To replace RTB, as he put it. I explained that wasn't quite how the bank worked . . .'

'That you'd backed us from the start.'

'With a minority holding, and a short-term loan. Yes.'

'And did he appreciate that forty-year-old, second-generation, fading agencies aren't quite the same thing?'

'Is that how you'd describe the company?'

'In the trade, it's know as Faintly Advertising. Bit unfair. It's not doing that badly, but thirty years ago it was one of the big names.'

'Built up by this chap's father?'

'Mmm. Hard man to follow, I suppose. Died ten years ago. Stuart's keen. Not untalented. Actually more of a creative man than a manager. Creative in the advertising sense, I mean. He's not aggressive enough.'

'He got in to see me,' Treasure chuckled.

'You mean he got lucky? He doesn't really understand business.'

'Age?'

'Oh, late thirties.'

'Seems older. Tough, though. Looks like a well-heeled, middle-weight boxer. But one who's been losing bouts. He said they bill between eight and nine million.'

'Yes, and pretty static. No new business for years. They've lost some, which means they're only keeping up the billing figures through inflation.'

'He said he was looking for growth through JF until he heard the Crabtree news . . .'

'And assumed JF would switch to us if the deal goes through.'

'Precisely. I must say it seemed to me a daft time to try selling Fentley Advertising to a merchant bank as an exciting risk venture.'

'As I said, Stuart's not really a business man.'

'So it seems. On the other hand, I had the feeling there's a deal in there for someone. That he just needed to go away and put his act together.'

'They own the freehold, or a long lease on their premises.'

'Long lease,' Treasure confirmed. 'Quite valuable, he said. Twenty thousand square feet in a fairly classy bit of Belgravia. It'd make sense to separate that from the trading company, sell the lease to a property group, then merge the agency with a bigger one.'

'Is that what you told him?'

'Indicated gently would describe it better. There are some locked-in capital reserves, too. Cash.' Uttering the word produced an involuntary pause, but one born of speculation not reverence. 'You can always sell money at a discount if that's the only way to unblock it. I must say the family seems to have been badly advised, assuming they've been advised at all. Fentley seemed anxious to get out of running the show on his own. Got to the end of his tether. That's the feeling I got, anyway. The JF news must have signalled the end was in sight.'

'Did he tell you about the shareholder relatives who don't work in the business but rely on the dividends?'

'Yes. His mother and two married sisters. They have sixty per cent of the shares between them. Apparently they're breathing over his shoulder the whole time. It's why he wanted us to buy the company. Of course I told him he was in the wrong shop. I also said he shouldn't be so precipitate.'

'Taking our deal with Crabtree for granted?'

'Mmm. If it doesn't go through, or even if it does and Jebbit, Fowler don't change agencies after all, he'd be in a much stronger position as a seller.'

'And that's when you suggested selling the lease separately, and so on?'

'Yes. Heaven knows why I give away priceless advice to anyone who drops in.' The banker laughed. 'Yes, I do. It was because Miss Gaunt said he looked suicidal. Oh, incidentally, I told him since you were all such chums he really ought to chat things over with one of you. I got the feeling the idea embarrassed him. I said I'd have a word first. Hence this call. Is there any reason for his diffidence?'

There was a slight pause before Timms replied. 'No. I'll ring him. It was really very good of you . . .'

'No, it wasn't. It's put me in my secretary's good books. He obviously brought out the mothering instinct in her. Something else too. If the Crabtree deal does go through, and you pick up the JF business, you might persuade Crabtree to buy the agency to merge with you. We have a client who might be interested in first option on the Belgravia lease.'

'That could work, yes.'

'The lease sale should practically see off Fentley's mother and sisters in terms of their cash expectancy. The trading bit of the company, the agency, will be worth a lot less but the cash reserves may be enough to cover their sixty per cent holding in that. Fentley would probably settle for shares in Crabtree instead of cash. He'll get cash too from the lease, of course.'

'So Crabtree could get the agency for nothing?'

'In a manner of speaking.'

'It could pay them better to buy the company as it stands. With the lease, I mean.'

'Probably. Anyway, I didn't suggest merging with you to Fentley. If you and the others are interested, you should look into it. Tell me, how have things gone since our somewhat abrupt parting after lunch?'

'More or less as expected. We had the *Financial Times* and the trade magazines clamouring for information. I had to deal with them. Roger didn't come straight back here with me. He did address the staff later, though.'

'Reaction?'

'Not much. Wait and see attitude, really.'

'And the Crabtree duo descend on you in the morning. That's still on?'

'Yes, except Roger won't be here. Helen's promised to be. Peter Bander will make it, I hope. He's not back from OPD yet. Probably went straight home.' Timms hesitated. 'I've been wondering about my own situation. If Roger votes against selling, but Peter and the bank want to go ahead, and I stood with Roger . . .'

'It'd be stalemate. Except you're assuming too much about Grenwood, Phipps. With two of the shareholders against, I think we'd have to consider our position very carefully.'

'You mean change it? So there'd be no sale?'

'Possibly. It's Helen's opinion, and mine too, it'd be an opportunity missed. So let's hope Roger comes round. You're very loyal to him.'

'You think too loyal?' He didn't wait for a reply. 'Actually, there's more to it than loyalty. We complement each other. In our work. Peter's part of it too. If we broke up . . .'

'You're assuming Roger would leave the agency if it were sold against his wishes?'

'I'm sure of it. But you don't think so?'

'Your opinion ought to be better than mine. But . . .
no. I think he'd grumble a bit, then probably soldier on.
Discover later he'd made the right decision after all.'

'That's encouraging. It's such a pity the offer's come
like a rushing mighty wind.'

'The new translation of the Bible reads "strong driving
wind" — not nearly so apposite or evocative.' The banker
pouted. 'Frankly, I'd advise all of you to keep your
options open. Take time to draw breath. I must go.'

Timms sat for a moment after the call had ended.
Then he got up and walked over to Rorch's office steeling
himself to speak his mind. But Rorch had gone, and so
had his temporary secretary.

'Thanks again for waiting. You shouldn't have, you
know. Your holidays started over an hour ago.'

Treasure beamed as he spoke to Miss Gaunt. She
smiled back, and at the well-bred acknowledgement. The
smile was brief and, as always, rather toothy.

Both knew the length of the office day depended on the
pressure of work. A private secretary as conscientious as
the fifty-two-year-old tall, thin and greying Miss Gaunt
would not have had it any other way: any more than she
would have entertained being described as a personal
assistant.

Miss Gaunt stood by traditions and standards that she
seldom deserted, and then only by arrangement. On Ash
Wednesday she arrived at the office half an hour later
than her usual 8.15 because Lent had invariably started
for her with a morning Mass. Once every summer she
took an extra afternoon off to go to the opera at
Glyndebourne with Mildred Pitts, her friend in the
Investment Department whose boss provided the tickets:
he got them free from a client.

There were other — a very few — special dispensations.
They served to make Miss Gaunt properly tolerant of the
many more indulgences claimed by other people. Even
so, she drew the line at the bald advantage-taker.

Visits to the doctor or dentist, she considered, should

be arranged after work or on Saturdays—not that this involved any great inconvenience for Miss Gaunt. She hadn't needed to see a doctor in years. Her teeth, if somewhat obtrusive, were remarkably sound.

She deplored lateness, and harboured an especially low regard for those whose inexhaustible stock of aged relatives was depleted only when funeral attendances would coincide with Test Match days. Everybody in Emily Gaunt's own family who had reached the terminal age group had proved the point by passing on. Her own mother's 'happy release' after a long illness had prefaced obsequies on a Bank Holiday Monday: no one had been surprised.

So, all in all, it was unthinkable Miss Gaunt would consider a two-week holiday that began on a Wednesday invented privileges the day before.

'I think that covers everything, Mr Treasure.' She ran a pencil down the last used page of her notebook.

'I'm sure it does. So I hope . . .'

'If there should be anything.' She had no inhibition about interrupting what was clearly the start of a goodwill message when there were still business matters at stake. 'Miss Barnaby has my address and telephone number. Please don't hesitate to call me. Our hotel is in a quite developed part of Greece.'

He was pleased to hear it, although if put to it, no doubt she would survive the excesses of primitive Balkan plumbing with proper British fortitude. 'So you think Miss Barnaby will be able to establish a telephonic link without my help?' He smiled.

'Definitely,' she responded a fraction too promptly. 'She's young but reliable. Mr Oakley is very pleased with her. The number's also with the switchboard—' presumably against the possibility of the dependable Miss Barnaby losing it: or her grip. Young Miss Barnaby was all of thirty. She had been secretary to Cecil Oakley for nearly two years.

'Oakley gets back . . . ?'

'On September 8th,' she replied. 'The day after me.'

Treasure's eyebrows arched. 'Just when Port Grimaud might start to become tolerable.'

'Miss Barnaby will be entirely at your disposal throughout my absence.' She ignored his comment and completed her point.

Though offered the freedom of Miss Barnaby, picturing her, he knew his demands were unlikely to exceed the conventional. 'Good,' he offered between thoughts. 'And where is it you're staying?'

'The hotel is one of the Xenias. Between Athens and Cape Sounion. On the sea.' She closed her notebook. 'Every other day we, that is Miss Pitts and I, we shall be making coach expeditions.'

'Where to?'

'Delphi, Corinth, Mycenae, Epidaurus. And Athens itself, of course.' Her eyes had brightened with the anticipation. 'There's also a one-day cruise to Hydra and Aegina. That's optional.'

'Not included in the package?'

'The extra cost is reasonable. Miss Pitts is not a very good sailor.'

'Hydra and Aegina don't make for a very long or hazardous cruise. I'd go, if I were you. It'll be cooler than the bus trips this time of year.'

'The *coaches* are air-conditioned,' she emphasized for the benefit of one whose familiarity with that particular form of conveyance would be understandably slim. 'We've been warned about the heat. Miss Pitts can't take her holidays at any other time. For family reasons.'

'I see.' He didn't at all, and speculated on what kind of family reason would oblige a middle-aged spinster, a bit younger than Miss Gaunt, to vacation during school holidays. 'Well, have a jolly good time. You deserve it. Come back bronzed as well as svelte,' he added extravagantly. 'And watch out for the topless Greek beaches.'

She reddened, then gave a broad embarrassed grin: because of the teeth and a very large mouth, all Miss Gaunt's grins tended towards the broad. 'We're really going to improve our minds. But you never know,' she added nearly coyly and because she had surrendered to the holiday mood.

CHAPTER 10

Roger Rorch swung the white Mercedes out of the Bloomsbury Square car park, across Southampton Row, down to Holborn, then left on to Kingsway. The rush hour was nearly over, but the traffic was still quite heavy. He was too preoccupied to notice.

He would keep to his resolution: since the two telephone calls it made even more sense.

The Marketing Director of Carter Cousins had been friendly but firm. They would not be waiting to see if Jebbit, Fowler transferred their advertising business to RTB after a takeover. If Crabtree acquired the agency, the offer from Carter would be cancelled. The company had an inflexible rule: it placed no advertising through agencies that served any of its competitors anywhere in the world.

Rorch had refused the proffered opportunity to withdraw from competing for the Carter business immediately. He had insisted the takeover was far from certain — that the item in the evening paper had been premature.

There was still time for him to get the Carter Cousins appointment for RTB: he needed it — he needed it very badly.

The middle section of Kingsway was clear. He moved the car fast down to Aldwych, then waited, along with six buses — five of them number 68s and all nearly empty — as three people ambled over the uncontrolled pedestrian crossing, and well apart, as though perversely intent to extend traffic delays.

'Don't worry, old man. He doesn't want to leave us. Deep down, he values the relationship. Couldn't do without us. Just leave him to me.'

That's what Peter Bander had said about Victor Grimalt. Rorch had called him at home ten minutes before. Peter's speech had been slurred. When he drank too much it was usually a sign he had failed at something. So it was on the cards Grimalt would be shifting the OPD Foods account if the takeover went through. Did it serve them right for getting and keeping business on the strength of a kickback to a creep like Grimalt? Perhaps: but the work was good — good enough to be helping them towards working for other OPD Divisions. There was an even chance they would get a piece of the OPD Paints advertising next year: the Sales Director there had been transferred from the Foods Division. He had half promised RTB at least part of the account. And that would have nothing to do with Grimalt. It was just something else Bander could come to regret if the agency lost its present OPD connection through the takeover.

It could be the same with Carter Cousins. Making a success with a piece of their advertising now would positively underwrite more business from them. George Timms and Peter Bander would both remember that when the time came.

Rorch thought back to the way the three of them had determined to build the company at the beginning. It had taken more time than they had estimated — and more talent than some of them possessed, he considered with some bitterness.

He steered around to the north of the islanded St Clement Dane's Church, over Lancaster Place, then left into Savoy Street. He parked at the side of the hotel in Carting Lane. He stayed in the car for a moment.

At the start they would none of them have countenanced selling out at any stage to an American agency as good as controlled by the Dandy Corporation, and so obviously beholden to Jebbit, Fowler.

So what if they could turn their stakes into half a million each? Was it time yet to be churning out 'safe' advertising for clients they had to humour in case of

100

repercussions in New York, or Nashville, or wherever the ultimate control might lie?

That was what could be bugging Timms and Bander a year, two years from now. It was why Rorch felt certain in his mind as he locked the Mercedes.

'Mr Roger Rorch? Well, I declare, if this isn't the most incredible coincidence.' Her sharp, undulating voice pierced every crevice of the empty corridor. 'I'm Joanne Rutledge Jackson. Come right in, won't you?'

He had announced himself at reception, and had later been invited to go straight up to the suite.

She closed the door behind him, motioning him into the living-room. She was glad she had changed early—into the sleeveless little black dress Lee had kidded her was too sexy to go out in. That was after Howie had suggested they eat in the hotel. It was the kind of dress that made shy men uncomfortable. Mr Rorch was examining it—and her—with a composure she found pleasantly disarming.

'Can you beat that? We met earlier today. In St Paul's Cathedral,' she announced, still basking in the appraisal.

'I'm so sorry. I don't remember.' He shrugged. 'Obviously I should have done.'

'I do believe that was meant as a compliment, but there's no reason in the world why you should have remembered. We were in the south aisle, by the stairs to the galleries? By that "Light of the World" picture? The Holman Hunt? You were in a terrible hurry. We brushed together. It was my fault. I dropped my guide book. You picked it up.'

'Thank God for that. I think I remember. You must forgive . . .'

'There's not one thing to forgive. But can you beat it?' She half-expected him to volunteer what an advertising man with a takeover on his mind had been doing in St Paul's at three o'clock that afternoon. Maybe he'd dropped by for divine guidance, except he didn't look the type. 'I'm sorry Mr Crabtree and my husband are both out.' She beamed encouragingly and fluttered her eyelids several times.

'Then I shouldn't have barged in.'

'No such thing.' The last syllable started on a very high note, then descended and hung in the air. 'I just hate drinking alone. So name your pleasure, sir.' Coyly, as if in afterthought, she indicated the drinks tray.

He hesitated, glanced at the time, wondered if she served anything but mint juleps, but ordered: 'A gin and tonic, thanks. But . . .'

'No buts. You're a celebrity. I've been just dying to meet you. Properly, I mean.' She handed him the drink, clinking it with her own glass once he had hold of it. 'Here's to us. Lee was telling me all about you earlier. You-all made a big hit today.'

He judged her more intelligent—perhaps more calculating—than the affected behaviour and accent were meant to indicate. 'I'm glad to hear it. Will he be long, d'you think?'

'Shouldn't think so. Come and sit down. Tell me how you feel the talks are going.' She settled herself on the sofa, patting the seat of the armchair beside her.

He remained standing in the centre of the room. 'That's why I'm here. I've come to a decision. I wanted your husband and Howie Crabtree to know about it tonight.'

'Sounds ominous, Mr Rorch. Is it?'

'In a way. I've decided I'm against the deal. It needn't affect my partners or the bank, but as far as I'm concerned . . .'

'You pass?' She waited for his nod. 'That's a pretty quick decision.'

'No.' He paused, taking a large gulp from the glass. 'Sorry. It probably looks that way. A deal like this one is always on the cards for an agency like ours. One develops a view on the principle involved.'

'And you've been basically opposed? In principle?'

'It was marginal, but now the chips are down, I'm

certain in practice too.'

'You don't think we can change your mind? No matter how hard we tried?' She fixed a steady gaze on his.

'I don't think so. No matter how hard.'

It was the declaration Timms and Bander were intended to recall in the future. It was important Lee Jackson should hear of it too.

'Rorch isn't going to sell,' said Howie Crabtree with incredible prescience and two miles away from the Savoy Hotel.

'Which would still make it three shareholders for and only one against,' countered Jackson.

'He'll come round.' Joe Ziebal didn't like having the Americans here in Chester Terrace. It broke all the rules. But since he had brought it on himself . . . since they had insisted they had to see him . . .

'Don't see how you can be so sure. The newspaper report really riled him,' Howie put in pointedly, but without looking at Ziebal.

'It was meant to smoke out the prejudiced,' their host replied flatly from the depths of one of his leather winged chairs. He preferred being at his desk, not stuck in this nice-to-look-at 'conversation piece'. When he used the chairs they made him feel shorter than he was—as if his feet wouldn't touch the floor, which they didn't if he sat right back.

'It's smoked out Rorch all right. So . . .'

'So, Mr Crabtree, the quicker we can work on what ails him. Rorch had a cold threatening over the Carter business. Now he's got pneumonia. That we can treat. It's better people come to see the real problems sooner not later. We only have two weeks. At least we know the others are with us, like Lee says.

'If Rorch digs in, you don't think any of the others will join him, Joe? There's no chance of that?' This was Jackson.

'None. Anyway, Rorch will change his mind. I know it. In the end, there's only one decision he can make.'

'Or drop out?' suggested Jackson.

'We have to offer more money quickly,' said Howie, producing his pipe.

Ziebal nodded. 'It was part of the strategy. Because of Rorch's attitude we can move up the timing.'

'I think we should also be looking at the second choice agency,' Jackson put in flatly.

'That's really why we're here,' came back Howie with a determined expression. 'Uuh jun ow . . .' He took the empty pipe from his mouth and started again. 'I don't go along with that. Not unless we tell Mark Treasure and the others. We made a promise. There were . . . considerations.' He blinked, then looked mildly perplexed at his own show of decision.

'The considerations being a peek tomorrow at the RTB financial projections we've already seen.'

'Mr Treasure doesn't know that, Lee.'

'It isn't necessary to look at the second agency,' said Ziebal.

'I think it is,' countered Jackson promptly.

'I think we ought to call my father.' For half a century this had been Howie's reaction in a difficult situation. Immediately he felt guilty.

'Be my guest,' offered Ziebal with unexpected enthusiasm.

Howie deduced at the prices they were paying Ziebal could afford to be magnanimous over transatlantic calls. In any case, Howie was doing battle with his ego about consulting HJ: his ego lost. He got up and made for the telephone.

Jackson was ignoring the actions and intentions of his titular boss. 'Joe, you seem pretty certain Rorch is playing games,' he said slowly, holding the other's gaze.

'Certain as tomorrow's Wednesday.'

'Is this what you get from your insider?'

'It's my view. From all sources, Lee.'

It was easy to tell from his expression that Jackson accepted that view — also that it didn't please him.

Howie was sitting comfortably in Joe's womb-like chair,

sucking his pipe, and dialling his father.

At 7.15 Roger Rorch was letting himself into his sub-leased apartment on the top floor of Tudor Reach, a newish ten-storey block of flats on the south bank of the Thames above Lambeth Bridge.

The outline of the building was unconventional. It rose in exaggerated counterbalanced stages. Each floor over-lapped the one below on two sides, the relevant sides alternating. There were four apartments on each floor except the top, which had only one. The single apartment there was joined to the block's service units—the water tanks, the lift gear, and the complicated and cumbersome components of the experimental auxiliary solar heating plant.

This penthouse apartment was marginally smaller than the others in the building, and the lift didn't ascend to that level. To reach it, the tenant took the lift to the ninth floor, then climbed the last flight of steps on the enclosed fire stairs—a concrete shaft at the rear, east side of the building where it offended no one who mattered. The Thames beside Tudor Reach runs almost due north down to Westminster.

Rorch had rented the flat furnished after the break-up of his marriage a year earlier. The owner, a wealthy friend in the Foreign Office, had been seconded to work at the UN in New York for two years.

The main hallway opened directly on to the low-ceilinged living-room down two wide, carpeted steps. The enclosed kitchen was to the right immediately beyond the raised dining area in the far corner. The two bedroom suites were to the left—one entered through a door in the living-room, the other down a short extension to the hallway. There was a wide terrace beyond the glass south-facing wall of the main room. The furnishings were bold and modern—a deep-cushioned sofa in off-white folkweave dominating. There were unmatched chairs, but in similar coverings, chunky tables in metal and glass, and practical steel lamps. The dark blue carpet and lighter coloured drapes helped the nearly white silk-papered walls to set off the eclectic selection of pictures—from stark abstract to sensitive small eighteenth- or nineteenth-century etchings.

'I'm late,' Rorch uttered quietly to the woman as she embraced him. She had come in from the terrace as he entered, and hurried to him across the room.

'Darling, I can't stay. I had to see you.' She pulled him closer to her.

She was a big-boned, handsome woman with a lot of animal attraction and some style. She wore her auburn hair shoulder length in loose and wanton waves. She favoured bulky, gold-coloured costume jewellery. Bracelets jangled on her wrists and her fingers explored the back of his head. The gleaming chains hanging from her neck pressed against the bronzed skin of a deeply exposed cleavage as she hung against him. The tight, slit-skirted green dress did justice to every contour of the well developed figure.

Her name was Gloria Fentley. She was thirty-two and married to Stuart Fentley, the Chairman of Fentley Advertising.

'I'm sorry about last night. Am I forgiven?' Her voice was deep and husky. 'Should have told you I'd be here. I tried phoning. Honestly.'

'You needn't have flounced out like that.'

'I didn't flounce. In the circumstances I was very collected. I just dressed and left when you chased after her.'

'It was so unnecessary.'

'So I should have hung on hoping for a round of three-handed bridge, or whatever else you might have had in mind?' She leaned back a fraction. 'Did you? My God, I believe you did.'

'Nonsense. I didn't even know you'd be here.' His tone was casual.

'So that was the brilliant Helen Wintly. You never said she was a beauty. I'm not jealous, you understand? Just surprised.'

106

'You're both. We're simply business associates.' He paused. 'You don't have time to share a joint?'

'Nor anything else, darling.' She frowned at the slim cigarette with the twisted end he had just taken from his top pocket. 'I wish you wouldn't. Not on your own.'

'Pot is stimulating, and it doesn't damage your health.' He smiled languidly. 'Fact is, I'm working tonight. Hell of a day. Need something soothing. OK, I'll save it. Want to get us drinks?'

'Mine's on the terrace. Gin?' He nodded. She went over to a trolley with bottles on it, coming back with a tall gin and tonic and ice. 'Did you and Miss Wintly do a lot of business?' She slipped an arm through his as they walked together to the terrace.

'I never caught up with her.'

'Never got her back? And I broke the spell. What a shame.'

'Was really. She's still very uptight about it. Can't imagine why.'

'Darling, you're so ingenuous. No, callous. The girl is obviously crazy about you. She nearly fell apart being brought to your lair just to meet a green-eyed redhead with a latchkey. Did she think I was living here?'

'Last night? Perhaps. Really, I don't know.'

'Or care.'

He shrugged. 'Perhaps I misled her. We'd had a working dinner. She wanted to see the view.'

'How corny can you be? But I'm sorry I bitched up your evening. It's something I try never to do. You know that. Just so I can have you to myself once in a while. That's all I ask.' She drew him down into the swinging garden seat: it had yellow cushions and a sun canopy.

'So why don't you get a divorce and marry me?'

'And lose my kids? Or tear them apart emotionally? No can do. Anyway, you're perfectly happy the way things are, and I promise always to phone in future.' She traced a finger down his cheek. 'You don't even like children. Stuart adores them.'

'I like you enough to . . .'

'Darling, we've said it all before. It wouldn't work.' She turned his face to hers. 'Why are you so edgy? I have to go in five minutes. I told you, I have to be home by eight-thirty. The sitter leaves then.' Home was a fifty-minute drive away in Berkshire. 'Stuart's dining in town with a client. Not like yesterday. I had an all-night pass.' She pouted. 'Said I was staying with a girlfriend. Went home in the end. You *are* edgy, which makes two of us. Tell me?' She stroked his hand.

He told her about the takeover bid—also that he was against it. He told her the last part in detail, as though it mattered she should remember. 'Anyway, I'm too busy to stay involved. I'm working on a creative job,' he added. 'The Carter prospect I told you about. I should have been on it today, but these Americans fouled up everything.'

She sat up. 'So I'll get out of your hair.' She looked at her watch. 'I have to anyway.'

'You sure?'

'Sure.' But she wished his entreaty had been warmer. 'Look, there's something I ought to tell you. Last night, Stuart and I, we had a flaming row.' She sighed. 'It's a shame the takeover isn't for Fentley's. Stuart thinks we're heading for the poorhouse. Says I'm too extravagant . . .'

'You know I'd gladly . . .' he tried to interrupt, but she stopped him.

'And you know I wouldn't let you. It's just that Stuart could do with a nice fat takeover cheque.'

'As a matter of fact, if it goes through, the Crabtree deal could hurt Stuart.' He told her about the JF complication, that the account would probably move from Fentley whichever London agency Crabtree bought. 'I'm sorry for Stuart,' he finished.

'Don't be till you hear what we rowed about.'

'You said it was money.'

'Only partly. Mostly it was about . . . about you. He's found out about us. He had to eventually. It doesn't matter. It doesn't alter anything.' The face she was searching showed more irritation than concern.

'What d'you mean, it doesn't matter? Doesn't alter

anything? The man's human. You're his wife. You belong to him, don't you?'

'Darling, don't be so old-fashioned. Nobody belongs to anyone any more. That's from the Dark Ages. What I mean is, it needn't alter any relationships. Ours. Or his with me.'

He looked away from her. 'If you believe that you'll believe anything. How the hell did he find out anyway?' Inwardly he blamed himself for treating the affair too casually: the episode last night with Helen, for instance.

'It just came out.' She stared into her glass. 'I was angry. It . . . it slipped out.'

'You mean you told him?'

'All right, I told him. It's nothing. In the end I made some silly promises. They didn't mean anything. Just to satisfy his manly pride. I thought you ought to know in case . . .' She hesitated.

'In case what?'

She shrugged. 'In case he rings you, or tries to see you, or anything.' She stood up. 'Look, darling, I have to go.'

CHAPTER 11

'But Katherine, Victor Grimalt is your sister's husband. For heaven's sake.'

'I know. It's awful. I . . . I shouldn't say these things about him. But I simply don't trust him. There, I've done it again.' She bit her lip in contrition, and absently stroked the cat so hard it woke up in protest.

The Banders were in the sitting-room of their detached neo-Georgian house on a small estate of neo-Georgian detached houses near Kingston-upon-Thames. They were waiting for the nine o'clock news on the BBC.

Katherine Bander was a quiet, comfortable little woman, proud of her home, and her three teenage children, but worried—always worried. If it wasn't an impending nuclear holocaust or the dog's suspected eczema (they had a dog too), there was always something to fret about in the wide disaster area open in between.

When her husband had got home at six in no fit state to have driven from Reading, it was his drinking that had occupied her. Now he had sobered up and, added to what Audrey Grimalt had told her on the telephone, she had switched to agonizing over the family's financial future.

'But Rog thinks Victor means what he says.' He wished his head didn't ache so much. He'd slept for an hour, taken a shower and several Alka-Seltzers—he couldn't remember how many. 'Rog thinks he'll take the account elsewhere if we sell. Rog seems to be against selling.'

She looked up from her knitting which was draped over the cat and roughly the same colour—serviceable grey. 'Roger has means of his own. I don't suppose it matters to him. Getting money now. He's younger than you. I expect he can afford long, expensive holidays.'

There was often no logical sequence or explanatory justification in her discourses with her husband. He provided the threads himself—except tonight it was a strain. 'We've just had two weeks away.' He took a deep breath. 'You said you didn't mind self-catering.'

'If we had half a million in the bank . . .' She sighed. What if Peter's drinking got worse? What if it made him ill? She couldn't go back to work with the children all at different day schools: expensive day schools.

'But it could be all we'll have. I don't want to go against Victor.' In the normal way he wouldn't have told her about the bid—not till it was all over. But Victor's wife had called Katherine while he had been asleep. She had pressed Katherine to urge him not to sell out, insisting Victor meant what he said.

'You mean if the agency lost OPD Foods you'd lose your job?'

'Not exactly.' Still, he had no illusions about Grimalt's business having bought him the partnership with Rorch and Timms in the first place. It was all a question of balance: the half-million and an insecure future with Crabtree, against things as they were with a future

110

dependent on Victor.

'But you're one of the bosses, aren't you? With shares?' She was never quite sure about these things: she had been a nurse before they had married—not in business. 'You could ask for a contract or something, couldn't you? What happens when Victor retires? Who makes sure you keep the account then?'

She was right, of course—not about the contract: Rog said there would be no contracts. Going against Victor was one thing: going against Rog as well, that was something else again. The solid thing was the money: if all else failed—and it needn't come to that, probably wouldn't—but if the worst happened half a million would see them through. He'd give up drink altogether, for a start. It wasn't as though he was an alcoholic. Somehow he'd got that reputation—just because he used liquor for courage occasionally. He wasn't even a frequent tippler. It was so unfair. Rog got away with hitting the bottle sometimes—and in a very big way. With Rog they said it was artistic temperament, including the time he broke up the furniture—and hurt his wife, his ex-wife. Only Bander knew about that: she'd told him herself.

'. . . Surely there are other accounts you're responsible for?' She was still talking. 'Are you listening, dear? Would you like the news on?'

'Not if you don't.' There was too much on his mind already without hearing about the latest disposition of ballistic missiles. 'Did Audrey say Victor was seeing Rog tonight?'

'Only that he was in London for dinner. He'd said he might call on Roger on the way home.'

'He told her to say that so I'd be sure to tell Rog what he threatened at lunch. Well, I've done that already.'

'What about George Timms? You said he's for selling. Couldn't you and he work on Roger?'

'I rang George just now. Twice. Line engaged. Probably talking to Rog.'

'See what he says in the morning, then.' She pulled at the cat's tail in mistake for the knitting.

Bander frowned. 'The way Rog was going on, tomorrow may be too late.' He wished he hadn't said that. Even the cat had stood up in her lap. They were both looking at him accusingly. 'Might be worth popping over to old George's tonight. I promised to tell him how I got on with Victor.' The Timms were only ten minutes away in the car. They lived in Putney, just the other side of Richmond Park. If Rog had told George he had sounded drunk on the phone it was a chance to prove he wasn't. 'Yes, that's what I'll do.' He got up with vigour — and a good deal of disguised effort.

'Sure you're all right to drive, dear?'

'Of course I'm all right. Just a bit tired earlier. You don't mind? Kids should be home from tennis soon.' He let the rest of his breath out, and gave her a quick, nervous smile.

'Sybil's ankle's still not right,' she called after him. 'I said she shouldn't be playing . . .'

At nine o'clock the Timms family was still at table — a large pine table in their massive 'countrified' pinewood kitchen. George was seldom home before eight. Tonight he had been later.

The house was a terraced Edwardian monster in red brick, but it suited. There was income from the rents of the basement and top floors. Both had been converted into flats. A good deal had been spent on the interior of the house. The Timms looked on the place as a solid investment.

Fay Timms had a doctorate in economics: she ran a market research consultancy, working at home so they charged a lot of domestic expenses to tax. So far they had accumulated no real capital: only mortgages and a ten-year plan. A disproportionate part of the quite substantial family income was lavished on Adam, the only offspring and a child prodigy. At ten and a half Adam was already 'into' composing computer programs. Ensuring Adam's voracious intellect was properly fed was an expensive process.

'It'll be difficult for you to go along with this offer without Roger, of course,' said Fay.

She was pale, dark and serious—a tallish, skinny thirty-five, who cared little about her appearance and a lot about the benefits of margarine, raw vegetables, and the philosophies of Erich Fromm. A liberal in all senses, and a searching agnostic, she was also a Samaritan counsellor.

She finished her fish salad after speaking, glancing at Adam to indicate it was time he finished his.

'He could say the same of me.' George took a sip of the white Rioja wine. The Timms drank no spirits and served only white wine: Fay understood red wine was bad for the arteries. They were trying a new brand of white. The sip had been tentative—like the statement.

'Not exactly, Daddy.' Adam had carefully digested the Crabtree story with his raw cabbage and carrots. He reached for his apple juice, unsweetened. 'It's only a semantic difference, I suppose.' He pushed his glasses back along his nose. He was a weedy child: in looks and build he favoured his mother. 'Mr Rorch isn't intending to go along with the offer. Your not doing so in a matching context would be less material. One has to consider the quality differential.'

'We have to consider the relative importance of Roger,' said Fay, clearing the salad plates. She placed a bowl of fresh fruit on the table and a carton of cottage cheese. 'Is that what you mean, Adam?'

'Yes, Mother. Entirely objectively,' he ended guardedly.

'Of course objectively.'

'And strictly in the context of the operating unit. The advertising agency.'

Timms knew what they were driving at. 'If I wasn't accepting the deal and Roger was, you think it wouldn't matter as much as Roger not accepting and my going along with it.'

'The last being the putative case in point, Daddy.'

'Roger and I are equal partners.'

'Define the unperceived input,' Fay commanded, to

avoid acknowledging the validity of the last remark—but implying it didn't have any.

'Client approbation?' Adam volunteered promptly.

His mother nodded. 'And without clients the unit cannot exist.'

'We'll have two huge new clients to make up for any old ones who pull out,' said Timms, afraid he'd missed the point.

Mother and child exchanged knowing glances: he *had* missed the point.

'Sustained or anticipated quality of output on historical data. It's the same with old or new clients,' Adam recited. 'Mr Rorch is Creative Director of the agency.'

'No, he isn't. People may think—'

Adam clapped his hands. 'Got you, Daddy. Mr Rorch may not be the titular Creative Director, but if he's perceived by the clients to be, then the concept of equal partnership is not sustained in reality.'

'Then clients will be in for a surprise if the quality of output is sustained if he leaves,' his father answered without emotion.

'George, you're not considering that as a possibility? Roger leaving, I mean.'

'What else?'

'That in the last resort he accepts the majority view. Or the rest of you accept his.'

'Since Mr Rorch is Chairman and the perceived . . .'

'Go to bed, Adam. Sorry I was late home. I've enjoyed the discussion.' It was Timms's trump card. The boy accepted paternal authority as a fundamental tenet: thank God.

'Very well, Daddy. I have something to finish on the computer. About ten minutes. OK?' The computer was in Adam's bedroom.

'You shouldn't risk it George,' said his wife when the boy had left. She got up from the table. 'Decaf?'

'Yes, please. And Roger shouldn't behave as if he owned the agency. I've been loyal enough to him.'

She turned from plugging in the electric kettle. 'But

114

there can be only one leader.'

'I'm not denying that.'

'So.' She returned to the preparation of the coffee.

He knew they were agreeing to different things. He accepted Rorch's leadership as indisputable: in her view it was indispensable. In practice he accepted she was probably right—but it hurt him: she was his wife. At a time like this he deserved more than cold logic from his nearest and dearest.

'Did I tell you Roger won't be in tomorrow? Perhaps not for the rest of the week. He's brainstorming on the Carter presentation.'

'And making up his mind about Crabtree?' She put the cups on the table and sat down again.

'Think he's done that already. Except there'll be a lot of new talk tomorrow. They may increase the offer. It's really not right, Fay.' He poured himself another glass of wine and drank nearly half of it. 'Look, I'm going round to see Roger. I know he'll be in. Working. We need to have it out. He can't just disappear.'

'Why not phone?'

'He should have phoned me. He hasn't, of course. Unless Adam was on the computer link for too long?' His wife shook her head. 'Anyway, if I call Roger he could easily cut it short. He left the office tonight without telling me.' He paused, fiddling with his wine glass. 'You know what could happen? Crabtree could walk away from the deal just because Roger *seems* to be against it.'

'If I were Crabtree, I'd want Roger.'

'Well, Barny Smith thinks we can manage without him. Laura Cray is a very fine creative director.'

'Mmm. Better than average. I'm not sure Barny Smith is omniscient.'

'Fay, you hardly know these people.'

'Well enough to know they're ambitious. Smith especially. What they lack is style. Roger has style.'

His sigh was more pained than exasperated. 'Sometimes I think everybody's in love with Roger Rorch.'

Her look suddenly became earnest. 'I think we all love

Roger a little.' She frowned. 'And hate him a little.'

'Roger Rorch is hungry, but I'm convinced you-all are
offering him the wrong appetizer,' Joanne Jackson
observed sagely. She smiled at the wine waiter who was
refilling her glass.

'More money won't do it.' Howie nodded as he spoke.

'More money will do almost anything. It depends how
much more,' Jackson snapped.

It was ten o'clock. The three were finishing dinner in
the Grill Room at the Savoy.

'Still wish we'd been there when he dropped by.' Howie
helped himself to more Perrier water.

'I sure did my best. All dressed for the part and all. But
he definitely isn't seduceable.' She enjoyed shocking
Howie, except it was her husband who frowned. She
wondered if what she had said was true.

'If we'd been here, it still wouldn't have been the
moment to up the ante,' said Jackson.

'Wasn't suggesting that. Joanne's right. It's what HJ
figured when I called him from Ziebal's—' so she almost
had to be right. 'Rorch isn't primarily concerned with
money.'

'Which kind of separates him from the rest of the
human race,' Jackson put in cynically.

'Seems to me he has enough money for the moment,'
said his wife. 'No family obligations. First wife remarried.
Penthouse apartment all to himself.'

'He gave you the address. It's close by. What was it
again?' Howie interrupted.

She told him, then continued, 'His ambition is for RTB
to make the big time on its own, with him leading.
Heading up Crabtree's London office doesn't qualify. Not
as of now. If RTB was already a whole lot bigger it might
be all right.'

'So we should wait around ten or twenty years till high
and mighty Roger Rorch builds the place up?' Her
husband snorted.

Joanne shook her head. 'I don't think it'd take him that

116

long. But he still has to pass up our offer. Could be it's the right decision for everybody,' she added pointedly, looking at her husband.

'HJ thinks we should get him over to New York.'

'And keep him there, maybe.' Joanne was still staring at her husband.

'You gave him quite a build-up to HJ on the phone, Howie. You figure he'd fit in our . . . our management structure Stateside?' questioned Jackson, who respected Howie's possible influence with his father a lot more than he respected Howie.

'Could be,' was the guarded answer. 'I just don't see where Roger thinks he's going from here . . .'

'Ziebal says he's bluffing. Using his influence on the others. Trying to swing them against us. When he fails, he'll come back into line. At the highest price.' There was no enthusiasm in the voice.

'So we just need to be extra nice to Timms and the other man. Increase the price while Roger's out of the way.' Howie spoke ruminatively, almost to himself. 'I'm glad we saw Mr Ziebal.' He looked at the time. 'Well, I'm going to bed. Been a solid day.'

'I'm certainly ready for bed,' announced Joanne, loud enough momentarily to capture the whole attention of three male diners at an adjacent table. 'Now are you-all sure I can take the car to Wilton in the morning? You don't need me for anything?'

'Not a thing, Joanne,' Howie volunteered promptly, glad to get rid of her, the chauffeur and the ostentatious car. 'Guess we'll be walled up all day at RTB. Is Wilton far?'

'Julian says Wilton House will take an hour and a half. That's where we're heading. Built for the Herbert family by Inigo Jones. My great-great-grandpappy was a Herbert. I expect the relationship was remote' — but the tone implied not overly so.

Lee Jackson scribbled a signature on the bill, then followed the others from the table. 'Why don't you go on up? I'm pretty wide awake still. Guess I'll get some air.'

117

He turned about and left by the street entrance to the bar. A moment later, Joanne chose to tarry before the windows in the Savoy shopping arcade, leaving Howie to go on alone.

'No, no. Perfectly convenient. Truly,' Treasure lied into the telephone.

It was 11.20. The night was getting warmer. He was standing stark naked in the master bedroom of his elegant home in Chelsea's Cheyne Walk. He had a charged toothbrush in one hand. In the other he held both the telephone and an open tube of toothpaste.

'You did quite the right thing,' he continued in the same conciliatory tone. 'Puts you in an awkward situation in the morning, of course. Irritating, too. Anyway, if he doesn't answer the phone, probably means he's left already. Wherever it is he's going. You'll have to play it by ear. Tell 'em what he said. Hmm. Bit enigmatic. You know the bank's attitude.' He listened for a moment to the voice on the other end of the line. 'If Crabtree pull out on the strength of his intention, that's it. Otherwise, go ahead as planned.' There was another pause. 'Not a bit. Quite understand. Good night . . . er, sleep well.'

'Must have been the Prime Minister,' observed the celebrated Mrs Treasure, better known as Molly Forbes the actress. She swivelled around on the stool in front of her dressing-table, spotting blobs of Pond's cream on her face and neck. She looked cool and serene in a simple white negligée, even allowing for the cream which she now began rubbing vigorously into her skin.

'Not the PM,' Treasure answered absently. He stayed eyeing the telephone for some moments after replacing it.

'Then stop standing to attention and tell all. Which lesser mortal's been keeping you from doing your toothies, and your Canadian Air Force exercises?' The high forehead lined and the eyebrows arched in wholly contrived, winsome anticipation.

Molly was not an outstanding beauty. The aquiline nose was a touch too pronounced, the long chin a shade too pointed. She was tall and shapely, but there was always the suggestion she had to strive to be gainly. This had been a necessity in gangling adolescence and cultivated in maturity as an endearing distinguishing characteristic. As a handsome patrician with a genius for underplaying comedy, on stage she personified the studied gracelessness and clipped articulation of confident women in the British tweeded classes.

Treasure stepped back into the bathroom. 'One of our executives taking the initiative,' he called through the open door. 'Anyway, I've done my exercises. You weren't looking.' There followed the sound of keen teeth-brushing and rinsing.

'Then you've been cheating on the schedule. You won't get into the Canadian Air Force *that* way.' She stretched her neck before the looking-glass, pawing the skin under her chin and staring at herself disconsolately. 'And lesser executives should be instructed not to harass greater ones in the middle of the night.'

'I wasn't harassed. It's assumed we're night birds because of your profession. Anyway it's not that late.' The last point was tentative.

'Stuff and nonsense. My profession has nothing to do with it,' she snorted amiably. 'And the way you say it, you'd think I was on the streets.' She wandered over to the bathroom. 'Perhaps she knew I might be away.'

Treasure was in the act of weighing himself. 'How did you know it was a she?'

'I didn't, but I do now, darling. Thrusting young female banker making time with big white chief while aging actress wife rests in the country.' Molly was thirty-seven. 'Is she pretty?'

'Passable.'

'Which means ravishing. Bet she'd checked I wasn't working tonight.' Molly was currently playing in a Shaw revival at the National Theatre. The play was alternating with another in the repertory. This had been her third night off. She had returned that afternoon from staying with friends in Hampshire.

119

'Your imagination's too active.' He stepped into the shower — wondering.

'So are my wrinkles,' she answered, studying her face in the brighter bathroom light. 'Anyway, wouldn't blame a girl for trying. You're very good-looking still.' She considered his appearance before he closed the half-door on the shower.

'And known to be very much married to you,' he shouted over the noise of the cold jet.

'I wasn't thinking of lifelong or enduring relationships.' She was silent for a few moments. 'What's this?' She had been into his dressing-room, returning with the menu card he had pocketed after lunch.

'It's for you.' He was towelling himself.

'Big deal. See what I missed by not lunching today at Grenwood, Phipps. Smoked salmon, grilled lamb chops Reform . . .'

'On the other side.'

'A doodlebug!' she exclaimed. 'Good one too. You are a darling.' She collected other people's doodles. 'Someone important? And an artist. These are brilliant sketches, not doodles. Who did you have to lunch? Hugh Casson?' He shook his head. 'Paul Reilly?'

'Wish it had been. Either of them.' He had put on a white bathrobe. She had gone over to the dressing-table for her glasses. He followed, looking over her shoulder as she studied the scramble of overlapping drawings. 'Chap called Roger Rorch. You met him once. We dined . . .'

'Advertising man. You financed his agency.'

'That's right. Now someone wants to buy it.'

She seemed not to hear. 'That's an Oribi.' She pointed to the antelope head in the centre of the card.

'How clever of you.'

'Not really. He's written it underneath. I wonder why?' She looked up. 'D'you remember Oribi Gorge? It's a nature reserve below Durban. We went there.'

He nodded. 'That's a sort of Palladian Bridge. Nice. And that's the west front of St Paul's, upside down.'

She turned the card around. 'And that might be the

120

auditorium of the Olivier Theatre.'

'Bit of a theatre in the round, anyway, with part of an antelope's head obscuring the view.' He smiled. 'Don't know what that is.' He pointed to one of the drawings.

'Inside the reading room of the British museum?'

'No. And I've been there.'

'Show-off. It's a dome anyway. Inside St Paul's?'

'Too shallow. Unless he was running out of space. Turn it the other way.' She did, as he went on. 'Extraordinary what helps people concentrate. While this chap was doing these, he was apparently engaged in a taxing discussion about the takeover of his company. Nothing remotely related to what he was drawing.'

Molly turned the card again. 'Look, there's a tiny sketch of the Hollywood Bowl. And I've performed there, so yah-boo to you.' She paused. 'Funny, they're not like most doodlebugs. I'd say they're much closer to what your Mr Rorch was really thinking about — and it wasn't the sale of his advertising agency.'

'You could be right. Funny chap.' He frowned. 'Talented and competent, but highly irritating traits.'

Later, Helen Wintly, still fully dressed, sat at the bureau in her living-room. She rewound the tape on her telephone answering machine once again. It contained only one message.

She pressed the replay button and listened to the voice. 'Helen,' it said, 'Roger here. In a way I was counting on the machine. Makes it easier . . . but . . . but still inevitable.' He had stumbled over the last word. 'I've made up my mind. I'm much better out of it. Better out of it altogether. Thanks for everything. Sorry to let you down. You see . . .'

The message ended abruptly in mid-sentence. The machine allowed only fifteen seconds for each caller.

CHAPTER 12

'We had the advantage of the early start,' said Emily Gaunt enthusiastically to Mildred Pitts. 'Still only half past nine at home.'

They were seated together in a stationary hotel minibus at Athens Airport. Miss Gaunt had been purposely impressing the benefit of their dawn departure since the two had met at Victoria Station to catch the 5.30 train to Gatwick Airport. At the beginning, Miss Pitts had not been much conscious of the compensations latent in her having risen at four.

'If we'd taken the other tour, we shouldn't have been here till six in the evening, with the two-hour time difference. That's the whole day gone, really,' she now advised, much to Miss Gaunt's inward satisfaction. 'It's quite warm, isn't it, Emily?' Miss Pitts continued, peering at the directional ventilators in the luggage rack above their heads. 'Not working yet,' she almost whispered as though loath to instigate a round of protest — or to induce a sense of impending asphyxia in others similar to the one she was experiencing herself.

'They'll start with the engine, I expect,' offered Miss Gaunt. Air travel made Mildred chatter, even after landing: something to do with nervous tension. 'Why don't you open that window a bit more?'

'It won't. They only go half way.' Even so, Miss Pitts rearranged the packages on her lap so that she could lean forward and give the glass panel another push.

It was a pity about Mildred's plastic carrier bags. There was one from the Gatwick Duty Free shop, another that advertised Marks & Spencer, and a more substantial affair in pink, incongruously provided by 'The Under-25 Store' and containing Miss Pitts's needlepoint. Miss Gaunt had never brought herself to mention the matter — not directly — in all the years the two had

122

holidayed together, but these inevitable appendages gave their possessor the appearance of a dumpy and overburdened refugee. This effect was heightened, in Miss Gaunt's view, by the tour company's label Mildred insisted on attaching to her plastic raincoat for fear she might ever be parted from that singularly unattractive if utilitarian garment.

'They only go half way,' boomed the elderly, red-faced, military-looking man with the white moustache. He was in the seat in front.

The two maiden ladies nodded their thanks for this confirmation.

'It's boiling in here,' said the military man's ample, jolly wife. She produced a fan from her handbag.

'Of course, it's half past eleven local time,' offered Miss Pitts, but quietly to her companion.

'What? Yes. Changed your watches have you?' asked the military man. He consulted his own. 'Twenty-five to,' he went on. 'Been on Greek time since last night. Best way to acclimatize.'

'Ask them why we're waiting, Bill,' urged his wife. 'We're missing the best of the day.'

The bus had seats for twenty, but so far only eleven passengers. 'Bill' heaved himself into the gangway, made for the door at the front, but became involved in a kind of quadrille with a young couple and their small boy who was fully equipped for instant snorkelling.

'Been to the Lagonissi Xenias before, have you?' asked Bill's wife, turning to the pair behind and allowing agreeable disturbances of air from her vigorous fanning to waft in their direction.

'First time,' volunteered Miss Pitts. 'You know it, do you?'

'From three years ago. My old man likes it. Got one of the beach bungalows, have you? Very nice. Place has got everything, really. Cape Sounion's very close. Athens too, for serious sightseeing. Not too close. Bit of a trek if you're going further afield, of course.'

'We're doing a lot of coach trips,' Miss Pitts responded.

'Oh. Well, I expect you'll be all right,' said Bill's wife, but doubtfully. 'We did that the last time. Delphi, Corinth and so on. It's just the hotel is twenty miles the wrong side of Athens. You have to get up before dawn for the hotel's coach that takes you into Athens centre so you're in time for your tour coach. The hotel does a smashing breakfast at six. It's a buffet.'

'Twenty miles isn't far,' said Miss Gaunt firmly.

'That's right,' replied Bill's wife cheerfully. 'Don't worry, you'll survive. It's rather romantic too, seeing the dawn coming up after you've had breakfast.'

'We did that this morning,' Miss Pitts observed ruefully.

'It's better here. Bill, you're a terrible fellow,' his wife continued, switching her attention as he returned. 'Think of my ruddy waistline.'

He was advancing up the aisle holding in both hands a pyramid of freshly baked croissants, each loosely wrapped in thin paper napkins.

'Keep us going for a bit, what? They fill 'em with hot cheese, remember? Forget what they call them. Try one?' He offered them to the other ladies after his wife had taken one. Miss Gaunt politely refused. Miss Pitts gingerly detached one from the pile, with many professions of gratitude.

'There'll be a slight delay,' continued Bill. 'Waiting for people off a German plane to collect their baggage. Half an hour, I'd guess.' He bit into the flaky delicacy. Hot, liquidized cheese ran on to his hand. 'Good, aren't they?' He beamed at Miss Pitts from where he was still standing in the aisle, knees slightly bent, feet well apart and flatly attached to the deck. 'Better get something to drink too, I suppose. Bloody hot. Midday sun, you see.'

'It's not right, really,' said Mildred Pitts whose plastic bags were now covered in a light fall of pastry. 'I mean, we're losing the advantage of the early start.'

'Afraid they don't open till eleven, Mrs Jackson.' The chauffeur had walked back to where he had left the

Jaguar at the entrance to the Wilton House car park beside the A30. He had been to read the notice on the main gate. It was exactly 10 o'clock.

'Not your fault, Julian. You said eleven. I just figured it might be earlier.' She got out of the car clutching the architectural tome she had been reading on the way down. 'Should have stopped to see Salisbury.'

'It's only three miles back, madam. We could . . .'

'Will you just look at that entrance, Julian?' she interrupted. 'Triumphal arch, actually. By William Chambers. Seventeen-fifty-five. They moved it here from some hill in the park around eighteen-two. The gates themselves came later. They're Italian . . .'

'Excuse me.' A well-dressed, well-spoken, middle-aged lady carrying some papers had approached them from the general direction of the house. 'Are you by any chance with Mr Rorch? Mrs Rorch perhaps?' She beamed at Joanne. The chauffeur had stepped back out of hearing—just as he supposed a well-trained retainer ought to do. He had once understudied the lead in *The Admirable Crichton*.

Mrs Jackson held out her hand. 'I'm Joanne Rutledge Jackson. From the USA,' she added, on a point beyond question. 'We don't have Mr Rorch with us, but if it's the same one, I was with him last . . . er evening. Mr Roger Rorch?'

The lady nodded. 'Of the advertising agency? Let me see.' She pulled a paper from the sheaf in her hand. 'Rorch, Timms & Bander of Red Lion Square?'

'That's the one.'

'You've come in his place, perhaps?'

'No. And he didn't know I was coming. You mean he's due here? This morning?'

'Definitely. By special arrangement. Nine-thirty. I assume he's been delayed, but there's been no message. It's the Earl's policy to give every cooperation in such matters.'

'That's the seventeenth Earl of Pembroke? Henry George Charles Alexander Herbert.' She recited the name like a litany, and just as reverently. After a nod from the other she went on: 'You say he cooperates in such matters? What kind of matters exactly?'

The lady's face clouded. 'Now there you have me. You see, the appointment was made some days ago, and not with me. The private secretary is on holiday, and the guide who was to have met Mr Rorch has sprained an ankle.'

'You're one of the docents here?'

'That's what we'd be called in your country. We just say guides.' The lady smiled. 'I usually take parties round in the afternoons.'

'But Mr Rorch was getting special treatment?'

'The arrangement was he should be allowed into the double cube room before the regular tours started.'

'I guess that's just about the most famous room in England.'

'We think it deserves to be, certainly. It's extremely beautiful . . .'

'And unique,' insisted Mrs Jackson. 'Sixty foot long, thirty foot wide and thirty high. Designed by Inigo Jones and finished after his death by John Webb, his nephew, in sixteen-fifty-three . . .'

'Or thereabouts. You're very well informed, Mrs . . . Jackson. So many of our American visitors are. You probably know the room was primarily intended to house the family collection of Van Dyck paintings.'

'Isn't that the truth? And, did you know Philip Trammell Shutze designed a museum wing for Swan House, that's in Atlanta, Georgia, using the same dimensions as the double cube here? Of course he planned the house in the first place. They never built the wing.'

'Indeed. Was that perhaps in the eighteenth century? We know Thomas Jefferson . . .'

'No, nineteen-sixty-eight. Mr Shutze was eighty at the time he designed the wing, though. I just can't wait to see those pictures. My family, way back, were Herberts. A common name, of course.'

126

The other made the usual expressions of interest before asking: 'You were with Mr Rorch last evening, but you didn't know he was coming here too?'

'Pure coincidence. He'd called to see my husband on a matter of business. We're staying at the Savoy Hotel. I didn't mention my trip.'

'And you don't know the purpose of his? I'm fairly certain it must have had a cultural connection.'

'He's head of an advertising agency,' Mrs Jackson reminded.

'A business and cultural connection, perhaps. Commerce and the arts are nowadays so often interlaced. We . . .'

'Come to think of it, I met Mr Rorch in St Paul's Cathedral yesterday afternoon. Except we didn't know each other then. I remembered when we met formally, later on.'

'I see,' said the lady, though she didn't really.

'He could have been there for the same reason he was coming here. I mean, he wasn't attending services or anything. Architecturally there could have been a connection.'

'Most of Wilton House is a generation older than St Paul's.' It wasn't put as a boast: just a statement of fact. 'The gothic additions here, of course, are a good deal younger,' came after, in mitigation.

The two ladies had fallen into step, and were moving slowly towards the main gate in close converse. Julian returned to the car. He calculated, correctly, that Mrs Jackson would not have to wait until eleven before being allowed inside.

Mrs Nibb had her own key to the main door of Tudor Reach. There was no porter living on the premises. Tenants normally admitted visitors by entry-phone. Mrs Nibb did cleaning for two of the tenants— two hours each weekday morning for Mr Rorch, and the same for a couple on the second floor whom she did first. They had always breakfasted by eight, when she arrived. Mr Rorch sometimes got up much later.

This morning, as usual, she took the lift to the ninth floor just after ten o'clock, climbed the stairs, and let herself into the penthouse, again, with her own key.

She rang the bell as she entered. It was a habit — and a bit of a joke she had with Mr Rorch, he being a bachelor — well, a divorcee, which amounted to the same. Once, when he'd had a lady staying Mrs Nibb had given her a turn appearing unexpectedly around the bedroom door after Mr Rorch had left. Mrs Nibb was over sixty, a widow with a broad mind and grown-up children: what her employers got up to didn't bother her. After the incident with the abandoned lady, though, she'd taken to ringing the bell to announce, as she put it, 'ready or not, I'm coming.'

Mr Rorch must have left in a hurry. The Chubb lock was only pulled shut, not double-locked. The curtains in the living-room were closed, and the lights were on. He sometimes left the curtains — if he was in a hurry and went without breakfast. Leaving the lights on was unusual, and wasteful: he'd only had to flick the switch by the door when he left. Mrs Nibb hated waste. She didn't care much for the smell of the room either.

Still, you couldn't complain. Mr Rorch was very clean and tidy usually. It was just whatever it was he smoked left this smell that hung about in the upholstery and the curtains: Turkish tobacco, as like as not. Mrs Nibb vaguely remembered Turkish cigarettes from after the war. For some reason they were easier to get than the other sort. Wouldn't give you a thank-you for them herself: not that she smoked any more — not that Mr Rorch did on a regular basis. It was just occasionally this sickly smell hit you when you came in of a morning.

There were no breakfast things to clear, so she gave more time to polishing, dusting and vacuuming the living-room. He hadn't left the lights on in the bedroom, but he had left the phone off the hook — there was a squarking noise coming from it when she went in. She replaced the receiver. She could see the bed hadn't been

128

slept in before she opened the curtains. So he'd been home the night before, gone out later, and not come back. She looked for his overnight bag: it was in its usual place. His work desk—in the bedroom—was tidier than usual. The cover was off the typewriter and there was discarded paper, but all in the waste-basket. She replaced the cover and emptied the basket.

Mrs Nibb left at twelve after a glance around the living-room at a job well done—and a small snort of Gordon's gin from the bottle on the tray. She always used a glass, and washed it afterwards: not like some with the same opportunity who'd swig from the bottle. If she said so herself—which she did quite frequently—you wouldn't find a fingermark in rooms just cleaned by Gerty Nibb.

She had already cleaned the bit of carpet between the door of the flat and the one to the fire stairs. She wasn't paid to do the stairs, though she sometimes swept them down if they got too bad—as far as the next floor. It was really the job of the maintenance people, but they only came once a week. Tenants paid good money for the upkeep of 'common parts' and got too little for it, was Mrs Nibb's opinion.

Now she looked at it, she could see the dust on the steel balustrade on the top landing. Even at a distance it had obviously only been half cleaned: shocking it was, really. She stepped across to do something about it, rummaging in her shopping-bag for a makeshift duster. Mr Rorch should complain. It was probably the same all the way down the stairs. There'd be light enough to see from the windows on every landing. She looked down into the deep stairwell.

'Oh my God!' she gasped.

Sara Lang-Beedle was a better than average temporary secretary. She was a big, hearty girl with an upper-crust background. Instead of trying to master other people's office routines, she invariably applied her own in the places she went to work, and rarely got complaints. She considered herself a natural 'temp', enjoying the variety of jobs: usually. After ten days with Roger Rorch she had decided the two-week commitment would be more than enough.

He was a nice man, glamorous, and evidently brilliant, but totally unpredictable and impossibly elusive. He had forgotten the letters she had left for him to sign the previous evening after telling her to go home. They were still on his desk. He had scribbled a note, tucked into her typewriter, saying he wouldn't be in the office today, or possibly the rest of the week. It gave no indication of where he was going, only that he'd ring in, and that she was to cancel all appointments, with 'suitable excuses'.

Of course, yesterday had been special: a takeover bid was bound to set a company on its head. But Miss Lang-Beedle had expected an exciting interlude as a result: she had certainly not expected the Chairman to go into hiding.

She had coped with the cancellations, also the morning's mail—though the last had produced some urgent requests and queries which she had had difficulty farming on to other senior people. All the directors had been at the meeting in Rorch's office with the two Americans since nine.

The telephone message from Karen Gradely of Sale, Manchester she had typed out and placed in a sealed enveloped marked 'confidential'. It could await the Chairman's return: she had definitely decided not to pass it on to anyone. It read:

Miss Gradely reports she is not in any trouble. She did as you instructed, and the result has been exactly as you predicted. You can ring her on the same number as before. She refused to enlarge. Said you would understand why.

Well!

Since no one had emerged from Rorch's office during the previous hour or so, at 12.30 she decided to go in and ask if they wanted arrangements made for lunch. George

130

Timms's secretary, who didn't seem very bright, had called several times on the internal phone to find out if they had asked for sandwiches. The same phone rang just as she was getting up. She took hold of it, meaning to tell Timms's girl to stop fussing, but the call was from reception. There was a police sergeant downstairs wanting a private word with the Managing Director.

She fetched Timms out of the meeting: Peter Bander had been closer to the door but in the time she had been at RTB he had never seemed to her to be a very convincing MD.

A few minutes later Timms came back looking solemn. He rejoined the meeting, interrupting Miss Lang-Beedle as she was reading out Howie Crabtree's sandwich order.

'There's been an accident,' Timms announced. 'Roger. He's . . . he's been killed in a fall. The stairwell at his flat. The police want me to identify the body.'

CHAPTER 13

'In short, I am bound to express misgivings before attempting to pronounce on this distressing case.'

The coroner sounded—as he appeared—both venerable and learned. He was a slight figure—small, bald and formally dressed in black jacket and striped trousers. He had retired from holding the same office in another place some time before, though he still practised medicine.

He had been impressed to hold the fort here, in South London, for several weeks. The regular coroner was on holiday. One of his deputies had contracted appendicitis just after the other had succumbed to a serious virus infection.

It was fortunate the backlog of work was not overwhelming, since the ministrations of the stand-in coroner were doing little to reduce it in real terms. He had always been meticulous, patient, understanding, and given to thorough explanation. Age had done nothing to diminish his commitment to any of those admirable attributes: it had, perhaps unconsciously, served to strengthen his conviction that speed was not the essence when it came to matters legal.

His grave gaze searched those assembled before him in the panelled and carpeted courtroom. He sat alone at a small table set on a dais. Behind and above his head was a facsimile of the Royal coat-of-arms—an emblem heavily out of proportion to the room, but which still affected an appearance more ominous than merely ponderous.

'It is clear enough the deceased was a highly intelligent young man, and in the opinion of those who should know, a talented luminary in the world of . . . advertising.'

The slowed and hesitant delivery of the last word did nothing to reduce the estimation of the character described. Only by implication did it reflect adversely on the seemliness of that character's chosen trade.

Treasure raised an eyebrow at Howie who was sitting beside him. Helen Wintly was on his other side. The banker had several times marked the coroner's careful way of implying reservation about the advertising business.

'He was subject to deep, and sometimes sudden fits of depression,' the elderly official continued. 'Did he suffer such an aberration a week ago last Tuesday night?' This was Friday. 'The evidence I have heard would seem to suggest as much.

'The day had been full of drama and incident. The late Roger Rorch seems to have been put upon to a degree. The fact that he outwardly showed to none, save one, the stress he was under is consistent with the character that has been drawn here by those who knew him.'

The coroner fingered the bridge of his gold half-spectacles, then glanced down at his notes. 'Both Mrs Joanne Rutledge Jackson and Mrs Gloria Fentley were in the company of the deceased for short periods during the early evening.' He paused, then slowly scanned the benches for the two women. Both had left after giving evidence. 'Each was of the opinion in retrospect that Mr

Rorch was slightly on edge. Each at the time ascribed his condition as consonant with the burden of the problem he admitted to carrying. I feel sure neither of these estimable ladies did anything to exacerbate his troubles.' Having prepared the compliment he had evidently considered it too handsome to waste.

'Mr Stuart Fentley was excused attendance today. He provided a deposition through my officer.' The coroner absently held up the document as if to prove there was no deception. 'He called upon the deceased at Tudor Reach at eight o'clock, shortly after Mrs Fentley had left.' The speaker hesitated as though for the first time considering some special import in the words he had just uttered: he grimaced, sniffed, and then continued. 'He left fifteen minutes later, having found Mr Rorch—' and here came a reading from the deposition—' "more than just edgy. Also impatient to be working," or so he assumed. The first indication of a deeper disquiet than had been exhibited to the ladies.'

The coroner fidgeted in his seat and adjusted his trousers beneath the table. 'I am indebted to Mr Fentley for coming forward to tell me of his visit. His statement is a valuable link to what followed.'

Treasure wondered whether the offer would have been forthcoming if Fentley had not run into another tenant of Tudor Reach at the lift as he was entering the building. Fentley's short visit had been over an innocent matter of business. The court had been left to believe that both Fentleys were friends of Rorch's who had dropped in on their separate occasions. The coroner had not sought further elucidation.

'I am obliged to Mr George Timms whose testimony was as clearly painful as his loss has been heavy to bear.'

This, at least, was a genuine statement echoed in the murmur put up by some of those present. At the funeral, three days earlier, Timms's tearful grief had been undisguised. His evidence to the court had been nearly as distressing for him as for those who understood his situation.

133

'Mr Timms was the last person to see Mr Rorch alive. The constraints the deceased allowed to temper his demeanour with others were abandoned in the company of one of his oldest and closest business associates. This may have been a natural enough event. It could nevertheless, and in aftermath, be something that weighs deeply on the mind of one who came to be the vent, the funnel of release for Mr Rorch's pent-up frenzy of distress.

'As the one on whom the deceased unburdened it would not be unnatural for Mr Timms to persuade himself to the feeling that he was in some way responsible for that burden. In the last analysis, this must be something decided between Mr Timms and his own conscience. For my own part, and on the strength of the evidence I have taken, I do not believe Mr Timms had more responsibility for what led up to the tragedy than had numerous other persons. I would go further and aver that the responsibility lay not with the deceased's friends and associates but entirely with the deceased himself. In the circumstances, I thought it proper to make these observations at this stage.'

There was more murmuring of a sympathetic kind, with numerous overt and kindly glances in George Timms's direction.

The coroner reverted to his notes. 'Mr Timms visited Mr Rorch in his flat at nine-fifty, and left at around ten-twenty, returning directly to his own home. In the words of Mr Timms, the deceased was angry and explosive during the whole time they were together, accusing Mr Timms, among other things, of being disloyal, and a money-grubber. In addition, he launched into un-founded and defaming accusations concerning Mr Timms's professional competence, his intellectual capacities and his moral integrity.' He looked directly at Timms. 'It was evidently and understandably hurtful for the witness to have revealed these unpleasant facts. He did so only after I had urged him to give as accurate an account of what took place as he was able to provide. This

134

frank and painful disclosure gave me the clearest conceivable picture of the deceased's state of mind.'

George Timms rose suddenly from his seat, then stood for a moment staring at the coroner, as if about to say something. Then, without warning, he hurried from the room.

The coroner made no audible comment, but nodded at Peter Bander, who, after a whispered comment to Treasure in front, followed Timms out.

'So,' the coroner resumed, 'Mr Timms had arrived expecting to enjoin Mr Rorch in analytical discussion concerning the merits or otherwise of the business opportunity facing them. Instead, he was effectively forced to leave. In his own words—' and the speaker looked down to read them—' "There never was any point in arguing with Roger when he got in one of his frenzies. Much better to let it blow out and catch him when remorse had set in." ' The coroner stopped reading and observed gravely, 'The judgement of an experienced intimate. Empirically, no doubt, accurate enough. In this instance it appears the frenzy never . . . blew out.

'At ten-forty we know that Mr Victor Grimalt and Mrs Jackson encountered each other, by coincidence, at the door to Tudor Reach. They had arrived separately. Both were seeking brief but urgent conversations with the deceased. Brief because of the lateness of the hour. Urgent because the common subject was the takeover bid. Both were to be disappointed. Mr Rorch either did not hear their summonses on the entry-phone, or else he chose to ignore them. The third possibility, that he had left the flat, is circumstantially unlikely. A point we shall come to in a moment.'

Treasure's eyes strayed to the seat occupied earlier by Grimalt. The Marketing Director of OPD Foods had been given permission to leave immediately after giving his evidence. He had nodded sharply at Bander, who had followed him out but returned a few minutes later.

Treasure concluded that neither Grimalt nor Mrs Jackson would have volunteered being at Tudor Reach if each hadn't had to suffer the other as witness to the fact. If they had known and trusted each other better they would almost certainly had agreed to wash the event from their minds, saving trouble and possible embarrassment.

Grimalt had evidently offered the attractive woman a lift back to the Savoy before he had found out who she was. He had certainly come to resent the whole episode, remarking — gratuitously and churlishly — in evidence that the Savoy had not been on his route home.

'My officer has tested the entry-phone mechanism. It is in perfect working order,' the coroner went on. 'The likeliest explanation for the failure of the deceased to respond to his callers was, in my opinion, a determination to receive no one else, most particularly — and this is Mr Timms's own view — Mr Timms himself on a second visit. He seems also to have decided not to answer the telephone. As Mr Grimalt testified, he called the deceased several times from the Institute of Directors, in Pall Mall, where he had been spending the evening. The last time was only a few minutes before he arrived in person at Tudor Reach. Then, as with another slightly earlier attempt, the line was busy. It's possible Mr Rorch was engaged in a prolonged conversation on the telephone, or in a series of conversations. No one has come forward who was party to such exchanges. Is it not more likely that Mr Rorch had purposely taken the telephone off the hook, as we say, to ensure he would not be disturbed? As we know, Mrs Nibb found the bedroom receiver in just that condition next morning.'

The speaker paused, then shook his head from side to side in answer to the question he was about to pose.

'Is it possible Mr Rorch left the flat between ten-twenty and ten-forty? Possible, but, in my view improbable. I am more and more drawn to the conclusion that he spent the time between Mr Timms's departure and the moment of his demise purposely alone and in a state of morbid introspection.'

Timms and Bander reappeared and quietly resumed their seats. The coroner made a just perceptible gesture of acknowledgment at the two. 'There is no way of knowing the exact time at which the deceased recorded his melancholic message on Miss Helen Wintly's telephone answering machine. We know only that it was done after seven-thirty when she went out, and before eleven-fifteen, the approximate time of her return.

'Again, it would be quite purposeless for Miss Wintly to blame herself in any way for failing to perceive the ominous nature of the message, in the context of its receipt.' The speaker smiled directly at Helen in a fatherly kind of way. Treasure turned to her also where she sat beside him, almost unmoving since giving evidence.

The coroner adjusted his spectacles. 'As we have heard, the phrases "I'm much better out of it. Better out of it altogether. Sorry to let you down. Thanks for everything", were all capable of explanation a good deal less fearful than the one I now judge was intended.

'How easy it was to misunderstand the portent of the message, most particularly by someone not nearly so well acquainted with the deceased and the vagaries of his disposition as some others. It should be a solace to Miss Wintly that Mr Mark Treasure, to whom she immediately relayed the message by telephone, should have been as nearly unsuspicious of any deeper meaning in it. Again, Mr Treasure was not numbered among the deceased's real intimates. At the end of his evidence he said he had felt a momentary qualm on hearing the words of the message, but a qualm that quickly dispelled itself because it had no basis in logic or common sense.' The speaker shrugged. 'It was not for Mr Treasure or anyone else to surmise that the actions presaged by Mr Rorch's words would lack precisely the reasonable foundation he had credited to them.

'Since Miss Wintly telephoned Mr Treasure at eleven-twenty exactly, and since I deduce Mr Rorch met his death at eleven-seventeen, whether or not Mr Treasure had decided to act on the momentary misgiving could not materially have affected the issue.'

Now the coroner adopted his gravest manner and tone. 'Mr Rorch fell to his death down the open well of the fire staircase at Tudor Reach. As the post-mortem examination showed, death was instantaneous. It also indicated the deceased had inhaled an unspecifiable quantity of cannabis, probably over a period of not more than an hour, and that he had consumed forty-two centilitres of gin in the same period.'

The speaker frowned, removed his spectacles, and blinked several times before continuing. 'None of Mr Rorch's friends had admitted to being aware he smoked cannabis. One, Mrs Fentley, has suggested he may have been experimenting with the drug to improve his imaginative capacities. He was ostensibly working that evening, devising an advertising campaign. Mr Timms has a similar theory, with the added suggestion the deceased might have been hoping the drug would calm his temper.' Some scepticism had crept into the tone.

'I am dealing here with speculation. However, no unsmoked cannabis has been found in the flat. Mrs Gertrude Nibb has sworn under oath that while she noticed an unusual odour when she arrived to clean on the following morning—an odour she now accepts may have been the atmospheric residual from burnt cannabis—she had never before encountered this smell about the place.'

Mrs Nibb shifted slightly in her seat at the back of the room, nudging her friend Else who had come to hear her say her piece—and very good Else said she'd been: clear as a bell, and no mumbling like some. There hadn't been any way of going back on admitting about the smell on the Wednesday morning. She'd already heard they'd found drugs in the body: the man who'd done the post-mortem had said so, and he was a professor. But there hadn't been any point in saying she'd smelt it before in the flat—oath or no oath. Let the dead rest: that was Gerty Nibb's motto. She had liked Mr Rorch. What she'd said—or hadn't said—in a way made up for kindnesses enjoyed—including the nips of gin: well, everybody had his little weaknesses.

'It is not impossible that this was the deceased's first experience with cannabis, and that this, combined with the alcohol, materially affected his subsequent actions.' The coroner nodded to himself, before continuing. 'Mrs Nibb discovered the body at two minutes past noon. There seems little doubt death occurred at eleven-seventeen the night before. As the police evidence states, the case of Mr Rorch's quartz wristwatch burst open on impact with the concrete, the battery was dislodged, and the mechanism stopped at eleven-seventeen. The post-mortem report corroborated this nearly enough . . .'

'No, it didn't,' whispered Howie to Treasure. 'The pathologist said left to himself he might have gone for a slightly earlier time.'

'Except he knew about the watch,' Treasure whispered back.

'That's cheating.'

'Not really. Weather conditions. Hot night spoils the body cooling rate. He's saying so.'

'. . . affected by the temperature of the environment,' offered the coroner, on cue, 'and serving to confuse pathological determinations.'

'Told you so.' Treasure glanced at Howie knowingly, then leaning towards him again added, 'Wonder how much longer he's going to take?'

The coroner took two minutes more making it even clearer to all what his decision would be before actually declaring it.

A disturbed, sensitive and overworked mind had succumbed to stress. The resort to drugs and alcohol, expected to alleviate a fraught condition, had served—as was often the case—to do the opposite. The deceased had been alone and determined to remain so for what was to prove the last hour of his life. What torments assailed him during that period could only be guessed at. The fundamental difference of opinion with his business partners seemed to have loomed in his thoughts massively out of proportion to its size and importance. Yet, one could only assume at the last that he felt he had let the others down, regretting it most terribly. Surrender to agonizing remorse, even momentarily, and one could pay an awful penalty—so the coroner advised gratuitously.

Was the recorded message in any sense a cry for help? The speaker believed not. In aftermath, it was clear enough notice of determined intention. The stairwell had beckoned.

'A coroner must speak as he sees.' This one was now staring at an empty spot in the centre of the courtroom. 'Would it be charitable to pronounce that an accident had occurred? Of course it would. But does the evidence support such a contention? It does not. Is there anything to suggest the deceased was taken ill, overcome by dizziness? Did he faint?' The speaker slowly shook his head. 'He was in sound physical health, and conscious before he fell. The drug and the alcohol may have made him unsteady. But, had he been hovering over that stairwell in danger of falling into it by accident, the instinct for self-preservation would surely have brought him to his knees before allowing him to fall.

'Is there the vestige of a suspicion that foul play was involved? There is not. Were any other persons present? They were not.'

The coroner put on his spectacles and shifted his gaze, as though involuntarily, in the direction of George Timms.

'My verdict is that Roger William Rorch died through injuries sustained by falling one hundred and ten feet on to a concrete floor, and that he killed himself.'

CHAPTER 14

'Best to get down to some meaningful activity, don't you think?' said Peter Bander breathily. He flashed an earnest smile, to go with the vacuous advice, at everyone standing

140

on the pavement outside the court.

His contribution as a witness had been limited to his recounting the gist of the last telephone conversation he had had with Rorch, the one that took place before Rorch left the office on the night of his death. Later, Bander had missed George Timms whom he had called on at home. Although he had intended catching up with Timms at Rorch's flat, he had 'stopped for a drink somewhere' on the way, then realized he had left it all too late, and gone home. Most of his associates took the view he had stopped for more than one drink that night. Significantly, none of them had seen him touch alcohol since the tragedy.

'You fellows really feel like keeping to the schedule?' asked Jackson carefully. 'How about you, Helen?'

She nodded, but her face lacked the sparkle that usually accompanied comprehension. 'Peter's right,' she said quietly. 'The lawyers would like us to be at Red Lion Square for two o'clock. It's twelve-forty-seven . . .'

'There'll be sandwiches waiting there now,' put in George Timms unexpectedly — Timms the stage manager with the sandwich-prone secretary, his voice and manner indicating the show would go on.

'The Jaguar's across the road. It can take four of us.' Jackson turned to Howie as he spoke. 'Were you aiming . . . ?'

'I'm going with Mark,' the other American volunteered. 'Don't believe I'll come to the meeting, Lee. If it's OK with you . . .'

'Routine stuff, Howie. Has to be got through, of course. Doesn't need full attendance from the front office.'

Howie nodded, then moved towards Helen and not very deftly took her hand between both his. She showed surprise. He cleared his throat. 'As that coroner said, it wasn't any way your fault. I believe that sincerely.'

'Thank you. I'll try to believe it too.' She withdrew her hand and glanced at Jackson. 'Are we ready?'

141

'Like to get in my car, Howard?' Treasure put in briskly.

Pink had the Rolls parked immediately outside the court.

'Won't take us five minutes to Tudor Reach,' the banker remarked as the car moved off with the two of them in the back. 'We're on the right side of the river.' He paused. 'Wish I were as convinced as that coroner about what happened.

'Other people didn't seem too surprised,' Howie offered tentatively.

'No, they didn't. I thought I knew the man better.' There was a touch of professional pique in the attitude. No banker would take pride in having advanced money to an enterprise with a potentially suicidal chairman.

There was silence for a moment. 'Still a good agency,' said Howie, this time on firm ground—or at least, he hoped so.

'I'm sure. Your price of two-and-a-half million seems entirely equitable.' Treasure smiled. 'Even if the bank has to throw in a full-time chairman.'

'You think Helen will accept?'

'It's a unanimous choice. I think she'll accept, yes. This afternoon probably. Very astute of you and Lee to propose her in the first place.'

'It was my idea.' Howie blinked several times. 'Good business woman. Very creative approach. We figure she'll know how to go about getting new business. That is, when the time comes . . .'

'Her accent's suitably transatlantic, and she won't upset the existing management balance in your new London office. I was mildly surprised that Timms agreed so readily.'

'Lee talked him into it. You know he's to be Deputy Chairman as well as Joint Managing Director? HJ, my father, he needed reassuring RTB wouldn't be putting in a second teamer after Roger died.'

Treasure's eyebrows lifted a fraction. 'Timms being a second teamer?'—and someone who had impressed

Jackson a good deal more than Howard. Surprisingly, it seemed Howard was making the decisions.

'In the sense of taking over the chairmanship, I guess. Mr Ziebal . . .' Howie literally put his hand to his mouth when he realized his error. 'That is . . . er . . . our advisers suggested Helen would get better headlines.'

'And be a more imaginative choice from the viewpoint of the clients and staff, perhaps.' Treasure affected not to have marked Howie's slip. 'Could it be she'll also make a better fall guy — or girl — if anything goes wrong over the next year or two?'

'I don't believe that's been comtemplated, Mark.'

'Except perhaps by Timms,' was Treasure's opinion, but he didn't express it.

The car crossed St George's Circus into Lambeth Road. The banker pointed to an AA direction sign. 'If you take on Roger's flat, you'll be quite close to the famous Oval cricket ground. Getting late in the season, of course. Interested in cricket, Howard?'

'Don't believe I am,' said Howard predictably.

'Nor me. Can't stand the excitement.'

The American wasn't sure whether he should smile. 'Tell me frankly, Mark. You don't think it'll be inappropriate . . . in bad taste if I take the apartment?'

'Not at all. Just hope it suits.' He shrugged. 'With eleven months of a furnished lease to run, and paid for, I imagine Roger's executors will be glad to get rid of it.'

'That's about the period I'll need to be in and out of London pretty often. While RTB and I are getting the Dandy show on the road.' Howie spoke with unusual confidence. 'I'm pretty close to the Dandy management. Closer than Lee. A lot closer.' It was difficult to tell whether he was telling the banker or convincing himself. 'I don't much like hotels. The Savoy's very nice, but this place sounds perfect. Lee won't be over so much. I guess he'll go on using hotels.'

'Your wife will be joining you from time to time?' It seemed appropriate to ask.

'Oh, I think so. Oh, certainly.' But the tone was

anything but certain.

'I wondered whether Roger's mother would keep the flat herself. Stay on for a bit.'

'She left right after the funeral, Monday.'

'For Palm Beach, and her third husband.' Treasure grimaced. 'Roger's father died a long time ago. I gather his mother's married two mountebanks since then.'

'It's hot in Florida this time of year.'

'She told me she likes it. Everything air-conditioned, including, I swear she said, the tennis court.' He shook his head. 'Anyway, it didn't bother her Roger left her only his school presentation Bible, and a loving message in his will. Charming, she called that. Seemed to mean it, too. Incidentally, she was quite sure he'd committed suicide. Told me he'd always been brilliant but unstable. That they hadn't been close since he went away to school at seven.'

'Seven?' Howie repeated incredulously.

'That's the usual age in this country — not to become remote from your mother, just to go away to school. If your parents can afford it, and subscribe to the system.' He decided not to elaborate further. Americans seemed never to understand the tradition: he wasn't sure he did himself any more. 'The family home was in Durban at the time. She was on her second husband. It meant young Roger had to be shipped to and from Britain several times a year. Bit unsettling, probably.'

'He left his RTB shares to be divided equally between the junior working directors. That just excludes Timms and Bander,' said Howie slowly. 'It's usual for quite young men to make wills over here?'

'It varies, as I expect it does in the States. In Roger's case I gather he wanted it made legally plain his ex-wife was intentionally excluded from benefiting. That's if anything happened to him. She left him for someone else. There were no children. The rest of the estate tots up to between twenty and thirty thousand, or so I'm told.'

'Peter Bander says it goes in trust for the existing

children of Gloria Fentley?' Howie's interpolation was questioning.

'Mmm. Which presumably means also the children of Stuart Fentley. Odd way of putting it. I believe the Fentleys have only ever been married to each other.'

'Could suggest . . .'

'All kind of things. I had the same uncharitable thought. Mrs Fentley's quite a looker.'

'She called alone that night. Ahead of her husband.'

'Mrs Jackson also called alone.' Treasure looked for a reaction.

Howie reddened. 'You know that was without Lee's knowledge? Or mine? It seems her intentions were in the best corporate interests,' he ended without much conviction.

'Meaning she hoped to persuade Roger to take a neutral attitude on the offer?'

'That's about it. Joanne's very supportive of her husband. Sometimes too much so.'

'Meaning?' When anyone mentioned 'supportive', Treasure's mind went inexorably to hernia belts: he couldn't help it.

Howie kneaded one hand inside the other. 'I guess it didn't bother her too much if Roger wasn't coming with the agency.'

'Because he might have been a threat to her husband's advancement? And that was conceivable?'

'From my short exposure to Roger, I'd say highly possible.' Howie was still kneading.

'But Mrs Jackson didn't want Roger's pulling out to influence the others to turn down Crabtree. Jackson must have felt the same way.'

The other nodded. 'The difference was, Joanne took some kind of shine to Roger. I don't believe Lee liked him. He liked him on paper. In the flesh . . .'

'So the Jacksons had the same end in mind. Funny if they'd met at Tudor Reach, neither having told the other . . .' Treasure paused. 'No. Pity one of them—anyone—hadn't got Roger to open that door.'

145

'Lee didn't go there. He'd have said so. You know Joanne ran into Roger at St Paul's that day? After lunch. Before they knew each other.'

'She told me. Near the entrance to the galleries. Can't imagine why Roger . . .'

'And she was at Wilton House when he was the one expected there. She found the coincidence pretty uncanny. He'd made the date some days before. She hadn't mentioned to Roger she was going there. Otherwise he'd surely have told her his plans. Or maybe that he'd cancelled them.'

'Not to put too fine a point on it, Howard, by that time he may have cancelled all future engagements.'

'Of course,' answered Howie solemnly. 'Fact is, as I started to explain earlier, Joanne isn't an officer of the company. I think she takes too much on herself that way. HJ is beginning to agree with me. At last.' His head twitched twice from the strain of the evident un-burdening, then he added, 'Lee thought Joanne was making for bed after we finished supper that night.'

Treasure swallowed the first and indelicate riposte that came to mind. Instead, he said, 'Anyway, she didn't see Roger, but she did . . . er . . . establish communication with an RTB client.'

'Yes. Mr Grimalt. Peter Bander and Helen had lunch with him early this week. He wasn't too happy about the merger at the beginning.'

'But he's coming around to it?'

'Peter thinks so. Says he's susceptible to female influence — Helen's I guess, not Joanne's,' Howie replied stiffly.

'Incidentally, where was Lee after you finished supper that night?'

'Walking by himself till . . . till around eleven. He didn't know Joanne was out. She told us she'd been to Tudor Reach when we were taking breakfast next morning. It was after Peter Bander had phoned us. Mr Grimalt had called him, saying he'd run into Joanne.'

'And she didn't mention her visit till then?'

'I suppose she forgot.'

'It's a big building to forget,' Treasure offered, nodding through the window.

The car had drawn up in front of the wide marble step that led up to the elaborately carved, wooden double doors to the apartment building. The doors stood wide open.

'It seems they're expecting you, Howard.'

'I don't believe so,' said the other seriously. 'I have the keys.'

As they entered the building a gangling, genial West Indian switched off the electric floor polisher he'd been waltzing with near the door. He was fortyish and dressed in clean white overalls.

'Welcome, gents.' He beamed broadly. The words had come out as a husky murmur emanating from lower neck level. 'Laryngitis. Damn fool time of year to have that. Shouted meself hoarse at a cricket match.' He unplugged the polisher. 'The name's Marcus, by the way. Have to ask who you are. Only leave the door open if I'm working in the hall.'

'It'll do very well,' announced Howie, ten minutes later. 'I like to cook,' he added, then as though this wasn't enough to explain why a red-blooded American male had been quite so long in the kitchen: 'I put the clock right in there. The one by the cooker. Complicated digital. They're all different. Had to work it out.'

'Good,' said Treasure firmly, because Howie seemed always in need of assurance. The American had just joined him on the penthouse terrace. Both men were now leaning on the metal rail that rose to elbow height from stanchions in the low surrounding wall. 'Marvellous view of London,' the banker went on. 'Westminster Abbey, Houses of Parliament up there.' He pointed to the right. 'River here runs almost due north. Much better view this side of it.' He turned his attention to the left. 'You could see my place . . . if it wasn't for the 'ouses in between,' he joked.

'Which houses do you mean?'

'Sorry, that's a line from a nineteenth-century ditty. Edgar Bateman, I think,' and since this seemed only to confuse his companion, he went on quickly, 'In fact you *can* see where Helen Wintly lives.' He pointed out Dolphin Square over the water. 'You could send signals to her from here. This terrace is very commanding — and pretty conspicuous, come to think of it.'

'Is Helen wealthy?' Howie inquired.

'Well, if she wasn't, she is now. Or comparatively so. She comes into eight hundred and thirty-three of Roger's shares. The other two non-shareholding directors get the same, of course.'

'It was generous of Roger to leave the shares to colleagues.'

'Mmm. Academic gesture at the time, I expect. His only relative appears to be his well-off mother. If he'd left the shares to her or anyone else outside RTB they couldn't have kept them. Shares have to be held by employees or the bank. Leaving them to people he'd agreed — possibly arranged — to have on the board was sensible and practical. Must have done something for good-will too. I gather he'd told them about it. Of course, you have to remember that up till fairly recently, those shares were worth about a pound each. Par value.'

'You mean our deal . . . ?'

'Obviously thumped up the value. Of course, when the deal went through, he'd have had no shares to leave, so the generous legacy would have ceased to apply. With or without your deal, he might have made a new will anyway with the company starting to prosper. Might have spread the largesse a bit wider. The present will has all the marks of something done in haste to spite his ex-wife — perhaps until he acquired a new one. Wife, I mean. Incidentally, those shares will pass on to Helen and the others still at their pre-bid price. There'll be no estate duty to pay.'

'Except your Revenue Department will revalue the shares, surely? There's a bid pending.'

Treasure shook his head. 'Pending is the operative

word. The deal doesn't count because it hadn't gone through. That's the marvellous part for Helen. Your offer values the shares at £250 each.'

'With no death duties to be subtracted?'

'Right. Her holding will be worth something over two hundred thousand.'

Howie screwed up his face. 'Two hundred and eight thousand, two hundred and fifty exactly,' he remarked, almost absently.

'Sounds about right.' Treasure smiled. 'Since the shares are to be sold on to Crabtree almost immediately, and since she got them for nothing, she'll have to pay capital gains tax at thirty per cent on the lot.'

'Leaving her with . . . one hundred and forty-five thousand seven hundred and seventy-five.' The pause for the calculation had again been impressively brief.

'I'll take your word for it, Howard.' The banker realized he hadn't mentioned the initial, modest tax-free allowance on capital gains, but it seemed churlish to spoil the results of such immaculate mental arithmetic with peccadilloes. 'Not bad after only six months' involvement. Three as an outside director,' he mused instead.

'And to be made Chairman of the board.'

'That's right.' Treasure was moving back to the glass doors into the living-room. 'Place is certainly spotless. Credit to Mrs . . .'

'Mrs Nibb. She said in court she did a thorough job. Not a fingerprint anywhere.' Howie had also walked over. 'Same in the bedroom. Guess I'll keep the desk in there. Good place to work. Saves clutter in here.'

'You could use the second bedroom.' The banker paused. 'Curious there was no evidence here of the work he was supposed to be doing.'

'Kept a good deal in his head, apparently. Especially concept work. George Timms was here last week to collect everything belonging to the office. Went through the desk drawers, even.'

'Mmm. He told me. Said he found nothing on the Carter Cousins project, for instance.'

'If Roger put anything on paper, I guess he'd thrown it away.'

'In a wastepaper-basket dutifully emptied by Mrs Nibb.' Treasure frowned.

The two men hadn't lingered at the top of the stairs when they arrived. In truth, Howie had purposely avoided doing so. Now, when they were leaving, as they came through the fire door, instead of going down the stairs, Treasure walked across the upper landing. The other man followed.

The stairwell looked to be about eight feet by six, with a sheer drop into the basement.

'Unofficially I hear they'll be casing this eventually. Putting in another lift,' remarked the banker.

'An elevator? Just for my apartment?' Howie responded on reflex, like a typical, soon to be enraged tenant expecting to be surcharged for an amenity he could do without. 'But it's practically a new building. Less than half the apartments are taken. Why didn't they put it in . . .?'

'It's a bit complicated, Howard.' It happened Treasure had heard the story from a property crony. 'Your flat wasn't in the original building plan. The local Council originally approved a nine-storey block. When the developers volunteered to install a new form of auxiliary solar heating, the Council allowed an extra apartment on the roof.'

'Why would they do that?'

'The plant was too costly, too experimental to try out on municipal housing, but the Council was anxious to know if it worked.' He shrugged. 'Putting in the plant increased the height of the building. By roughly one floor.'

'Seems fair.'

'Better than that, Howard.' Treasure gave a wry smile. 'The developers were pretty certain the solar plant would warm nothing more than the hearts of a few keen environmentalists.'

150

'So why go to the expense . . . ?'

'After a decent interval the experiment will be quietly abandoned and the plant dismantled. Then there'll be room for three more flats up here. Hence an extra private lift in this over-sized stairwell—which wasn't in the original plans either. Only the stairs.'

Howie shook his head. 'Kind of a roundabout way of doing things.'

'Not at all,' pronounced the other, a trifle sententiously. 'Expectations of the authorities and the developers, though quite different, have been perfectly reconciled. Tribute to the marvellous powers of commercial expediency. May even work too.' He turned about and tried the handle of a door that evidently led on to the roof. 'Locked. Pity. I'd like to have looked at the fancy equipment out there. Can't see it from the flat.'

'I have a key to that door, gents.' The disembodied voice seemed to come from close by: its hoarseness identified its owner.

Marcus, the maintenance man, now appeared on the basement floor of the stairwell.

'Want me to come up? Won't take a minute.' He stared up from more than a hundred feet below. 'Sounds like I'm there already, doesn't it?' he wheezed. 'Trick of this shaft.'

He disappeared, emerging shortly after through the firedoor on the landing below them.

'Used to tickle Mr Rorch, that one. On Fridays, that's the day I'm always here, if he saw me on the stairs, he'd stand right where you are now and talk to me as quiet as he could. And I'd talk back the same way. Like today I couldn't talk no louder, anyway.' He pulled a bunch of keys from his pocket. 'Mr Rorch said it was crazy. The way your voice carried out here.'

'Acoustical oddity,' murmured Treasure, testing the phenomenon and still considering the drop. 'Can you tell us when the refuse is collected from the building?' he asked.

'Wednesday mornings, regular. Goes down bagged in a

chute from the flats. There's a hopper in the basement. Good system. Works.' The speaker's gaze followed Treasure's. 'Terrible thing last week. If it'd been Friday, I'd have found him. Always here early. He was such a great guy, Mr Rorch. Made time for jokes. Gags. You know?' He swallowed with effort, making towards the locked door. 'Accident, huh?'

'We just came from the inquest. The coroner's verdict was suicide,' said Treasure.

Marcus shook his head in disbelief. He looked from Treasure to Howie. 'You friends of his? You buy that? Suicide?'

'He left a message. There was other evidence,' Howie offered.

'Well, I don't buy it, gents. That man had everything going for him. Everything.' He swallowed again. 'Remember the last thing he said to me. Two weeks ago today. He was in the basement getting his car. I was up here dusting that rail. I thought he'd gone, but then he steps out. Where I was just now. Where you saw me. "What you forget, Mr Rorch?" I called down loud, not thinking. But he was just having fun. "Relax, man," he says, real quiet. "Relax, man," he says, again, even quieter. "You don't need to shout when you can whisper." '

CHAPTER 15

'I'm not requesting. I'm insisting,' said Emily Gaunt severely, but not nearly so sure of her ground as she sounded. 'Please make that absolutely clear to your superiors in Athens. If they won't cooperate, I shall report the whole matter to — to Thomas Cook.' She paused to afford proper emphasis. The name of her own one-man travel agent in Islington, she felt, wouldn't have carried nearly so much weight. From the look on the girl's face, Thomas Cook's didn't carry much either.

'There's a room available,' Miss Gaunt continued. 'We shall wait here in the lobby while you telephone. Please be as quick as you can. My friend should be in bed.'

Tina, the pretty young guide from the tour company, had quite lost the good-humoured sparkle she had shown all day. She was a third-year language student at Athens University. She had never before faced losing tour passengers en route. She was not sure whether the company would deduct something from her pay, which wasn't very much to start with.

The coach driver had said he wouldn't be responsible. As for the other passengers — assorted, but all English-speaking, and grouped around the coach outside — their sympathies lay with their suffering fellow traveller, Miss Mildred Pitts.

Neither Miss Gaunt nor Miss Pitts had much enjoyed lunch at the open air taverna in Nafplion: that had been four hours earlier. Nor had that been the start of their discomfort. By that time they had already suffered a blisteringly hot journey from the wrong side of Athens, visiting Corinth and Mycenae and beginning at 6.45.

The cooling system in the coach had broken down just after 11, when the need for it had become greatest. There had been a strong smell of diesel fuel, even when the windows were opened — especially when the windows were opened and the vehicle was moving slowly behind a lot of other coaches, which it was a good deal of the time.

By lunch-time Miss Pitts had been visibly and progressively wilting, only rallying at brief intervals. For her own part, Miss Gaunt had summoned all her stoic reserves.

There had been compensations. The ladies had marvelled at the chasm of the Corinthian Canal, and at Corinth itself. The pagan Temple of Apollo had been predictably less awesome for Miss Gaunt than the touch of the very rock from which it was alleged St Paul addressed the citizens before writing them all those epistles. The Lion Gate at Mycenae had been a powerful sight. There had been time for the museum there, too—blessedly cool. Miss Pitts had even at last got over her tiresome inhibition about having to view starkly naked male statuary while she was still moving, and affecting to be looking at something else.

Culturally, it had been a rewarding morning.

The two companions had been hungry when the coach party had been deposited at the taverna. At first sight, they had applauded with the others when the chefs had brought out the roasted whole sheep carcases. It was the barbarous dismembering of those carcases that had begun to turn Miss Pitts's stomach. Stout men had done the job with flashing cleavers on wooden slabs just in front of the guests. Seated very close to the butchery, Miss Pitts had been in fear of getting spattered: her chair had been continuously bumped by the shouting, bustling waiters as they distributed pyramid piles of plates filled with ragged lumps of the rough-hewn mutton.

'Quite Bacchanalian, don't you think, Mildred?' Miss Gaunt had offered cheerfully at the time, adding, 'I wouldn't have too much of the wine. Bit sharp.'

The shame was Miss Pitts had ignored the last advice. But she had been very thirsty: the wine was free, and they had kept filling up her glass: she had asked for water, but it never came. She remembered thinking the alcohol would act as a kind of antidote if the small amount of meat she had consumed proved as noxious as it looked.

It was later, on the road to Epidauros, that Miss Pitts had thrown up: just outside the picturesque village of Ligourio. She was quite sure that this event had 'settled' things: it had passed off with the minimum of embarrassment. She had had a Harrods plastic bag ready in good time. She always carried a few small bags against this specific emergency: it was a pity to have 'lost' this particular one, though she had another like it: her boss bought his socks at Harrods.

She had felt a bit groggy again when they got off the coach in Epidauros where they now were. She had still insisted on setting off along the partly shaded broadwalk in the park to see the famous amphitheatre. It was here

154

that she had literally fallen by the wayside — specifically beneath a tree against which she had been propped up for some time, gulping bile and moaning quietly. Eventually Miss Gaunt had got her to her feet, and steered her to the lobby of the small hotel. She insisted, there, that she felt much better — then fooled everybody by throwing up again.

It was Miss Gaunt who had made the decision they would remain in Epidauros for the night. The coach tour company operated a daily service. It was only necessary to ensure places were reserved on the Saturday coach for the two passengers who were now deserting the Friday one.

But Tina, the guide, after close consultation in conspiratorial Greek with the coach driver, had been ready to risk the bilious Miss Pitts on the two-hour journey back to Athens. It was the height of the season. She could not be sure there would be empty places on the coach tomorrow — and if there were, who would have to pay for using them?

'The company must make sure there are seats for us tomorrow,' Miss Gaunt had announced, just prior to her point about insisting, not requesting in the matter.

'We don't absolutely have to stay, Emily,' confided Miss Pitts as soon as Tina was out of hearing. She was absently fingering the Austin Reed bag in her hand. 'I'm feeling much better. Truly I am.'

Miss Gaunt surveyed the pallid countenance with the patches of raw and peeling skin — the legacy of the previous week's over-exposure to the sun: Mildred learned the hard way. 'Yes, and you'll be right as rain tomorrow if you go to bed now.'

'But Emily, what about the expense?'

'Bother the expense. Anyway, we're insured for this sort of thing.' Miss Gaunt wasn't completely sure on that point. She meant to read the small print on the form when they got back to their own hotel. Still, the information helped to cheer her friend a little. 'This place seems clean and cared for.' Miss Gaunt looked approvingly at the scrubbed tiles and the hand-lettered notice 'no credit cards' exhibited on the reception desk: Miss Gaunt disapproved of credit cards.

'It's quite small. Do you think we'll have our own bathroom, Emily?'

'And loo. Of course. I wouldn't have booked otherwise.' There was more relief on the other's face. 'Pity we didn't do the Corinth and Epidauros two-day tour in the first place. It was only a thousand drachma more.' And it had only been Mildred's diffidence at paying the extra that had prevented them: Miss Gaunt allowed herself this mild recrimination.

'Do you think we'd have stayed in this hotel if we had, Emily? Is it the hotel the tour company uses, perhaps?'

'No. That's back in Nafplion.'

'Oh.' Miss Pitts's expression glazed. The mention of Nafplion stirred memories of flaying meat cleavers.

'If you're better in the morning, and I'm sure you will be, we might get up early and see the sights.'

'Before the buses get here? Before it gets so hot? Oh, that would be nice. To be honest, I . . . I've found the crowds a bit much today. Worse than last week on the Athens Acropolis. Worse than Delphi . . .' The sentence was allowed to peter out on the return of Tina.

The young guide's bonhomie seemed mostly repaired.

'So it's OK. There'll be two places on tomorrow's coach for you. No charge. But the company won't pay for this hotel tonight. You understand, we have no arrangement here?' the girl continued in her good student English. 'If you'd decided to stay at Nafplion . . .'

'It doesn't matter,' Miss Gaunt broke in quickly with a glance at Mildred Pitts.

Treasure had been surprised to get the call — and on his private line: the number was not in general circulation. It came shortly after he'd returned from lunch with Howie who he'd taken to his club after their visit to Tudor Reach.

From what he knew of Joe Ziebal — which wasn't a great deal — he was even more surprised at the request for an urgent and confidential meeting, and intrigued enough to grant it.

Exactly on time, at five o'clock precisely, the rotund Mr Ziebal bounced into the banker's office.

The two shook hands.

'Mr Treasure, you ever do things on impulse?'

'Mmm . . .'

'Neither do I. And we're both right. Think first. This visit is probably a mistake. What I have to say is probably a mistake. But to live with yourself, sometimes you have to . . .'

'Break rules?'

'Trust reputations. That's a compliment. You don't know why I'm here.'

'Unless it has to do with the Crabtree RTB business. Do sit down.'

'You figured I was involved in that?' Ziebal settled himself on one of the two facing sofas. 'You were right.' He took off his tinted glasses and put them away, squinting for a moment at the banker who sat opposite.

'It was a reasonable guess' — also one that relieved Treasure of having to dissemble over Howie's slip.

'The deal went through this afternoon?'

'I understand the letter of intent was signed.' The banker nodded. 'The lawyers have worked very fast.'

'So, no problems. No complications. Nice marriage. I set it up. Mind if I smoke?'

Treasure indicated the silver cigarette box on the marble-topped table between them, but the visitor produced his own packet. 'You've stayed in the background?'

Joe froze in the act of lighting the cigarette. He snapped the lighter shut and snatched the unlit cigarette from his lips, hiding both objects from view in clenched fists, like a conjuror. 'Invisible!' For a moment he didn't move any part of his small but substantial anatomy. 'And when I decide to be invisible on a deal, that's the way I stay. That's why I'm not here now. Why we've never met. OK?'

157

'If you wish.'

'That is my sincerest wish, Mr Treasure. And I respect your word as a gentleman. It's a nice temperature in here. I came in a cab. Phew!' He blew air at his nose from his protruded lower lip. Then he lit the cigarette.

'You said a personal matter. I take it the Crabtree involvement is incidental.'

'Right again.' Joe stubbed out the cigarette. He smiled knowingly. 'Way to stay sane *and* healthy.' Now his right hand was feeling for his hairline. 'See, I work in different ways. Horses for courses. Lot of the stuff is personal.' The hand dropped to rest on the podgy knee. The torso was bent forward.

'You're in executive recruitment.'

Both palms shot out towards the banker. 'Head-hunting. Which is entirely personal. You'd understand, of course.' Pleasure registered at the assumption of a higher comprehension. 'Not to say arranging company marriages isn't personal too. It's all contacts, Mr Treasure.' He leant even further forward: it was difficult to credit any part of his rear was still in touch with the seat. 'And sometimes the personal relationships are transitory. Sometimes enduring. Never shallow, though. Not for me. Come to the point.' It was a statement not an injunction. 'I have friends in Crabtree. I have friends in RTB. Otherwise I couldn't have put them together.'

'No exaggeration?' This came with marked good humour.

'For most people saying such a thing, there might be.' The tone, too, admitted grounds for disputation. 'For me, I have to know and like people in both companies.'

'Very commendable.'

'OK. Trade secret coming. If I stay invisible on a deal, it's because I have a very influential friend in the candidate company.'

'The company you pick for your client to acquire? So he does covertly . . .'

'But objectively.'

Treasure pouted at the interruption. 'All right, and

objectively, what you could only do . . .'

'With as much apparent objectivity as a brush salesman with two feet in the door.'

'You share your finder's fee with the inside man?'

'Depends. He does the work. Sometimes if he's a shareholder it's . . . it's not necessary.'

'Or especially ethical.'

'You took the words out of my mouth.'

'He's a Trojan horse.'

'Let's say a merchant bank couldn't use the tactic. In case anyone found out.'

Treasure smiled tolerantly. 'I'm not sure . . .'

'So why quibble over the niceties, Mr Treasure? In ten years in this business, I never handled a merger that didn't work. OK? I operate in one industry only. Communications. Mostly advertising agencies. So I'm putting pairs of agencies together. American with American. American with British. British with British. British with German. So on.' He shrugged. 'I don't handle public companies much, and usually not the top five or six. Anything below that—and privately controlled. That's for mergers, you understand? Executive placement is different. That's across the board.' He lit another cigarette.'

'I understand but . . .'

'Hear me out, Mr Treasure. Most times on a merger I'm right out there, foot in the door, like I said. And everybody knows Joe Ziebal's running the show. No ethical hang-ups, you'd say. No Trojan horse. Everything kosher. When I'm invisible it's only so I don't cramp the style of whoever's inside rooting for the deal . . .'

'On the inside of the candidate company. And he's identified as that to the principals of the other company.'

'No, sir.'

'Not till after the deal?'

'Not ever is my advice. It's usually followed. If there's an insider, I tell the chief company officer on the other side. Never who. Only if.'

'The chief officer being at liberty to tell others. Probably does.'

'Sometimes yes. Sometimes no. In the case of Crabtree there's three of them know there was an insider.'

'The two Crabtrees and Lee Jackson. I appreciate the confidence, Mr Ziebal, but frankly I don't see . . .'

'To the point, like I said.' Joe drew deeply on the cigarette. 'I hear they decided at the inquest Roger Rorch committed suicide because of pressure over the deal.'

'I was there. Yes, that's what it boiled down to. Verdict was pretty predictable. He was obviously on a tighter string than anyone suspected. These things happen. I suppose everything seemed to be going against him.' Treasure paused. 'Is your insider taking it hard?'

'Very. He's dead.' Joe stabbed the cigarette into the ashtray, breaking it in two. 'His name was Roger Rorch.'

'Roger was your inside man? But that's impossible.'

'Impossible he killed himself over the deal? I think so. He and I set it up three weeks ago. Day after I got the word from Crabtree to start searching. We even agreed the price. Three million. Meant the shareholders would get top dollar. The maximum. No one lost because Roger was working on the inside. Except me. I usually get a bonus if I bring the price in under my maximum estimate. But Roger insisted.' The eyes twinkled. 'So I fixed my basic fee nice and high.'

'But Roger gave every indication of being against.'

'And he'd have gone on that way. Past the point where Peter Bander would be pressing they let go of OPD Foods, if necessary. Past where they'd all have got used to being the Dandy house agency—and working for Jebbit, Fowler, the account everybody loves to hate.'

'You mean he didn't want to be the one seen to be leading?'

Joe nodded. 'Roger was seeing further ahead than the others. To the time of repenting. Recrimination. Know what I mean?'

'He thought the others would come to regret the deal?'

'Right.'

160

'So then he could say I told you so? You brought it on yourselves? You forced me into it?'

'Almost. I guess he'd have gone easier on them than that. You've got half the picture. Come the time the others would be regretting—say a year from now—Roger would be President of Crabtree, world wide. Jackson wasn't getting the job. I had two briefs from the old man. Find a British agency, and find the corporation a new executive leader. The second brief was strictly between HJ and me. It was luck RTB gave both answers.'

'So Roger was to be put in over Jackson?'

'Provided Howie liked him when they met. He did. It was mutual.' Joe laughed. 'Howie was certain his father would go for Roger too.'

'And they met just once? Here, at lunch. And Howard Junior didn't know you had Roger pencilled in for the New York job?'

'Still doesn't. And I had him inked in. The old man was accepting my judgement. That included Howie and Roger liking each other. After they'd met, I was to brief Howie on the plan. Never had the chance. Would have done it Wednesday. I saw Howie on the Tuesday evening, but he had Jackson with him. Incidentally, HJ never did think much of Jackson. Prefers Joanne, his wife. If you follow me?'

The banker's eyebrows lifted. 'I think so.' He paused. 'And Roger affecting to disappear for a bit? That was to give you the chance to clear his appointment with Howie?'

'It fitted. Along with other things. Roger needed that confirmation. You got to understand he wouldn't have gone for just the sale of RTB by itself. He still had too many dreams about where the agency might be going. Except, deep down, he had this gnaw in his gut they'd missed it.'

'Missed the boat, you mean?'

'Sure. Know something else? Especially he figured Timms and Bander weren't going any place. They weren't giving him the back-up he needed. But he was stuck with them. Nice guys. He couldn't drop them. Not

161

in his nature. But he could move up while they stayed level. So the way things were planned, heading up Crabtree in the US was a better base for a guy with a busting ambition to be top.'

'And Carter Cousins?'

'Roger's *pièce de résistance*. He needed to land that fish. First to prove his ability. Second, so he could make the big sacrifice throwing it back. He guessed Carter would pull out after the takeover. But he wanted them as clients first. The timing was off, that's all. Roger still figured to get them in under the wire.'

'Which is why he was devoting himself to producing that campaign.' Treasure frowned. 'And passing up Carter Cousins would have appeared a bigger personal sacrifice than either of the other partners suffered.'

'Come the time for repenting.'

'Curious. The Carter affair seems exactly to have reflected the way Roger said RTB should grow. He seemed so thoroughly earnest about it.'

'Great actor. But don't think he didn't have doubts. Right up to the last minute. With me, that is.' The cigarettes came out again. 'It was the girl who tipped it. Helen Wintly.'

'She was made Chairman this afternoon.'

'I guessed. That was Roger's idea. Now brought forward. He figured she'd be outstanding.'

'For when he went to the States? And he didn't expect opposition? For instance, from George Timms.'

'Categorically not. Said when the time came, Timms would say he wanted the job. Then be happy to be talked out of it. Looks like Roger was right. I've had to pressure Howie a little over Helen. Wasn't so difficult. Her getting the top job here tied up the twin package. HJ was happy to go on my judgement — especially when Lee Jackson made reservations about Roger. That did it for HJ.'

'The package you speak of involved Roger Rorch eventually moving to New York. But he's dead. He committed suicide.' Treasure showed his perplexity. 'Mr

162

Ziebal, why are you telling me all this? Your client is Crabtree.'

'Nice people, Mr Treasure. But foreigners,' was the preposterous reply, considering the accent it came in. 'Understand me? The deal's through. The client's got what he wanted at below the price expected.'

'But without Rorch.'

'Who Howie didn't know was tagged for New York. It's HJ who's especially grieved.'

'Because although he's getting an adequate London agency . . .'

'With the Chairman we eventually planned on, there's no new guy for the States. That's right. For him we have to go out looking again. HJ is waiting on me for that. Meantime, Jackson isn't too upset.'

'But surely he has no idea he's not going to be promoted?'

'Only suspicions — shared by his wife. He thinks time's on his side.'

'That he'll be made President when the founder retires next year . . .'

'And Howie becomes Chairman, with no one else in the running for President. Except the old man could postpone going. He'd done it enough times already.'

Treasure nodded. 'You still haven't . . .'

'I want to thank you for your time, Mr Treasure.' Joe abruptly stabbed out the hardly smoked cigarette. 'Talking with you takes a load off my mind. That coroner's verdict. I couldn't have lived with it. Thinking British, the way I do, I couldn't be the only one knowing Roger couldn't have done what they said. That he took his life because the Crabtree deal bugged him. OK. He had something else on his mind I didn't know about. Something so bad, he couldn't go on. Whatever.' He stood up.

'And that's it? You're not intending to tell anyone else?'

'What's the point? Like they say in the movies, it won't bring him back.'

'You're not expecting me to tell anyone? In the

circumstances, I wouldn't without your concurrence.'
Treasure also now got up.

'That's what I figured. Also, when you've thought about it, you'd maybe see there's no point in it going beyond the two of us. Maybe.'

'It might make the younger Howard feel easier in his mind.'

'Howie doesn't feel responsible. I know it.'

'I think you're right.' The banker nodded slowly. 'He believes . . .'

'That Roger must have been heading for a crack-up anyway. Also, it won't help Timms and Bander any to know Roger was conning them over the deal.'

'That he was your inside man? No. That would do very little to burnish Rorch's memory.' Treasure held out his hand. 'Let me think about it. You prefer to see yourself out?'

'You bet.' Joe had already put on his dark glasses.

A minute later, after his visitor had left, Treasure was still debating why the man had really come to him. He hadn't seemed the kind whose conscience would prey over what, when you analysed it, was a hair-splitting issue. Rorch had committed suicide either for the reason offered by the coroner, or else for an unknown one. Could it have really mattered that much to Ziebal?

The man had admitted to being devious. You could almost say his transparent deviousness was refreshing: but you could hardly call him naïve.

Treasure recalled some words of Ziebal's at the end—when he had nearly said his piece. Had he been divesting himself of a responsibility, rather than sharing it? Was it now up to Treasure to conclude from the new evidence not just that *maybe* there was no point in sharing it, but that *maybe* Rorch hadn't committed suicide at all?

And if it hadn't been suicide, and if it hadn't been an accident, how had Rorch come to die? And why?

CHAPTER 16

'I believe you know our new Chairman,' said Peter Bander to Treasure with mock earnestness.

'Not nearly as well as I'd like. And now it's too late,' replied the banker with matching joviality. He took Helen's hand. 'Congratulations.'

Most of the RTB staff was assembled for drinks in the basement conference room. Treasure had agreed to look in at 6.30. It was a short notice party to announce the merger was going ahead, and to mark some boardroom appointments.

'Thank you. You've been so understanding. It's what I really want to do. I feel . . .'

'Hi, Mark. Glad you could make it,' interrupted Lee Jackson, who had pushed through the knot of people near the door. He had a glass in each hand. 'You'll have champagne? Compliments of Howard J. Crabtree Incorporated.'

'Thank you. Can't stay long, I'm afraid. Have to leave at seven.' There was no especial necessity, but he put limits on courtesy visits.

'Buying another advertising agency?'

'No. Putting together a loan to build a bridge, as a matter of fact.' This was true. He had the details to read over the weekend. 'So your meeting was concluded satisfactorily?'

'For starters, we voted Howie and me on to the board, Helen into the chair, and George to be Deputy Chairman,' Jackson went on. 'Plus a few other un-important details like resolving to sell all the stock to Crabtree, paying off the bank's loans. That kind of thing. Your lawyer was there to see fair play.'

'Good.' Treasure smiled, then turned back to Bander. 'And I understand Mr Grimalt is proving more cooperative,' he said, dropping his voice.

'He's pretty well committed to leaving OPD Foods with us for a six months' trial under the new ownership. We sweated too much over that one. Really thought it was a goner. It was Helen won him over.' Bander took a very deep breath, then quickly blew it out again. 'I can tell you, the day old Rog . . .' He hesitated in mid-sentence.

'The day Mr Grimalt heard about the merger, he wanted out,' Jackson filled in. 'Guess we've all helped to change his mind since then,' he added immodestly. 'He was uncomfortable about certain arrangements being changed. We've straightened him out on those. Now he'll stick with the agency. The six months is just to make sure we stay on our toes.'

'Is Howard here?' asked Treasure, stepping back from the tight little group of top management. He looked around at the sea of faces. A good many curious gazes promptly turned away from his: some — mostly female — lingered.

'Be along later. Bringing Joanne. Some of us are having dinner,' answered Jackson. 'Glad to have you join us.'

'Sorry I can't, Lee. Good evening, George.' Treasure went across to Timms, the focus figure in a large group. 'Congratulations, Mr Deputy Chairman.'

'Thank you, Mark.' Timms seemed unaccountably pleased for someone who had just been passed over for higher office. 'Don't think you know Laura Cray, our Creative Director, and Barny Smith, Media Director.'

The banker shook hands with the stout, amiable woman wreathed in cigarette smoke which she was doing her best to disperse. 'Nice to know you, Mr Treasure. This is Barny. Sharp as he looks.'

It was Laura who saw to it Treasure was introduced to as many people as was practical, bringing some over to meet him, moving him about between groups, making sure always he wasn't stranded with bores or belligerents. She behaved altogether like someone charged to shepherd a royal personage — a status Treasure began to feel he had temporarily acquired. The reception from some was obsequious and nervous, from others intelligently

166

inquisitorial, and — in a very few cases — smoulderingly hostile. When Laura noted the last reaction she promptly moved her charge onwards.

Barny Smith had stayed close by. Later, when Treasure had said it was nearly time for him to go, he found himself engaged again just with these two younger directors.

'Reckon everyone deserving's had his or her fair share of merchant banker,' pronounced Laura, lighting a fresh cigarette. 'Good of you to show. Puts the seal of respectability on what's happening.'

'Can't please everyone, of course,' offered the well-groomed Media Director, a touch of apology in his voice. 'A few are against the sell-out,' he added quietly.

The banker nodded. 'So you're both of you substantial shareholders now. Helen too.'

'For a few days, anyway,' Smith answered. 'The accountants are finding out if instead of taking the money for the RTB shares, we can exchange them for Crabtree shares.'

'Called a roll-over deal,' said Treasure automatically. 'Should endear you to your new masters.'

'Me, I'll take the money,' pronounced Laura. 'Don't trust them damn Yankees,' she called across genially to Jackson.

'But we're good to our women,' he called back.

'Maybe, but you're not rolling me over. Well, not all of me.' She raised her glass in Jackson's direction. It was clear good relations had been established between the two.

'It'd delay your having to pay capital gains till you sell your Crabtree shares,' offered the banker to Smith. 'That could be a long time ahead. Meantime you'd have the use of the money, and eventually you might spread the final sale over several years to reduce tax.'

'You'd recommend it, sir?'

'Yes, but it's unlikely the Revenue will allow it. Worth trying, though.'

'I'm spread out enough already,' quipped the Creative Director.

'It's an ill wind, of course,' said Smith solemnly.

'You mean Roger Rorch?' questioned Treasure.

'His shares. His generosity. His death.' The woman was suddenly serious.

'You knew he was leaving you shares?'

'Yes. It was a kind of joke, though. One night, over drinks, he said, very casually, he'd made a will to spite his bitch of an ex-wife.'

'He also said we shouldn't get heady about it,' Smith took up the story. 'It was only a temporary sort of will. Till he got his life sorted out . . .'

'But meantime we'd be his undeserving beneficiaries.' This was Laura again. 'That's how he described us, the darling. Oh God, I keep expecting him to walk through the door. He loved champagne.'

'Except when flying,' cautioned Smith. 'Said you shouldn't drink anything aerated in high altitudes. Even Perrier water.'

'Oh, and no coffee after five. Keeps you awake. Have to be five in the morning in my case. Live on the stuff,' Laura added. 'Roger had a lot of fads. Didn't smoke. Well . . . not tobacco.' She coloured slightly. 'Not anything, really.'

'And he practised what he preached,' Smith chipped in quickly.

'It's why we'll never know about the smashing idea for Carter Cousins,' said Laura. 'No one will. It died with him.'

'Keeping what you call a creative concept to yourself. That's the right way to play it in your business?'

It was the woman who answered Treasure. 'Roger didn't see it that way. Creative people are expensive. If he had an idea he reckoned it was cheaper for him to worry at it round the clock till he was satisfied it was right. Not to involve others at the "iffy" stages. Matter of fact, used to burn me sometimes. That he didn't share. Even with me. I'm supposed to be the Creative Director. I told him.

168

Often.' She paused. 'He was still a marvellous fella. And he got some great ideas.'

'Carter's have given us the boot,' added Smith, very down-to-earth. 'Inevitable, of course. Plenty of compensations, though.'

'And you approve of Helen as Chairman?'

Both the others nodded vigorously at Treasure's question.

Smith had voted in the new Chairman as enthusiastically as the other directors, while still keeping his own counsel. It was obviously something the Americans had wanted. He wasn't yet in the confidence of Howie Crabtree or Lee Jackson, but he intended to be so soon. He saw the prospects for his own advancement as now considerably augmented, provided he pleased the new owners.

'Probably the job should have gone to George,' said Laura, who was totally unconstrained about the frank airing of views. 'But we're used to Roger's methods. Helen's won't be much different. So we'll each of us go on with doing what we're good at.'

Treasure noted that no one had considered Peter Bander for Chairman — including, presumably, Peter Bander.

'Roger didn't care for management meetings or committees,' said Smith. 'Consensus is no substitute for leadership or decision. End of quote. One board meeting, once a month, to keep everybody in the picture. That was it for Roger. He wasn't a collectivist. Neither is Helen.' Barny Smith was volunteering his views loudly, and not waiting to be counted.

'It's true, under Roger you always knew who to blame.' Laura chuckled. 'And it was often Roger.'

'And if it was, he really took it out on himself. That's why I think . . .' The Media Director's voice tailed away.

'If you really have to go, can I beg a ride? Have to change before dinner.' Helen Wintly had joined the trio: her words were directed at Treasure.

*

'I wanted to thank you properly. For your support. Being made Chairman. Clearing my release from the bank. Oh, everything. Another drink . . . Mark?' They both smiled. It was the first time Helen had used his first name.

He shook his head, turning away from the living-room window of her fourth-floor flat.

Their conversation in the car had been mostly about business. He had accepted her invitation for one quick drink, and sent Pink home with the car. The short walk along the Embankment later would do him good.

He had hardly noticed the furnishings which came with the service flat — a smallish one in the south-east section of Dolphin Square, but probably quite pricey. He was mildly surprised the tenant had done nothing to stamp the place as her own, even after six months. She had explained she had taken it on a temporary basis, but never got around to finding anything more permanent.

The walls and coverings, he now became aware, were in agreeable enough light pastel shades: quite feminine. He had already remarked on the pleasing view across the river — though it was not nearly as spectacular as the one from Tudor Reach, a building that was clearly visible.

'Cecil Oakley is sorry to be losing you. But he wouldn't have stood in your way if he'd been here. Might have put up a fight, of course. Serve him right. I told you I rang him? They're giving up Port Grimaud after this year. More crowded than the Norfolk Broads. Anyway, you're in the clear.' He nodded over the double satisfaction.

'You're very kind. I promise to make a success of it.'

'I'm sure you will. The thing was awfully well received. I mean, people went out of their way to say so to me.' He paused. 'To be frank, I was surprised . . .'

'About George Timms? So was I. It might be, of course, Jackson figures on moving him to the States after he's been made President. They've become great buddies.'

'You mean it'll now be less traumatic for clients and staff if that happens? Not to have another change of executive chairmanship at RTB, I mean.'

'Could be.'

170

Treasure hadn't mentioned the other possible and discouraging reason for Timms's acceptance of Helen's promotion—the one he'd raised with Howie. Nor could he hint he knew from Ziebal it was far from certain Jackson would be succeeding to the Crabtree presidency.

'You didn't find the champagne and congratulations at the office tonight in bad taste?' she asked suddenly, her eyes opened especially wide. She still had on the simple black sheath dress she had worn for the coroner's court. Treasure found it, and her question, and her whole demeanour, all very becoming.

'You mean so soon after . . . ? Certainly not. Life goes on. People don't like being held in suspense. No, I think it was right to get everything straightened out today. There must be other clients besides the dreaded Grimalt who'll need reassuring.'

'It's just that I was so fond of Roger. He did so much for me. Today's been kind of unreal. I'd hate to have done anything that might have seemed at all callous.'

'There are tears in your eyes.' He beamed. 'How reassuringly female.'

'You mean I'm not usually . . .'

He walked over to her and put his hands on her shoulders. 'I mean you do so very well in what's still largely a man's world, one could forget to make allowances for feminine sensitivity. Tell me, were you in love with Roger?'

'Probably. If I was, the feeling wasn't returned. He respected me as a colleague. End of romantic possibilities.'

'That's an unusual admission for a woman as . . . resourceful as you. I'm not even sure it's an accurate one.'

'You mean I couldn't have been trying hard enough?'

'I think you may have misjudged his feelings.'

'Except Mrs Fentley was the one with the key to Tudor Reach. Did I tell you she was there in the flat the night before he died? He'd forgotten. Asked me up for . . . for a drink. Without thinking.' They both knew she hadn't mentioned the incident before. It seemed to Treasure it

171

was something she needed to disclose. 'Without thinking,' she repeated.

'Of her, or you?' He dropped his hands. Otherwise the two figures remained close. 'Perhaps Mrs Fentley was an old habit. They're quite the most difficult to drop. I doubt many men would find her more attractive than you.'

'Thank you, kind sir.' She lifted her gaze to meet his directly. Now there were no lurking tears. She was smiling, and this time it was her arms that reached up to him.

Treasure cut the top off his boiled egg. 'After eleven at night I suppose most people are home in bed, and can prove it,' he mused aloud.

'Proving it might be difficult for some. People living alone, for instance.' His wife looked across at him over the top of *The Times*. She moved her glasses half way down her nose. 'Reason for asking?'

'None, really.'

'I see,' she responded slowly, meaning she knew there was one, and was now guessing at its character. The two were taking their Saturday breakfast in the sunshine on the patio. 'For instance, you'd have to take her word for it your Miss Wintly was all tucked up at Dolphin Square. If she said so. If the question ever arose,' Molly continued brightly, still regarding her husband across the prettily laid, circular ironwork table. 'Did you see her bedroom last evening?'

'No, I didn't see her bedroom. I went in for a drink, not to make an offer for the premises.' He turned over the still folded *Financial Times* that lay on an empty chair beside him, and wished he hadn't asked the question—or troubled to mention he had driven Helen home.

'You might have wanted to wash your hands.' She made a brief, inquiring smile.

'You'd do that in the bathroom, not the bedroom.'

'Don't they interconnect?'

'I've no idea. Wouldn't think so. I told you, it's quite a

172

small flat. Why are we talking about Helen Wintly's bathroom?'

'Bedroom. Because you raised it. Indirectly.' She wrinkled her nose at him. 'I really do believe she fancies you.'

'I expect so. Really! She just wanted to express her gratitude.'

'How deliciously old-fashioned of her.' Molly arched her eyebrows. Then she asked brightly, 'Love me?'

'Unswervingly,' he answered.

'That's all right, then.' She pursed her lips in a kiss, then went back to her paper.

'I've been thinking,' he offered ruminatively a little later. He had finished his egg. 'Almost everyone closely involved with Roger Rorch has gained handsomely by his death. Predictably or, as some of them still think, inadvertently.' He turned to study a bluetit making stabs at the water in the birdbath.

The walled garden was up a stone step from the patio: it was narrow, and not very long, but full of colour—roses and herbaceous plants, mostly in bloom. There were two old apple trees at the end. It was not a tight, dull oblong: more like a pretty arbour through which a wide grass path had been allowed to stray in a much bigger garden—someone's favourite spot.

Molly finished the paragraph she had been reading. 'You can hardly blame Mr Rorch's chums for coming into the loot he left them.'

'No, of course not,' he answered absently. 'Excepting . . . This chap Ziebal's knocked quite a hole in what everyone took as the suicide motive.'

'So Mr Rorch had other reasons for doing away with himself. Reasons not to do with business. Or d'you think it wasn't suicide?' She lowered her paper. 'More coffee?'

'Yes, please. If it wasn't suicide then it has to have been an accident.'

'Or murder. And don't look so surprised. It's what you've had at the back of your mind ever since you saw this Mr Ziebal.'

173

'Not seriously.'

'Because no one involved would have been so beastly?'

'Right. It's just that a lot of them *could* have . . .'

'But not the ones in bed at the time, covered in witnesses.'

'Mmm. Or something like that. For instance, Lee Jackson had been out walking by himself, but Howard says he heard him in the living-room of their suite around eleven.'

'You said Jackson didn't hit it off with Rorch. He looked harmless enough at the funeral. His wife is very . . .'

'Supportive,' Treasure offered involuntarily. 'She was asleep by the time her husband went to bed. From what they said at the inquest, Timms and Bander must both have been home at the time Rorch died . . .'

'And Miss Wintly rang you at eleven-twenty from her flat. At least one assumes from her flat. Pity she hadn't asked one of the others up. For a drink. She didn't, I suppose?' Molly added her most practised, understanding smile.

'I doubt it. Anyway, it's nonsense to speculate about any of them.' He took another piece of toast. 'This isn't Oxford marmalade?'

'Hasn't been for years. It's Tiptree.'

'It's very good.' He applied more of the earlier suspect confection to the toast, then picked up the paper with his free hand. A moment later he put the paper down again. 'You see, he just could have been planning a trip. "I've made up my mind. I'm much better off out of it." That's what he said.'

'Mr Rorch? On Miss Wintly's answering machine?'

'Mmm.' He was watching the birdbath again. 'That Palladian bridge. Could have been the covered bridge at Wilton House. That's where he intended to be on the Wednesday morning. Then there was St Paul's. Mrs Jackson met him in St Paul's. Oh, and it wasn't the British Museum. It was the Central Library, Manchester . . .'

'Are there prizes at the end of this dawn acuity test?'

174

Molly inquired. 'Ah, I know. It's my doodlebug, isn't it? So how do you know it was the Manchester . . .'

'The Creative Director at the agency told me. Rorch probably intended going there himself on the Tuesday. The shuttle flight he never took. He was so secretive about it all. He got someone else to go to the library. Local girl who's joining the staff soon. She had to read some poetry there. Out loud.'

'Why?'

'No idea, and I didn't pay too much attention when they were telling me. It was a kind of joke. Rorch's secretary had misunderstood a message, but the girl rang again when she heard he was dead.' He frowned. 'What else was there?'

'The Oribi antelope head.'

'Durban. That's where he might have been going. Lived there for a bit. As a child. The Johannesburg flights are all early evening. He'd have plenty of time to drive to Wilton. But he'd have made a reservation. That can be checked.' He paused. 'There has to be a connection.'

'From Johannesburg to Durban? Of course there is. Dozens of them.'

'No. Something linking the places he drew. What did we see at Oribi Gorge? At the nature reserve?'

'It was two years ago, darling.' Molly frowned. 'Ah, I remember Baboon's Castle . . .'

'That's right. And what they called Horseshoe Bend . . .'

'And . . . and Echo Valley,' she added triumphantly.

'Echo Valley,' Treasure repeated. 'You know, I think you've got it.'

It was then that the telephone rang.

CHAPTER 17

'It was so thoughtless of me, Mr Treasure,' crackled the familiar voice over a very bad line from 1500 miles away. Miss Gaunt was standing in the cramped wooden booth that housed the only telephone available for use by guests at the small hotel in Epidauros.

'I took the message while you were on the line to Mr Timms,' she continued. 'The telephonist thought Miss Barnaby was already working from my office. I explained to the caller, Mr O'Leary, that Mr Oakley was on holiday. He asked then if you could call him. It's so very unlike me to forget such a thing. It was because he had asked for Mr Oakley in the first place. It was such a busy afternoon. There's no excuse, of course. I am so sorry.'

'My dear Miss Gaunt, stop worrying. If the Managing Director of Carter Cousins wanted me that much, I'm quite sure he'd have rung back the next day,' answered Treasure, standing at the kitchen phone. 'If it'll make you feel better, I'll ring him at home this morning. I think I have his number upstairs. Lives in the country. Great buddy of Oakley's. Probably wanted a four for golf.'

'Oh dear, you're in the kitchen. I've interrupted your breakfast. It's eleven o'clock here.' There was no end to the mortifications Miss Gaunt was heaping upon herself.

'Two hours ahead of us, yes. Anyway, we're in the garden and we've finished breakfast.'

'It was when I heard of Mr Rorch's death. It all came back to me. I believe the advertising agency was hoping to work for Carter Cousins.'

'So it was, but not any more.'

'Oh dear. I hope . . .'

'Couldn't possibly have been affected by my not phoning O'Leary,' he uttered firmly. 'You say Miss Pitts was taken ill. Better today, I hope.'

'Quite herself. We were out before breakfast, at six. To see the amphitheatre.'

'Best time. Must be crowded in the day, and very hot. Did you have it to yourselves?' He had no constraint about prolonging the conversation. The hotel owner had made Miss Gaunt reverse the charges: it was a house rule for overseas calls. She had opened with a grovelling apology on that count as well.

'Not quite to ourselves. You see, that's when we came upon Mr Fentley.'

'Stuart Fentley? The head of the advertising agency?'

'Yes. He came to see you that same afternoon.'

'Very woebegone.'

'He appeared quite ebullient this morning.'

'Was he on holiday?' Treasure recalled Fentley had been excused appearing at the coroner's court.

'No. Making a film. An advertising commercial. It was how I came to remember about Mr O'Leary. The amphitheatre was temporarily closed to the public when we arrived. It was hired out to the film company working for Mr Fentley. They had been there since before dawn apparently. We shouldn't have had to wait long. Their time was nearly up, but the man who let us through mistook us for Carter Cousins personnel.' Miss Gaunt gave an audible, irritated sigh. 'Miss Pitts happened to be carrying her things in a plastic bag with Carter Cousins' name all over it. She's never without plastic bags.'

'I see,' put in Treasure. 'And the commercial was being made by . . .'

'For Carter's,' Miss Gaunt emphasized. 'I don't believe there were any people from Carter's there. Only from Mr Fentley's company, and the film production people — there were quite a lot of those. All British. Miss Pitts fell into conversation with one of the men working the arc lights. Though why they needed lights it was difficult to comprehend. I mentioned Rorch, Timms & Bander, since it was an advertising film they were making. It was the electrician who told us about Mr Rorch's death.'

'Did you speak to Fentley?'

'Unfortunately no. He left rather hurriedly. I waved, but I don't think he saw me. The amphitheatre is quite overwhelming. It tends to dwarf . . .'

'The auditorium of any theatre in the round.' Without meaning to, Treasure repeated aloud his words of some days before.

'I'm sorry? Oh, I think it rather better than most. It has that reputation. Acoustically . . .'

'Of course, it's ravishing,' he interrupted. 'Tell me, did you see what they were filming?'

'Indeed we did. They had a very beautiful girl alone on the circular stage . . . what the Greeks called the orchestra, as you know. There was one other actor, a young man standing. He was silhouetted at the very back of the . . .'

'The cavea? He was up in the gods?'

'That's right. Above the gods, really. The girl was in a white Grecian gown. We were well to the side, a very great distance from the stage, but in the auditorium — a part that wasn't being used in the filming. There was a great deal of equipment besides the lights. It was all extremely interesting. We were lucky to have sneaked in.'

'And they weren't recording sound?'

'Oh, but they were. I thought I'd mentioned it. That was what was so marvellous. We could hardly believe how clearly we heard the actress's lines. Line really. She only had the one. The man had none at all. He just had to turn around. We heard her say her piece several times though. She said . . .'

'Can I guess, Miss Gaunt?' Treasure interrupted. 'Was it something like . . . "You don't need to shout when you can whisper"?'

'You knew?'

'Sort of. Was that it?'

'Not exactly, but you were extremely close. She said, very quietly, but we could hear her every time, she said, "A woman shouldn't shout when she can whisper." '

Ten minutes later Treasure was in his study dialling

O'Leary. Before that he had called four airlines.

'It's Mark Treasure. Got a minute?'

'Always for the head of a merchant bank. You're only keeping me from my second dip this morning.' The youngish, celebrated and unmistakably Irish Managing Director of Carter Cousins lived near Gerrards Cross, deep inside the swimming-pool belt. 'What can I do for you?'

'Accept an apology for a start. You rang Cecil Oakley a week ago last Tuesday. He was away. Still is. My secretary promised you I'd ring back, but the message got fumbled. Was it important?'

'Not at all. It was a tip-off, actually. Don't you own or finance Rorch, Timms & Bander?'

'We have a large interest. Some Americans are relieving us of it.'

'That was it. It was in the paper that afternoon. One of our divisions was on the point of using the agency for a new product range . . .'

'But the takeover produced a conflict. The American agency, Crabtree, handle the Jebbit, Fowler account.'

'You're very well informed.' O'Leary chuckled. 'I don't imagine RTB can be one of your consuming interests.'

'Temporarily.'

'I see. Well, I happened to hear the story. Thought it'd be a charitable act to let Cecil know the undoubted reaction of our marketing people. They're quite firm about not using agencies that handle competitors. It just might have had a bearing on the way the bid went.'

'Very thoughtful of you.'

'It's an Irish characteristic. Seriously, it might have saved somebody making a wrong guess about Carter Cousins. Most probably, though, the die was cast anyway.'

'I know RTB were sorry they had to pass up working for you. Perhaps you knew Roger Rorch, the Chairman, died that day?'

'Suicide. Somebody told me. I'm sorry. We hadn't met. Cecil had mentioned him a couple of times. So that was

179

the reason for my call. In case Cecil thought I could influence things. I couldn't have. Not without putting a lot of noses out of joint.'

'I understand.'

There was another chuckle from the other end. 'We're still relying on Grenwood, Phipps to chip in on our new loan stock, by the way.'

'No prejudice to that, I assure you.'

'Good. Incidentally, it was somebody connected with RTB that suggested the agency our people have switched to. It was a recommendation we were glad to use. All very civilized.'

'Would that be Fentley Advertising, do you know?'

'Right again. Seems it was a good choice. Fentley are keeping to the same schedule RTB had. I see all important advertising presentations myself. The original dates haven't been altered. It's a ground-floor project. All the agency has to work on is blank packaging—and raw product, of course. And no doubt you know what that is.'

Treasure decided to push his luck. 'At a guess, scent,' he said, confidently.

'Fragrances, we say in the trade. It's a new field for us, but not entirely unrelated to other things we do. The retail outlets will be the same. As always, too, we're going for volume at low prices.'

'Cheap and nice.'

'In a nutshell. Perfume, *eau de toilette*, talc, the lot. Our chemists were sure they had the smell right. The market research confirms it.'

'All still on the secret list?'

'Till Monday. We're making an announcement about intentions then. Creates a bit of interest in Carter Cousins, as I'm doing now. Pre-empts competition too. It's too late for anyone else to launch a new fragrance range before Christmas. We'd like to be the only ones doing it in the spring.'

'Provided Fentley's deliver . . .'

'A name and a theme. We're not dependent on them, of course. I think there are two other agencies short-listed to be briefed if necessary. And there's time enough. It's just that our people were so confident about RTB in the first place. Someone's done a hell of a good job getting Fentley in solo. As sole substitute, I mean.'

'Particularly as they're Jebbit, Fowler's UK agency.'

'Ah, that I know about. It worked in their favour. They resigned the JF business a week ago. Hasn't been formally announced yet. Legally they could be made to serve out three months' notice. Actually, your RTB boys will take over more or less immediately. I'm told Fentley's know the fragrance business backwards. They've worked on JF for so long.'

Even so, the banker thought, Stuart Fentley had to be supremely confident of producing work that would secure the Carter account. It was an opinion he left unspoken.

Later, Treasure drove himself down to the country. He had followed the lady's directions: off the M4 at Windsor, eventually to a side road posted to Ascot, through a lot of crossings whose clearest markings were horse droppings, and two villages that seemed to be made up entirely of outskirts. Most other road traffic in the area consisted of confident, upright and immaculate women on nervous, shying stallions, the riders acknowledging motorists' courtesies with a touch of the crop to the peak of the hat, usually during controlled equine lunges at the defenceless radiator grilles of stationary motor cars.

He had found the house — approached through gateless gateposts and a curved, loose gravelled drive. To the left the view was blocked by overgrown bushes and to the right by a continuous, high red brick wall behind a grass verge run to moss. Half way, he glimpsed an untended orchard through an arched ironwork gate in the wall.

Beyond the main building was a wide entrance into a cobbled yard with open wooden garages and loose boxes, the first sagging from over use, the second spruce but empty.

There was a Mini in one of the garages, a gaggle of small bicycles in another, and an ancient Bassett hound on watch who barked at Treasure's arrival—but only in a token kind of way.

The house was substantial mock Tudor: early 'thirties, the banker reckoned, more agreeable in decay probably than it had been when new. Wistaria mellowed the façade, and disguised the crumbled pointing. The thatched roof was patched—aesthetically one of the least seemly advertisements to rural impoverishment, and one of the loudest.

'Roger certainly never told me about any ideas for Carter's. Frankly, I wouldn't have been in the least interested. More to the point, he never ever talked about his advertising projects. Anyone would tell you that.'

Gloria Fentley had looked attractive—if uncomfortably subdued—both at the funeral and in court where he had seen her before. Here, in jodhpurs, blouse and riding boots, she was relaxed and stunning.

The two were standing in the sunshine on the flagged terrace. There were weeds between the paving stones. The huge lawn showed green because clover, yarrow and moss were flourishing: grass had given up.

'Is it possible he'd have discussed the campaign with your husband? They were together that evening.'

'Wildly unlikely, Mr Treasure.' She grinned. 'I know exactly what they discussed. I'm bloody sure it wasn't advertising ideas for Carter Cousins. Still, you can ask Stuart yourself if you like. He lands at Heathrow at twelve-thirty. Been to Athens. I don't know why. You could ring him here after lunch. He'll hurry back because the boys are all at home.'

The look that went with the remark supported the implication that Fentley wouldn't make the same effort just to be with his wife.

Treasure checked the time. It was 10.50. 'How many boys,' he inquired, smiling. 'And where are they?'

'Three. The twins are eight. The older one's ten'—facts that tended to weaken, if not entirely to eliminate an hypothesis. 'Stuart's mother is staying. She's driven them to their riding. Cuts the time she has to spend with me.

We don't get on. Never have. She thinks I'm a vulgar baggage. And that's the genteel description.' She looked down at her clothes. 'She does approve of my riding, except nowadays I just get to exercise friends' horses when they're away. Like today. I had my own mare till last year.'

'I'm keeping you?'

'No hurry. Really. You said it was important. If you were ready to come out of your way, I'm ready to listen.' He had said earlier on the telephone that he was playing golf at Swinley Forest, not far away. 'Sure you won't have coffee? A drink?' she added.

'Positive.'

'We do run to the basic necessities, despite appearances.' She moved across the terrace to a group of wide, white garden chairs with plastic raffia seats, dropping into one of them. 'Sit down, at least.'

He did, taking the chair opposite. His back was to the sun.

Her pose was languorous—legs splayed, arms draped loosely over the sides of the chair. Her head was bent backwards, the auburn hair falling away from the tautened neck.

'You probably wonder why we keep on a place this size when there's no money. We've had it on the market for years. No one's interested. Stuart insists we don't have the lolly to paint the windows, so it gets even less attractive as time goes on.'

It was true that the southern aspect of the house looked a good deal more weatherbeaten and dilapidated than the entrance front.

'He told me he'd been ploughing everything into the business.'

'Fattening it up for sale.' She bent her head forward while she plucked at the blouse. It was unbuttoned well below male passing interest level. A long, single-strand gold necklet shimmered in and out between the folds of white nylon and the brown flesh beneath. There was no jewellery at her wrists today.

She brought her glance up quickly, and caught his straying. The deep green eyes registered the event. 'Roger gave me this.' She fingered the necklet. 'You said on the phone a chat might save Stuart and me embarrassment later. The Carter Cousins business . . . ?'

'Is part of it. Something's happened that could suggest Roger didn't take his own life. That the phone message was misunderstood. You don't seem surprised.'

She shrugged. 'I said an accident seemed more likely to me. But the coroner went a bundle . . .'

'On what the others said about his mood, and on the recorded message. Precisely. The coroner will have to be told.'

'About this new evidence? He doesn't know already? So?'

'He didn't think it was an accident. If he believes the new evidence puts suicide in doubt, he may consider what they call foul play. Then he'd have to hand the thing over to the police.'

'Murder?'

'Perhaps. And if you'd rather, we can stop there and I'll leave.'

She sat up, shaking her head. 'Murder I can't believe. But go on. Who'd want to murder Roger?'

'Nobody, probably. Not your husband, for instance? Could he have had a reason? Did he know you had keys to the flat? That you were there the night before?'

She showed no surprise at the questions. 'Stuart knew Roger and I were having an affair, if that's what you mean. That's the bit Miss Wintly might not have known.' The last words carried a good deal of bite. 'If she's your only source of . . .'

'She's not the reason I'm here.'

'And murder wasn't the reason Stuart went to see Roger. In any case, George Timms was there later. Roger phoned . . .'

'Your keys?'

'Were in my handbag. Stuart was at his office when I left Roger. I came straight down here. You're suggesting

184

Stuart could have gone back later if I'd spirited him the keys . . .'

'Or left them somewhere. Of if he'd had duplicates . . .'

'Let himself in and, consumed with jealousy, pushed Roger over the banisters. He didn't. To begin with, he didn't have a motive.'

'Good,' seemed the most appropriate comment on this forceful declaration. 'I'm trying to eliminate, not implicate.'

'Stuart went to see Roger because I sent him. All right. He knew about the affair. I'd told him. The night before. When I was angry with him. Later on, we made it up. It was then I said I wanted to break it off with Roger, that I didn't have the heart to tell him myself, that I wanted Stuart to do it for me. It's why he was there. Gave him quite a kick. That was the idea.' She paused, allowing her tongue slowly to run across her lower lip. 'It was mostly true, too. I'd seen the red light just once too often. Your snap, crackle and pop Miss Wintly did it for me.'

'You met her there the night before. I did hear about that.'

'I'll bet you did. It wasn't the first time that kind of thing had happened either. When he'd forgotten I might have been around. And it always involved younger, more available women—more available in every sense. Doesn't do much for a girl's morale. I'm a realist, Mr Treasure. I was very fond of Roger, but our relationship was—you might say—more physical than spiritual. And it was coming to an end. So I ended it. What I'm saying is, I may have bruised Stuart's friendship with Roger . . .'

'But you also gave him the satisfaction of seeing off an unwanted lover. The effect on Roger could have been fairly traumatic, of course. The suicide possibility . . .'

'Don't you believe it,' she cut in quickly, and with heavy conviction. 'Whatever happened to cause Roger's death had nothing to do with me. It may have sounded like grounds for suicide. To outsiders. It's why we kept it out of what was said at the inquest.'

'You're being very frank now. You realize, on the face

of it, what you've just said is hard to justify?'

'For someone who didn't know Roger well. So he was depressed, irritated, overworked, worried—about his job. Grounds there for suicide, perhaps. Except I told you, I didn't accept that either. But so far as his love-life was concerned. Roger couldn't have cared less. Basically he was selfish. At one time I was ready to divorce Stuart to marry him. He asked me to. Except he didn't want to know about my children.' She shrugged. 'It could have been a convenient way of blocking the marriage idea. Making it my fault. He knew how I felt about the boys. Actually, I believe he wanted to marry me. But just me. He was that selfish.'

'And losing you entirely?'

'Would have bruised his ego a little. He might have made an effort to get me back.' Her eyebrows lifted. 'Who knows, he might have succeeded. On my terms. For a while. But suicide? Over me? Any woman? You'd have to know Roger well to know the idea's so wild it's laughable.'

There was silence for a few moments. Treasure found himself not wanting to believe her, but having to accept she was possibly right.

'And at eleven-twenty that night?' he asked.

'I was here. Stuart got in just after eleven-thirty.'

'He'd been dining in town.'

'With that Victor Grimalt. You didn't know that?'

His expression had indicated as much. 'No, I didn't.' He wondered who else did.

'Stuart's a fast driver, but even he couldn't have made it from Tudor Reach in ten minutes. Robin and I—he's our eldest—we were just going to bed when Stuart got home. I remember, for a lot of reasons. Stuart and I had a big love-scene later. I owed him that.' She paused, smiling archly at Treasure. 'But strictly about the time, I'd let Robin stay up to see the end of a TV movie. It finished at eleven-thirty-five. Satisfied?'

'Roger left your children his whole estate.'

'Except the RTB shares. I gather Miss Wintly gets a

large chunk of those.'

'Like some other directors.'

'I know that. Don't be so protective.' She was wholly relaxed again. The long fingers were gently caressing her bare upper arms. 'Stuart and I were Roger's closest friends around the time of the divorce. That will was just to spite his ex-wife whom we neither of us cared for. It was written the way his lawyers wanted.'

'For easy administration, I expect. There was no significance . . .'

The hands went to fluff her hair. The upward movement of the arms tightened the fit of the white blouse. 'It didn't mean Roger was father to any of my children. None of us thought of that at the time—of the will.' A glance matched the nuance. 'You think the police will be involved?'

'I'm hoping not. It's possible.'

She sighed, then stared at him appraisingly. 'And I thought you were just making an excuse to come down to . . . improve our acquaintance.'

It was five minutes later when Treasure pulled the Rolls into the side of the Fentleys' drive, near the gate. The small estate wagon he was letting past stopped as it came abreast.

'Can I help you?' asked the imperious, grey-haired lady through the open driver's window. She looked a well-preserved sixty-five or so. There were three young boys inside the car with her.

'Thank you, I've been talking to Mrs Fentley,' he replied through his own open window. 'It's Mrs Fentley Senior, I imagine? I know your son. My name's Mark Treasure.' It was a reflex reaction to establish his acquaintance extended beyond the wayward Gloria.

She put a hand to her throat, and pondered for a second. 'Mr Treasure the banker?'

'That's right.'

'How d'you do, Mr Treasure. Stuart spoke of you a week ago. Had you come to see him—or me, perhaps?

I've a shocking memory, these days. Is it about the shares we've sold? My daughters and I? In the company? Stuart will be here this afternoon. My daughter-in-law isn't involved, you understand?' She stiffened slightly.

'No. Different bank, I expect.'

She nodded, smiled, then, peering carefully at the narrow gap between the cars, set hers moving again towards the house.

'Goodbye, then. Goodbye,' she called as she went.

CHAPTER 18

Traffic had been light, and Treasure had moved fast once he was back on the motorway. He had not, after all, headed for lunch and golf at Swinley Forest. That had been his earliest intention—that, and to drop in at the Fentleys' on the way.

He knew his wife had lunch scheduled with an American feature writer, followed by a matinee as well as an evening performance. He had arranged to pick her up from the theatre: until then he was wholly unengaged.

He had persuaded himself it was too hot for golf, that he had left it too late to be sure of finding someone to make a game, and that the Rorch business had not become an obsession. That he had failed in the last connection was confirmed when he had pointed the car to Heathrow Airport.

He swallowed a draught of the lager he had ordered at the bar in Terminal One, nearly oblivious of those about him, but thankful not to be one of the mighty throng of mostly holiday travellers.

'Don't be so protective,' she had said—the frank, unfaithful Gloria. She had made no bones about indulging her instincts—nor about affecting to spot similar indulgences in others.

But was he so evidently given to shielding Helen Wintly from being suspected of involvement in Rorch's

188

death? — a demise that more and more hinted at murder?

Facing facts, he had been immoderately disappointed at the way Gloria had demolished several hopeful preconceptions.

Fentley himself had benefited through Rorch's death, but it was difficult to see how he could have been physically involved in it. The same applied to his wife. Treasure had to admit a certain relief in her case — even if the reason wasn't wholly admirable, or even admissible! It was a good deal easier to dismiss the thought of physical involvement by Mrs Fentley than with Mrs Fentley.

It wasn't the Fentleys' capacity to vouch for each other that had convinced Treasure. A small boy allowed to stay up late to watch a movie would make a rock-steady witness on timing. Nor was it possible Gloria would suborn one of the children she clearly adored into telling a lie — when that lie might have to be told in court, during a murder trial, and when it wasn't a strictly necessary stratagem anyway.

But if the Fentleys hadn't been party to Rorch's death, then the field of those who could have been had reduced quite sharply. The pointer, too, had moved in directions Treasure had refused to allow that morning.

Gloria Fentley had left only one question begging in his mind. He had told her new facts had emerged that affected the tragedy. She had established that neither she nor her husband could have been involved — but she had never asked the nature of the new facts. Was it conceivable she was that indifferent?

Involuntarily, Treasure studied the purposeless expressions of others at the bar. It wasn't a crime to be incurious: it seemed almost to be a national characteristic.

He had expected the airport to be crowded and the car parks full on an August Saturday. He had left the Rolls at the Heathrow Penta Hotel on the perimeter and taken the courtesy bus to the terminal.

The indicator board still showed flight BA 509 from Athens was expected on time. It was due to land in five minutes. He returned to his lager and his thoughts.

The visiting Americans were all accounted for. Jackson would ordinarily have made a credible suspect for a variety of circumstantial reasons. But Howie, the ingenuous but palpably honest Howie, had vouched for Jackson's return to the suite at 11 o'clock.

It could be assumed Timms and Bander had been safely tucked up with their lawful wedded witnesses. Probably Grimalt had been too by the relevant time. Grimalt seemed to rate further consideration, though since he felt suspects ought to be beneficiaries, Treasure had no reason to believe the man qualified.

The other two young RTB directors — what were their names? — Laura Cray and Barny Smith, they had both benefited. Safe at home by 11 probably. They might have to prove it.

The word LANDED was logged against the Athens flight on the TV screen above the bar. He finished his beer and moved down to the concourse and the passenger exit. It was much too soon to be standing there but the compunction, as always, was not to risk missing his quarry. He hoped he would remember him. How had he described him to Timms that day? — a well-heeled, defeated middle-weight.

The banker wished he could get the thought of Helen Wintly's vulnerability out of his mind. It was simply that if suspects were likely to be beneficiaries, then, circumstantially, few qualified better. Of course there were holes in the indictment he had been compiling against her — almost subconsciously compiling, and not as accuser either, but yes, as protector. So the holier the better. He believed he knew the difference between driving ambition and ruthless ambition. It was a difference usually easier to discern in men than in women. Helen was an overt driver. Did her subtle use of her sexual attraction make her determination unsuspectedly more ruthless?

Gloria Fentley left very little to be imagined in the exercise of her primal instincts: Helen's technique was

190

quite different, but to her sex would more likely be a means rather than an end.

In a way, Treasure cursed Joe Ziebal for beginning the train of thought that had him standing here at the airport on a sunny Saturday lunch-time, concerned to limit the extent of a scandal which increasingly he believed was becoming inevitable. Of course, it was Miss Gaunt who had deepened and even confirmed that belief — and he never cursed Miss Gaunt.

South African Airways and Olympic Airways had both offered a gleam of hope when he had telephoned them: they had neither of them had a reservation from Rorch. But the hope had been promptly dashed when British Airways had confirmed that Mr Roger Rorch had booked a one-way ticket, first class, on their 1.30 p.m. flight to Athens on Wednesday, August 24th. He had made the reservation at 9 o'clock the evening before — and had paid for it, over the telephone, through American Express. The ticket had never been claimed.

In all respects, Rorch had been consistent, logical and rational.

Over the Crabtree deal he had decided to play diffident — to appear to be objectively opposed, while secretly he was in favour: to allow his partners to follow their instincts. He was satisfied they would do so, too, provided he removed himself from the scene at the point where his opposition might sway them away from the path he wanted them to take. It was a curious strategy, but Ziebal had made the sense of it clear enough.

With the Crabtree problem looking after itself, Rorch had been able to apply himself with genuine single-mindedness to following a creative idea. It was an idea that intruded on his every action and mood — that controlled his mealtime doodling, that impelled him to visit a cathedral when he was facing an impossibly busy afternoon, that made him perhaps less attentive to — indeed, wholly careless about — the susceptibilities of two females who at different times, and once at the same time, had expected to engage his exclusive interest.

191

That in the end his effort was fated to come to nothing seemed not to have affected him. He had remained determined to win the Carter business with his concept, even though he knew any agency appointment would almost certainly be shortlived. Did he perhaps feel circumstances would somehow intervene, and that, after all, if RTB once got the business, it would be allowed to keep it?

Certainly something had impelled Rorch to follow the route he had chosen, and also to justify his apparently purposeless indulgence to someone—the someone to whom, for once, he had exposed an unproved advertising concept.

Stuart Fentley hadn't appeared at Epidauros to film an idea that had expired with its originator. Fentley might have been the first to put it on film: Rorch, in cryptic fashion, had put it on the back of a Grenwood, Phipps luncheon menu.

'Mr Fentley. Hoped I'd run into you.' He thrust forward through the waiting crowd.

'Good lord. Mark Treasure.' It was difficult to gauge whether Fentley's reaction registered more undisguised apprehension than real surprise.

'But I knew absolutely nothing about Roger's plans for Carter Cousins. He was famous for keeping things like that from his colleagues, let alone competitiors. No, we never discussed it.'

Fentley was over the hesitancy he had shown when they had first met. He was still on his guard—though, unfortunately for him, he had just dropped it without knowing. He and Treasure were lunching off toasted sandwiches in the coffee shop at the Heathrow Penta. Fentley had driven them across from the airport in the car he had parked there.

'So you started from scratch with the client last week?'

'Prospective client. We don't have the business yet. But, yes. Word got around pretty quickly RTB would be scratched. It was just as certain we'd lose the JF account.'

Fentley shrugged. 'I decided to take the initiative.'

The bullish comment seemed scarcely to fit the character Treasure had first met a little over a week before: the man who had then been so certain he was facing corporate disaster.

'O'Leary told me he thought you approached his company through an RTB recommendation.'

Fentley's face clouded. 'That's not quite right. Peter Bander put in a word, I think.'

'Not George Timms?'

'George too, probably. It all happened pretty quickly. Carter's gave us the brief on the Wednesday afternoon. That's ten days ago. I've hardly slept since. Been so busy. We've put together a great concept, though. You know it's for a new product range—one we've even had to name. I decided we should go in with complete packaging and merchandising, as well as press and TV advertising. We shot a highly finished video commercial this morning. Did Gloria tell you?'

It was a question that didn't quite fit the facts. 'She only told me you were in Athens.'

The other paused. 'And you think they'll have to reopen the inquiry on Roger's death.' It was a statement not a question—a worried, inward conclusion spoken aloud.

'It's conceivable.'

'I can't credit it was suicide. Much more likely an accident. I mean, I saw him that evening.'

'I'm in a personal dilemma over it all,' the banker offered. 'Whether I'm obliged to go to the coroner with what I take to be several inconsistencies. If Roger had given you his ideas for Carter's the thing would have been a mite simpler to understand.'

Fentley swallowed, but there was nothing in his mouth. 'Would it? He didn't, though. As I told you, he didn't.' Was there a touch of regret in the tone? 'We discussed . . .'

'Advertising business, as you said in your written testimony. It was read out in court. I wondered if . . .'

'We talked over what you'd said to me earlier. About what could happen to Fentley's.' He paused. 'There was that, and . . . er . . . a personal matter. Very briefly. It wasn't important.' So much for Gloria.

'Nothing that could have upset him emotionally?'

Fentley's gaze narrowed, giving his round, well-nourished countenance a slightly oriental flavour. 'Gloria's probably told you they'd been having a . . . flirtation. She with him, mostly. It was nothing serious. Believe me. Nothing—not by today's standards. It satisfies her ego to have men make a fuss of her. Then she kids herself she's having important affairs. Involves me. Sets me up to tell what she calls her lovers it's all over. It's puerile, but fairly harmless. Especially in Roger's case.'

It was a curious admission, but in a way credible. 'Roger was very fond of you both?'

'Exactly. We're very old friends. Were, I mean.'

And in this case, the privileges of friendship seemed almost to have been boundless. 'He did leave his money . . .'

'To our children. Not Gloria. To the boys. She'll romance about that for ever. Say it was really her he was leaving it to.' Fentley sighed. 'Anyway, it was meant to be a temporary sort of will.'

'So I understand. Tell me, did Roger know you were dining with Grimalt?'

'No, he didn't. And I didn't tell him. I suppose you'll think that pretty snide. There was a message to ring Grimalt when I got back to my office after seeing you. He was steamed up about the RTB takeover. Said he'd probably move the OPD Foods account, and if I was interested could I see him that evening.'

'And you could hardly have told Roger.'

'You understand that? Happens all the time in advertising. It's a small industry. We all know each other. Some of us are close friends, but we're still competitors. Roger wouldn't have told me at that stage if the thing had been the other way around. My biggest client asking to see him . . .'

'Happens in banking, too,' offered Treasure.

194

'In fact, I don't think there was much to it in Grimalt's case. I believe he actually wanted the people at RTB to know we'd met. To frighten them. He insisted we ate at the Institute of Directors. That's the last place you'd go if you wanted to keep a meeting secret. Well, one of them anyway.' He looked at the time. 'I think I ought . . .'

'You must go. Sorry to have delayed you. I'm away next week. This seemed the most practical way of getting in a quick chat. And there is another point.' Treasure didn't care for dissembling—but he was very good at it. 'When we met before, you asked if the bank would be interested in buying a controlling interest in your company. I've been thinking more about that. Is it still for sale?'

So Stuart Fentley had proved as incurious as his wife about the alleged new evidence affecting Rorch's death. There was only one explanation for their strange reaction: both were observing a predetermined intention not to press for information if occasion arose. This could mean they were more at risk by asking questions than by appearing unnaturally indifferent. It also strengthened Treasure's unsupported deduction that they might some-how be involved in a conspiracy involving others—where questions might produce counter-questions, and thus embarrassing, unpredictable and uncommunicated deviations from an agreed party line.

The banker had taken the inner ring road at Earl's Court, and driven past his home at Cheyne Row when he reached the Embankment. He was making for Vauxhall Bridge and Tudor Reach.

Fentley had lied twice.

He had said he was still making up his mind about selling control of the agency, when less than an hour before his mother had indicated someone had already bought that control.

He had insisted, too, he knew nothing about Rorch's ideas for Carter.

Unfortunately for Fentley, there were two ways of proving the provenance of the advertising concept he had filmed that morning—Rorch's concept, the one that hadn't died with him. First, there would be the witness of Marcus, the maintenance man, who had innocently quoted the line that was so evidently the origin of the campaign theme. The other testimony—the menu card—was not animate but it was nearly as telling.

It seemed clear enough Rorch had decided 'Whisper' should be the name of the products—a seemingly sound and evocative enough name for such a range. Nor did you need to be unusually perceptive to accept the potentially persuasive quality of 'A woman shouldn't shout when she can whisper.' It seemed to Treasure to be sufficiently lyrical and simple—with some sort of message and some measure of promise—sufficient, anyway, to commend itself to a good many women. He tried to remember a better advertising line for anyone else's scent: off hand, he couldn't.

He did recall that regular nouns couldn't be registered as trade marks. Was there a way round that law? After all, Rorch had gone long past merely branding the products—and Fentley had done the same.

Once you figured what the places in the doodle had in common, it wasn't difficult to guess the drawings had all featured possible locations for advertisements—places where a beautiful woman could mark her presence with a whisper.

How many more such places Rorch had in mind one couldn't guess. How many of the ones represented on the menu card he seriously intended to use, again it wasn't possible to say. The point was, they all qualified. The probability was, he was engaged in checking out the suitability of each.

St Paul's with its whispering gallery was the most obvious. Joanne Jackson had bumped into Rorch close to the gallery stairs in the south aisle.

The Double Cube room at Wilton House was built to house the Pembroke family's collection of Van Dyck paintings. It was hardly incidental, though, that the dimensions of that most glorious and famous chamber served curiously to amplify the human voice—and in the most mellifluous way. There was little doubt Rorch had intended driving to Wilton, then back to Heathrow that Wednesday morning.

The acoustical peculiarities of the Manchester Central Library were known to almost everyone who had ever visited it—a company that happened to include Molly Treasure. It was she who had worked out the connection between the library, St Paul's and the eerie amplification she remembered witnessing in Echo Valley, Natal—all before her husband had rejoined her after taking the call from Miss Gaunt in Epidauros.

And Epidauros had completed the puzzle.

Treasure left the Rolls in the sidestreet next to Tudor Reach, not troubling to use the underground garage there, even though he had a key to it, as well as one for the main building and Rorch's flat. Gloria Fentley had asked him to take them all and get rid of them for her.

There had been little real purpose in visiting the place again, but he had given in to the impulse.

He stood on the top step of the fire stairs after walking up from the ninth floor. His back was to the door that led to the corridor of the penthouse.

The balustrade was relatively lower where he was standing because, like most balustrades, it bent to its descent angle where upper step fused with landing. For someone poised on the edge of the top step, there was at least four inches less protection from the handrail than there was at any other place on the landing. It was the spot Marcus had indicated Rorch had used when calling to him in the basement well.

It was logical enough. Anyone going down the stairs from the tenth floor was unlikely to preface the move by unnecessarily stepping across to the square of the landing: he would stand on the top step and lean over. Treasure tried it.

It was a small point, but someone the worse for drink, unsteady, tired, if he was going to overbalance by accident, and standing at this particular spot . . .

What he heard was the door springing shut—not opening. He sensed there was someone right behind him. He pushed himself upright, rolling his whole body to the left along the landing: then he thrust back hard with his right elbow.

And the person Treasure painfully jabbed in the stomach was Howard J Crabtree the Second.

CHAPTER 19

'My own fool fault,' Howie reiterated. 'More coffee?' He rubbed his middle again.

It was five minutes since the encounter on the landing. The two men were seated on the apartment terrace under a large sun umbrella. Howie had just been to fetch the refilled coffee-pot. As always, he was soberly dressed, though he had temporarily discarded the jacket of his dark suit.

'Teach you to come up behind people with your mouth full,' joked Treasure. 'I really am sorry,' he added seriously.

Howie had moved into Tudor Reach from the Savoy that morning. He had seen Treasure arrive as he had been contemplating the view and consuming a hamburger—freshly made by himself from the best ingredients. When there had been no buzz from the entry-phone he had hurried on to the landing on his way to look for the banker, receiving a sharp blow to the ribs for his trouble.

'So you're now sure it wasn't suicide?' asked the American, reverting to the main topic.

'Mmm. Except I'm diffident about saying so to the powers that be. There's certainly fresh evidence pointing in a different direction.'

Howie made a face at Gloria Fentley's keys which Treasure had placed on the table. Gingerly he picked them up—as though he feared they might be carrying some communicable disease.

'You're talking about the airline booking to Athens? The fact Roger was immersed in ongoing activity for Carter Cousins?'

'That, certainly.' In his own mind, the fact that Rorch had been Ziebal's inside man at RTB still outweighed the other considerations. But that continued as one confidence he wasn't free to share with Howie.

'So you think it must have been an accident or . . . ?'

'Something involving foul play.'

'That's a terrible thought, Mark. The repercussions . . .'

'Which is why I'm trying to eliminate possible suspects. Before going to the authorities. I'm sorry. That sounds very pompous. What I mean is, I'm trying to head off purposeless muck-raking. I also have a responsibility to Grenwood, Phipps. Banks don't care to be involved in scandals of any kind.'

'I can testify Joanne went through to her bedroom at ten minutes of eleven,' Howie offered in a businesslike tone. 'I guess Lee can vouch I came out of my room to speak with him when he got in. I got out of bed to do it. Hadn't been to sleep.' The last words came with less sureness. The speaker, sitting bolt upright in the aluminium and canvas chair, began kneading a clenched fist in the palm of the other hand. His eyes watched the process.

'And you mentioned Lee came in just after eleven.'

Howie began to rock his trunk jerkily. 'That involved a slight error.' He looked up. 'No, it didn't. It involved a fabrication. Truth is Lee came back at eleven-forty-five. He asked me to tell Joanne it'd been earlier. That's if she asked. In the morning. She did, too.'

'I don't understand. Why should . . . ?'

Howie shrugged. 'I guess Lee didn't want his wife to think he'd been out on the tiles. She's pretty . . .'

'Possessive as well as supportive?' Treasure put in wryly.

'All of that. What I was going to say was jealous. She usually travels with him. Whenever she can. He doesn't get off the hook very much.' Howie gave a discomforted frown. 'It seemed a little thing at the time.'

'Wouldn't she have known what time he came to bed?'

'He figured she'd have been asleep. From around eleven. She'd taken a pill to get over jet-lag. He said he'd stayed a while in the living-room after he got in. That was true.'

'So she wouldn't have known the difference.'

'That's right, Mark. I still told a lie, though. And once I'd told it—at breakfast—I kind of believed it myself. Told you, too. Seemed unimportant till now.'

'Probably the whole episode just means Lee Jackson is a trifle more henpecked than one would guess,' said Treasure lightly, but without wholly meaning it.

Howie sighed. 'I don't believe Lee had anything to do with Roger's death. But he'll have to come clean about where he really was at the time. Privately. Between the three of us, Mark?'

'Tricky thing for us to ask him.'

'Better us than a policeman.' Howie looked at the time. 'Did you know Helen Wintly and George Timms are going to New York this evening with the Jacksons?' Treasure shook his head as the other continued, 'They're having lunch with my father tomorrow, then going on to Nashville for meetings Monday morning. Helen and George will fly back Monday night.'

'After being approved by your father and the Dandy management.'

'That's about it. Formality. Has to be gone through, though. Decided last night. They have a team at the agency today putting together a capability presentation on RTB to show Dandy. It'll feature some of the agency's past work on TV and the other media, with slides detailing the company's organization, their operating philosophy and so on. It should be quite interesting. I'm due to see it in half an hour. Would you care to join me?'

'Why not? Let me make some phone calls from here first.'

'I've been thinking, there's something else you should know, Mark.' Howie's head twitched. Treasure noticed that this happened either when someone was giving the American a hard time, or, more often, when he was giving himself a hard time. 'The deal Crabtree have done with RTB. From the start, there was someone on . . . on the other side working for us.' The speaker looked up as though expecting to be admonished.

Treasure grinned. 'I assume you don't mean God.'

'Someone committed in advance to promoting our interest.' Howie looked grave.

'Not cricket, as we'd say over here, Howard.'

'That's right. I'm not proud of the arrangement. Don't know who the person was either. Seems to me, though, whoever it was, he could have been gunning for Roger.' He hesitated. 'Realize I've breached a confidence telling you. You could call us out over it too. There are probably laws . . .'

'Governing the exercise of covert influence in that kind of situation? Only if a shareholder's involved who stands to make a special gain as a result. One that could be seen as a bribe. Even that's a difficult one in law, more particularly in the case of a private company. I shan't call you out over it, Howard.' The revelation had even so presented Treasure with something of a problem.

'But if they suspect murder?'

'Could I suggest you confer with Mr Ziebal before you do anything else in the matter?'

Howie looked totally taken aback. 'Oh. I see,' he said with an inflection and expression indicating as much — but only just.

'Peter Bander isn't going to New York?' asked Treasure quickly, anxious to change the subject.

'Not so far as I know. He wanted to. I think they figured someone should be here minding the store.' As Howie spoke, he absently produced two sets of keys from his side pocket. He regarded them quizzically, remembered one set had been given him by Treasure. He held up the other. 'Got the keys to Roger's Mercedes this morning. Marcus brought them up. Said he had a private deal with Roger to clean the car early every Saturday. He did it last Saturday. Figured it didn't need doing today. Thought he should hand over the keys though, in case we were selling the car. There's another set of keys I found, hanging in the kitchen. The car's owned by the company. By RTB.'

'Then why don't you appropriate it, Howard? You'll need a car of your own for a bit. Is it a big Merc?'

'No. The Two-eighty. I don't care for large automobiles. It's well equipped, though.' Howie looked doubtful. 'Marcus said it's packed with gadgets he never touches. I could read the handbook,' he added, more or less to himself.

'Let's have a look at it before we go,' suggested Treasure with several purposes in mind. Rising, he picked up his empty coffee cup and went with it towards the kitchen. He paused on the way to remark to Howie, who was following him through the living-room, 'As we said before, not a fingerprint anywhere, by the look of it.'

Howie nodded. 'Mrs Nibb started working for me this morning. She really is very thorough. I have a little difficulty with her accent. Great talker.'

'Kitchen clock's keeping good time since you fixed it.' Treasure deposited his cup and saucer on a working top: Howie promptly placed both in the dishwasher. 'Where d'you keep the telephone directories?' asked the banker.

'In the bedroom, at the side of the desk. Look out for my bags. Haven't completely unpacked yet.'

Later, while he was dialling the Bander home, Treasure made a mental note to ask Howie and, if necessary, Mrs Nibb whether the bedside clock had required adjusting since Rorch's death.

All eight people present blinked as the lights came on. They were arranged on two sides of a long table set down the centre of the easily adapted basement room at the RTB offices. Members of the group had been sitting at different angles watching a videotape and slide performance on the TV receiver placed beyond the end of the table, and on the larger screen on the wall behind.

Laura Cray was furthest from the screens. It had been her job at one point to change carousels on the slide projector set on the metal stand just beside her. Jackson, Bander and Timms were further down her side of the table. Barny Smith was opposite, with Howie, Treasure and Helen Wintly.

Timms had been standing a good deal of the time, delivering a not very fluent commentary on what had been shown. He had worked the slide projector from a remote control switch in his hand: another gadget worked the videotape machine slung under the television set.

'Very impressive presentation. Very interesting,' said Treasure, who felt he ought to say something.

'And good luck to all who sail with it,' put in Laura heartily. She pulled a cigarette from the pack in her hand, grinding a flame from the lighter dangling around her neck. 'Sets new creative standards for your people, eh Lee? Have to watch it. Don't want all your clients insisting creative control moves to the Brits.'

'Guess we'll have to risk that,' quipped Jackson, sitting beside her. He was obviously pleased with what he had seen.

'I'll get the commentary polished,' offered Timms, a strong note of apology in his tone. 'Wasn't sure till this morning which ads we'd include.' He paused. 'Roger used to do the presenting.'

'The bit at the beginning on the agency's background, your working philosophy. Very convincing, I thought.' This was Treasure again.

'I was using Roger's script.'

'Fits well enough with our attitudes,' said Jackson.

'And RTB expresses them better.' This bold comment by Howie produced no echoing confirmation from the other American. 'What you say about accountability in advertising in this agency brochure. We should lift that for our own promotion material,' Howie continued. He held up a plastic-bound copy of the document in question.

'Roger used to insist that making advertising

accountable was an attitude of mind.' Helen spoke for the first time.

'I should have thought advertising a hopelessly unaccountable quantity,' offered the banker.

'And that's just the attitude of mind old Rog said advertisers had to avoid,' came from Bander, breathy and earnest.

'Negative thinking on my part.' Treasure smiled. 'I'll try to remember.'

'Direct response ads are accountable,' Bander went on, brow furrowed. 'That's when the advertiser invites the reader to order the product direct by post or phone. You always know whether that kind of ad has been cost effective.'

Helen took up the point. 'We aim to have all our clients benefit from the same kind of disciplines direct response advertisers enjoy.'

'Tall order, I'd have thought,' observed the banker, but impressed with Helen's assurance.

'Involves the intelligent use of sophisticated research techniques,' put in Jackson heavily.

'And research makes advertising accountable.'

'No, it doesn't, Mr Treasure.' Laura blew a smoke ring for punctuation. 'Just makes it less hopelessly unaccountable.'

'Dandy, anybody?' called Barny Smith. He had slipped out of the room and had now returned with a laden tray. 'Specially imported for your delectation.' There were glasses, ice, and a dozen bottles of America's fifth or sixth most popular aerated soft drink. 'Lee had a dozen cases flown over,' Barny continued. 'The drink we're determined to take to our hearts and bank balances, straight from our very own fridge. How about it, Mr Treasure?'

'I can hardly refuse,' He turned to Bander. 'So you're flying with the others tonight after all?'

'Seemed a pity not to have the complete trio on parade . . . It's a very short trip.' It was Timms who had answered. He and Bander exchanged glances as he spoke.

204

'And don't forget the Creative and Media Directors are promised the same acclimatization tour before Christmas. Never been to America.' Laura was gathering up the papers and other impedimenta in front of her as she spoke. 'Right now my union says I've done enough this Saturday to cement Anglo-American relations.' She pushed the two boxed slide carousels down the table. 'There are all your pictures, George. Don't lose 'em. Remember the videotape in the machine. Here's the cassette of the radio commercials.' She slid that towards him also. 'Want a lift anywhere, Barny? Car's outside. Give you two seconds to finish that rotgut.' She beamed at Jackson, who blanched slightly. Then she looked at Timms. 'You don't need us for anything else?'

Smith had risen, ready to leave. 'It's a very fine drink,' he exclaimed, downing his emptied glass, and making up for Laura's irreverence.

'Mark, do you need . . . ?' Howie didn't complete his question.

'No, I don't.' Treasure had broken in.

'Think I'll get going too, if you don't mind,' said Bander as the other two left. 'Still got some packing to do. See you at the airport.'

'Me too. The car should be outside. Can I drop anyone?' This was Jackson, document case closed and ready.

Treasure had already nodded his head in answer to Howie's further questioning glance. 'If you could both hang on a moment longer. Something's come up about Roger's death. It's just possible people with him on the night may have to answer some more official questions.'

'You mean the inquest's to be reopened?' asked Helen.

'Just possible. It won't concern Laura and Barny. Laura told me just now the two of them flew to Edinburgh that evening for a meeting there next morning.'

'That's right. Our unit-trust client is there,' Timms volunteered. 'What sort of questions?'

'Oh, where everybody was around eleven that night. I

205

thought it sensible to let you know.' The banker turned to Helen as he went on, 'The taped message may have misled, after all. Roger had arranged to fly to Athens the following morning. A few other things have come up which may . . .'

'So the police will be asking the questions?' Helen pushed away the glass she had been fingering.

'Not necessarily. That'll be up to the coroner to decide. It's possible, though.'

'Because he could believe the circumstances suspicious?'

'Let's see now, I got back to the hotel at . . .' Lee Jackson looked across the table at Howie. His gaze held the other's for a long moment, then dropped. 'I got back around eleven-forty-five. That right, Howie?'

'That's exactly right, Lee.' There was a good deal of relief in the delivery.

'Sure, I remember now. Dropped into a little night spot. In St James's, just up the road. Cab-driver recommended it.' Jackson had evidently decided to come clean about his timings, as well as the 'walk' he had taken after dinner. 'They had a short floor show at eleven. Watched it from the bar with . . . er . . . with some other people. Must have left around eleven-thirty.'

All of which meant that at 11.17 Jackson had been in a night club drinking with a hostess, watching a strip show, with possibly a barmaid to corroborate the story—or so Treasure concluded. It wasn't an especially wholesome alibi, but it was probably verifiable: the man would hardly have volunteered it if he had thought it wouldn't be.

'I was home in Kingston by eleven,' volunteered Bander, thankful it wouldn't be necessary to explain whether drunk or sober. 'Katherine will remember. She thought I'd been with George. Went to his house earlier but he'd gone to see Rog, of course. Missed him.' He looked around at the others. 'I say, I really think I'd better be off.' He got up. 'If your driver could take me on to Waterloo after the Savoy, Lee?'

'Sure thing, Peter.' Jackson turned to Treasure, speaking to him in a stage aside, while other talk was going on. 'Pity the Roger Rorch business isn't cleared up yet.'

'It may be. Quite soon,' answered the banker.

The American vacillated for a second, then went on in the same quiet tone. 'I'll let Howie have the name of that club. Happens I exchanged cards with one of the people at the bar . . . Got it somewhere.'

The hesitation prompted Treasure to the cynical conclusion that Jackson had taken the name and telephone number of a club hostess. In the way of such matters, it was doubtful there had really been anything so conventional as a mutual exchange of such detail. Still, Jackson seemed to have done the right thing—even if for a discreditable reason.

'Wouldn't mention this to Joanne.' Jackson continued in a normal voice. 'About Roger . . . and so on. Doesn't seem to involve us. Could upset her, though.' After this moving little speech, Jackson got up and shook Treasure warmly by the hand. 'Nice to be doing business with you, Mark. See you again before long. Ready, Peter? You coming, Howie?'

'No, I'll walk down later. See you and Joanne before you leave.'

'OK. Helen, George, see you at the airport.' Jackson waved as he neared the door.

'Don't be late, Peter,' warned Helen sternly. 'What's the time on your watch now?' She looked at the clock on the wall.

Bander turned back into the room, and ran a hand across his forehead. Bashfully he looked down at his wrist. 'Actually, it says twelve-thirty-six. I know it's six minutes past three. Fact is—' he gulped in a deep breath—'well, you know we all used to have a giggle at old Rog? Every time he went abroad—long distance abroad, I mean—putting his watch on half the time difference the day before? Well, the last time I went to America—on holiday it was, actually—I did the same thing. Helps bridge the five-hour gap. I'd have done it yesterday if I'd known. Did it today, anyway. Don't worry, I won't be late.'

'Have a useful trip,' Treasure called after him.

'As you know, Mark, I was home around ten-fifty the night Roger died.' Timms was on his feet, picking things up from the table, his demeanour implying imminent departure.

Helen spoke distinctly but quietly. 'I hope it's not going to be important. I guess I'm the only one in the group not accounted for by anyone else at the time Roger died.' She shrugged. 'I was at home. Been to a concert. At the Albert Hall. Oh, I rang you, of course, Mark. That was at eleven-twenty.'

'Which may not be as relevant as we first thought,' Treasure responded, still sitting beside her. 'Taking into account all the new facts, the authorities may conclude Roger could have died an hour earlier.'

CHAPTER 20

'And everyone knows Roger was given to eccentricity,' Treasure concluded. He leant back in his chair, elbows balanced on the arms, palms together.

It was an unfortunate coincidence he was between Helen and Howie on one side of the table, while Timms, to whom he was speaking, was the only one left opposite — and in the centre. Someone coming in at that moment could have assumed Timms was being interviewed by the others — or, judging from the expression on his face, being in some way interrogated by them.

All four had become quietly conscious of what the configuration implied: none had yet done anything to change it for fear of tacitly admitting it existed.

'I've never known him do his half-time change for short trips. For Paris or Frankfurt, say. Only for the States. The day before,' Timms insisted.

'And once when he went to Saudi Arabia recently. Someone mentioned it,' put in Helen.

'Yes. I'm sorry. I'd forgotten.'

'I gather he suffered badly from jet-lag. I can understand.' This was Howie, with feeling. 'But Paris . . .'

'Is only an hour different from London. I know that,' Timms interrupted. 'All right, Athens is two hours. Sorry, I still don't believe he moved his watch on an hour.'

'Didn't he alter his mealtimes too, George? Before he went to New York?' It was Howie again.

Timms sighed. 'Sometimes.'

'Half way to Greek time is one hour,' said Howie to no one in particular. He reached forward and spooned some ice into a glass which he then filled from an open bottle of Dandy.

'But he didn't tell anyone he'd altered his watch. That he was going to Athens.' Timms was showing more than impatience. The intonation fell somewhere between plea and protest. 'He didn't change his office clock. Or any other clock for that matter.'

'Afraid he did. Not his office clock, but we know of two others that were an hour fast,' said Treasure.

'Mark's right. I changed the one in the kitchen. We noticed the one in Roger's car just before we came here. Mrs Nibb, the cleaning lady, she remembers the kitchen clock was wrong on the Wednesday morning. Mark rang her about it. She didn't know how to change it.'

'You said it was complicated, Howard,' Treasure put in lightly. 'Howard's an expert with modern timepieces,' he added more thoughtfully.

Timms was listening carefully to the detail. 'But I didn't leave Roger . . .'

'Till around ten-twenty, you told the coroner,' said Treasure. 'After a row.'

'Mark, can you tell us more about this new evidence?' It was Helen who broke the following silence. She had stood up to reach the ice for her drink. Then, while speaking, she moved casually to the other side of the table as though to stretch her limbs. She put her glass down, and took a seat beside Timms.

'Yes. Can you tell us more?' echoed Timms.

'I can. Plus a hypothesis, George?' questioned the banker carefully.

'All right.'

'It's the one the coroner may arrive at, given the same facts.' Treasure paused briefly, glancing at the other three in turn. 'Roger wasn't against the takeover. It just suited him to give the opposite impression.'

'That's for sure,' Howie confirmed boldly: he had spoken with Joe Ziebal on the telephone before leaving Tudor Reach.

Both the others looked surprised — Timms more so than Helen: she made as if to say something, then changed her mind.

'Roger kept up the charade because he wanted to land the Carter Cousins account before the deal with Crabtree went through,' Treasure continued. 'He made no allowance for the upset he'd be causing other people — or the antagonism he might be building. He was thorough, of course, even in his perversities. He gave extra credibility to his anti-Crabtree pretence by breaking one of his own golden rules. He let someone in on his whole campaign concept for Carter's.'

'You mean so that person would say, "Great, wonderful, we should go for Carter Cousins not Crabtree"?' asked Helen with a frown.

Treasure nodded. 'Or at least accept Roger's apparent determination. The idea backfired, though. Roger died. The takeover went through, and it was Fentley Advertising that got the concept.'

'You talk as though the three were linked,' put in Timms sharply.

'They could have been?' It was Helen again.

'It's only a theory, but one that fits most of the facts,' answered Treasure. 'Fentley's have built a campaign around the product name "Whisper". That was Roger's name. It's also his advertising campaign they're using.'

210

' "Whisper"?' Timms repeated, then shrugged. 'Roger could have given his campaign ideas to Stuart Fentley. They were together . . .'

'Not a possibility,' the banker broke in. 'And I think we all know it. There was every reason why he should tell one of his close associates, and still more reason why he should keep it from any competitor.'

'Gloria Fentley.' Timms simply uttered the name. He made no attempt to go on.

'Could have been told about "Whisper".' Treasure nodded as he spoke. 'It's possible, but unlikely, George. And she was nowhere near Tudor Reach at the time of Roger's death. Nor was her husband.'

'Implying I was the one told about "Whisper", and present when Roger died. Also that he died at ten-seventeen, not eleven-seventeen.'

'Mark didn't say anything like that,' protested Helen.

'Getting close, though. Isn't that true, Mark?' Timms asked bitterly. 'Could I have it all? Right now? The rest of the hypothesis?'

'If you like, and if you're determined to believe it centres on you.'

'You've made it pretty obvious it doesn't centre on the Fentleys, or the Jacksons. You've dismissed Peter . . . oh, and Grimalt, because of the timing. Howie and Helen here . . .'

'Are friends who I'm sure will leave if you . . .'

'No. I want them to stay. Go on, Mark.'

'All right. When you were with Roger that night he made it clear he would go on opposing the bid. He showed you his idea for Carter Cousins to prove what a waste it would be to pass it up. You didn't agree. But that's only part of it.'

Treasure stood, then paced to the end of the table. As he continued speaking, he was standing just where Timms had stood earlier when making his commentary.

'You believed that without Roger's support the Crabtree deal wouldn't go through. You knew that without Roger you'd probably oppose it yourself. And you hated yourself for it. It was the ultimate confirmation that whatever the sign on the door here says, it's always been Rorch who made the decisions, and Timms and Bander who went along with them. And the Rorch with you at the time was rude, drunk, and on the downside of a marijuana drag.

'And this was the man, the footloose, high-living, womanizing divorcee, who was denying you and your family a cool half-million. Who you figured had been the real attraction for Crabtree in the first place. Something confirmed by the exchanges we had at lunch at the bank that day. And it didn't seem fair—nor a situation that would obtain if Roger was removed from the scene. Permanently.'

Treasure paused.

'There's more. So go on,' demanded Timms.

Helen sat still, upright and silent. Her face showed no discernible emotion. Only Howie looked uncomfortable, trying to avoid the gaze of the man the banker was accusing.

'Roger died at ten-seventeen, which is one good reason why he couldn't answer the door later. He either fell, or jumped, or he was pushed. When the coroner decided it was suicide, he'd already rationalized against it being an accident. Now, if you had been there—let's say as witness to an accident—there was nothing you could have done for Roger. Death was instantaneous. The post-mortem proved that beyond doubt. Sending for an ambulance might well have seemed purposeless. The police? Could you have gone back to the flat with the idea of sending for them, and on the way decided on a different plan?

'The possibility of anyone finding the body that night was pretty remote. Less than half those flats are occupied. Only Roger used the stairs at all. His watch stopped at eleven-seventeen.' Treasure glanced briefly at Howie. 'Did that watch give you the idea you should walk away? Avoid being involved in Roger's death—a death that might need a lot of explaining? Is that what you did?

'The recorded message to Helen was an unexpected bit

of luck. Or did Roger make it while you were with him? The "Whisper" campaign really was a bonus, though, and one very much under your control.

'It's curious everyone seemed to know Roger intended working on that campaign that night, but no one questioned why there was no evidence of the fact. No sketches, notes, bits of scripts. Nothing. Mrs Nibb just told me the wastepaper-bin in the bedroom was full of screwed up, discarded paper which she put down the garbage chute. She'd left the bin empty the day before. Had Roger rejected everything he produced on Tuesday evening? I don't believe so. I believe he showed it to you. Showed you the whole campaign, in the living-room, before he died. That you took the lot with you. That's how Fentley got something close to a complete campaign.

'Did you give Fentley the stuff? For a consideration of some kind? We all know the mess his company was in. You and I spoke of it that afternoon. I suggested various solutions to both of you. For Fentley to resign the JF business and take RTB's place for Carter Cousins wasn't one of them. O'Leary of Carter's told me he thought someone from RTB had smoothed the way for Fentley with his marketing people. I'd still bet no one there realizes they're getting the RTB original campaign.

'Finally, you didn't quite finish the course. You knowingly refused the last jump. After years of playing number two to Roger Rorch you could now have stepped into his place. But you let Helen here do it instead. Was that because succeeding him could to someone, sometime, suggest complicity in his death? It would fit. You've been so meticulously careful over that kind of detail. The Fentleys, for instance, are unnaturally incurious about the reasons for the possible reopening of the inquest. It's obvious they've sworn to ask and offer nothing that could point to the source of "Whisper".

'Or did you pass up the RTB chairmanship for the reason I understand Roger said you would, if ever it came your way? That you don't believe you're up to the job?'

For several minutes Timms had seemed to be staring at

Treasure without seeing him. There were beads of sweat on his forehead. His body had gone limp in the chair.

For his part, Treasure was relaxed. 'You asked for it, George,' he said, moving back to his seat at the table. 'It's the hypothesis I think they'll throw at you. Now, if someone would be good enough to hand me a glass and some ice . . .'

'Stuart Fentley asked me to ring the Marketing Director of Carter Cousins,' Timms began in a choked voice. 'If I'd realized, I wouldn't have done it.' He looked around at the others, then continued speaking in a low monotone.

'Brilliant deduction on your part.' Helen was seated behind Roger Rorch's desk in the office that had now become hers. 'But are you sure . . . ?'

'But hopelessly incomplete,' Treasure interrupted. He was sitting in the big armchair watching her arrange the contents of her document case which was lying open before her. 'And he denied everything.'

'Would have anyway.'

'Not necessarily,' the banker observed slowly.

It was less than ten minutes since George Timms had left the RTB offices after protesting his innocence. Howie had gone soon after, anxious to consult with Jackson after a rapid private conversation with Treasure conducted in the men's washroom.

'Howie didn't believe George.' Helen looked up as she spoke.

'Did you?'

'I don't believe he murdered Roger.'

'But you believe he was there when he died?'

'Accident. George saw his chance, and took it.'

'Out of character?'

'A bit.' She reflected for a moment. 'He'll never admit anything, of course. Chances are Roger fell as he was calling something to George when he was leaving. Roger could have been acting the fool . . .'

'And whispering, not calling. What time's your flight?'

'Six-thirty, I think.' She pulled the airline ticket folder

from the top of the case.

'And it's "Wisper" without the "h",' he said.

'Mmm.' She was studying the ticket. 'Yes. Six-thirty.' She looked up inquiringly. 'Is that how they're doing it?' she asked, wide-eyed.

'Because you can't protect a common noun as a trade mark, apparently.'

'Only if you register it as a distinctive design.' She frowned. ' "Wisper" without the "h" should be all right, provided no one else has it registered. I guess Fentley's have checked it out through trade mark agents. Roger may have done.' She sighed. 'If you go to the coroner, and he comes to the same conclusion as you about the new evidence, and if it really was an accident . . .'

'Is it worth putting George through the hoop?' He seemed to ponder the question.

'What if George is telling the truth, and can somehow prove it? Doesn't that put a whole lot of others under suspicion?'

'Who, for instance?'

'Well, all the others who might have called on Roger after George left . . .'

'And before Roger died. Assuming George had left a bit earlier than he thought in the first place. What he now says he must have done.'

'There aren't that many individuals involved, of course . . .'

'Some, like Peter Bander. Some pairs. Grimalt and Fentley,' Treasure suggested. 'They were together. Both had reasons for conspiring not to have been involved in Roger's death — even as witnesses. Laura Cray and Barny Smith. They could have been there and taken the night train to Scotland instead of the plane. Would they have volunteered Roger had died in the circumstances? Once you think of it as a conspiracy, there are many possibilities.'

'Maybe if you just told the coroner about Roger booking that Athens flight? That he was kidding us all about being against the deal? You haven't said how . . .'

'And nothing about his putting his watch forward? Nothing about George giving Fentley the campaign?'

Helen leaned back in her chair. 'Wouldn't that be enough to make the coroner change the verdict to accident?'

'Making the whole group of us conspirators.' He pouted. 'I think it would be enough, yes. Innacurate, though. Untidy, too, since Roger didn't put his watch forward, and George didn't give Fentley the campaign.'

'But you said . . .'

'That Roger could have advanced his watch. That was after you called attention to Peter doing the same thing. What you might call introducing your fall-back position.'

Her gaze became very calm. 'I don't understand.'

'I think you do. I'm told it was you who insisted to the Americans that Peter should go with you to New York.'

'As a reward for keeping the OPD business. Yes.'

'And after you'd had a call from Gloria Fentley that I'd been digging for information?'

'I don't . . .'

'Understand? Neither does Mrs Fentley. Except she must have been told by her husband to keep you informed if anybody inquired about the campaign while he was away. Oh, and not to ask questions that could lead to counter-questions about Carter Cousins. I think she rang you before lunch to say I'd been to see her.'

'I don't know what you're talking about.' She was cool and completely unruffled. 'This is another hypothesis?'

'No. This one really happened. This was why you had to enrol Bander in that New York party. You knew he'd emulate Roger's anti-jet-lag routine. So then you could have him admit to it in front of all of us, encouraging me to accept Roger would have put his watch on an hour if he'd been going to Greece.'

'Which he did.'

'No. Only what you've been relying on someone all along to conclude if necessary. If it came out the so-called suicide message was simply to tell you he was making a trip. So if the inquest was ever reopened, if there was

216

a change of verdict, whatever took the place of suicide — accident or something even nastier — the time of the event would be ten-seventeen, not eleven-seventeen. I assume you were with someone at ten-seventeen?'

'Not that it matters, but yes, I was. I left the Albert Hall just after ten. I was with a girlfriend. I dropped her in Sloane Street.'

'And you could have been home, alone, by ten-fifteen, not eleven-fifteen, played the tape, rung Roger, then driven over to Tudor Reach. Your purpose? To dissuade Roger — not from taking his life, of course. We both understand exactly what he meant by that message. You wanted to talk him out of being against the Crabtree deal. You may also have been taking advantage of the situation he'd created just . . . just to be with him.'

'That's the biggest lie,' she snapped, suddenly riled.

'You'd have arrived after Timms left.' He ignored the interjection. 'Ahead of Grimalt and Mrs Jackson. That's why Roger stopped answering the door to others. Who could blame him?'

Helen stood up, closing her document case as she did so. 'I don't have to stay and listen to this nonsense, Mark. I don't know why you're indulging a whim to . . .'

'I think you'd better.' He hadn't moved from his chair, but his gaze was as stern as the injunction. 'It's for your own good,' he added.

For a few moments she stood irresolute. Then slowly she lowered herself into the seat again, but she rotated it to the left so that her gaze was fixed on the window and the trees in the garden beyond.

'You didn't succeed in talking Roger into the deal. You couldn't have. He was committed to letting you and everyone else go on thinking he was against it. Instead, he deepened the charade by showing you the Carter campaign. Then, mildly doped, and more than a bit tipsy, he took you out on to that landing to demonstrate a girl shouldn't shout when she could whisper. Only perhaps that's all he'd been interested in . . . in showing you. Had he passed you up sexually for the second night running? Were you mad at him? Angry enough to push him over that balustrade?' He held up both palms, symbolically, to parry protest. 'I repeat, you'd better listen. The opportunity and motives are too strong for anyone to ignore. Anyone.'

'There *was* no opportunity,' she came back firmly.

'None? Not when you knew you had what amounted to a declaration of suicide on that tape? When all you had to do was alter two clocks—the one in the kitchen, the other in the Mercedes? You left the bedside one alone. Mrs Nibb would have remarked to someone if two clocks had been an hour fast. She wouldn't have seen the car clock. That was for the maintenance man, who, incidentally, happened not to notice it. Howard did, though. So the main ingredient of your fall-back story was safely in store if required, but not so prominent it alerted any single individual. Plenty of reason, too, why logically Roger wouldn't have altered the bedside clock. He hadn't been to bed.'

'Not with me, certainly.' There was undisguised acerbity in her voice. 'You seem to have forgotten . . .'

'That at eleven-twenty you telephoned me at home from Roger's flat, pretending to be at your own place. I've pondered a lot on that call. On balance, it was a bad mistake on your part. An over-emphasis. We were neither of us supposed to suspect Roger intended suicide. If he wasn't planning anything so horrendous, with proper protestations of modesty, why the hell did you have to ring me about his business affairs at that time of night? You could have done it in the morning.'

Treasure shook his head. 'It was smart to leave the receiver off after the call, in case anyone else had rung when you were talking to me. If Roger had died at eleven-seventeen, he could hardly have been on the phone three minutes later. No one had called between the time he died and your speaking to me. You'd have heard any ring. What you couldn't allow for—in your fall-back position—were the only other calls anyone knows about between ten-seventeen and the time you arrived at the flat. There you were simply lucky. Grimalt seems to have been the only caller, between ten-twenty-five and ten-thirty—precisely the time, I'd estimate, you were on the line to Roger yourself. So he got an engaged tone, supporting the belief Roger had taken the phone off the hook earlier, where Mrs Nibb found it in the morning. That was the good luck. The bad was Roger not telling you he'd actually booked his flight to Athens, assuming he told you he was going there.'

The banker paused. 'You want me to spell out the motives? The material ones are pretty numerous. The RTB shares, for instance. Who else would have realized what a coup it was, how critical it was, to inherit them—' he paused, then repeated—'to inherit them when you did? Then there's the chairmanship of the agency. I gather your contract with Crabtree is to be pretty generous. No more than you deserve, no doubt. Did you give the Carter campaign to Fentley in return for getting sixty per cent of his company's shares at a very special price? You knew the fix he was in. Brilliant of you to get Timms *and* Bander to commend Fentley to Carter's. Not difficult, perhaps, but astute. Did you have them thinking it was their own idea? Helping an old friend in a jam? Meantime you bought all the shares owned by Fentley's mother and sisters.'

'There is no way . . .' she began, then stopped speaking, shrugged, and swivelled her chair so that she was once again facing the banker.

'You were going to say the share deal was through nominees,' said Treasure quietly. 'But you also know it won't take long to find the name of the real buyer. You've had to borrow money. Quite a lot, and quite quickly. You knew how to cope with that bit, naturally. Poor George Timms wouldn't have had a clue. It's the main reason I found him a truly unconvincing suspect. Now you virtually control Fentley's, all you have to do is wait and see which way the wind blows. If they get the Carter Cousins business, they should grow handsomely. If they don't, you'll no doubt persuade Crabtree to buy the agency and merge it with RTB. Either way you stand to make another packet.

'As I said, the material motives are pretty impressive. The human one transcends them, though. "Heav'n has no rage, like love to hatred turn'd, Nor hell a fury, like a woman scorn'd." Congreve. A lyrical profundity. Sometimes abbreviated. Very durable. Was Roger really worth that much hate?'

There was silence in the room for more than a minute. Treasure was content to wait. A bus started up on the other side of the square. Some boys went by outside shouting to each other. A dog began to bark close by, then stopped abruptly on a whimper.

'I didn't hate him.' Her voice was steady and clear. 'I didn't love him either.' She paused. She made no movement, but she seemed somehow to be reaching out to him: for him. 'Mark, how can I make you believe me?' The question sounded wholly genuine. 'You see, it *was* an accident.'

CHAPTER 21

'Seems to me people get away with murder these days,' said Molly Treasure. 'Is that egg done enough, darling?' She peered across the pinewood kitchen table at the overflowing, decapitated embryo under review.

It was raining outside. In the two weeks that had elapsed since Treasure's confrontation with Helen Wintly, the threatened prolonged drought had been replaced by record-breaking downpours. The Treasures' leisured Saturday breakfast was being taken indoors.

'The point being, it wasn't murder,' replied the banker. 'The egg's just edible.'

Molly reverted to studying a report on one of the inside pages of *The Times*. 'I was speaking figuratively. All it says here is the coroner altered his decision after reopening the inquest yesterday. That it was accidental death.'

'And so it was.'

'You're satisfied . . . ?'

'That it's now established Rorch didn't kill himself. Never thought he was the type. I'm glad we got the record straight.'

'Hmm.' She put down the paper and stirred her coffee. 'And Miss What's-her-name . . . ?'

'Wintly,' he supplied.

'She gets off scot free?'

'She did go to the coroner of her own free will . . .'

'To say she'd lied under oath, failed to report an accident, altered clocks all over the place, hoaxed you on the telephone, pinched an advertising campaign, come into wads of money, the chairmanship of an advertising agency, and the control of another.' She took a breath. 'One law for the rich, that's what I say.' Unthinkingly she brushed away some toast crumbs lodged on the wide platinum bracelet at her wrist. They slid over the green silk Givenchy housecoat on to the kitchen rug.

'She didn't tell him all that. Wasn't necessary. She confessed to panic. Scared in the circumstances people might have thought she'd pushed Roger over the banisters. The coroner accepted her explanation. He ticked her off, then left it to the police to prosecute if they wanted. They didn't.'

'Doesn't say any of that here.' Molly sniffed at the deprivation.

'Because it's pretty run-of-the-mill stuff.'

'Indeed? So after a moment of panic . . .'

'Minute or two, to be exact.'

'After a minute or two of girlish tremors, she coolly sets up a *mise-en-scène* . . .'

'Perfectly consistent,' he cut in loftily. He'd abandoned the egg, and was spooning marmalade on to his plate. 'She's a highly intelligent woman. Having adopted a course, she followed through with it — with some later trepidation, and, I suppose you could say, courage.'

221

'No, you say it.' She gave an understanding smile.

He ignored the barb. 'The clock business, in the kitchen and his car. That was pretty cool thinking. Safety-net, you see. In case the result of the inquest had indicated foul play . . .'

'In which case she'd laid grounds so everyone would think poor Mr Rorch had died an hour earlier.'

'When she was pretty certain he'd have been alone as he'd intended. Also when she'd guessed everyone else who might have been suspected would have an alibi anyway.'

'Except when you started to stir things, you said she didn't balk at having poor Mr Timms put under a cloud.'

'Certain it'd come to nothing. Even so, it was something she hadn't bargained for. He was quite safe, though. Home at ten-thirty, and proved it. The tenant of his basement flat arrived home at the same time. Timms must have left Tudor Reach by ten-ten or earlier. It's a good twenty-minute drive from there to his place, even at night. He'd just got the time wrong in the first place.'

'And Mr Rorch hadn't altered his watch?'

'Very, very unlikely for such a short trip, and discounted altogether once Helen Wintly admitted to me it was she who'd changed the two clocks.'

'So he died at eleven-seventeen?'

'That's right.' He hesitated, then added diffidently, 'The clock business didn't come up with the coroner.'

'Indeed? How very convenient for Miss Wently. Wintly,' she corrected. 'You mean she just left it out of her true confessions?'

'It wasn't relevant. She admitted simply that Roger had been making a nuisance of himself.'

'You mean undesirable advances?' Molly modelled her mouth in a circle of shocked surprise, and kept it there expectantly.

'That's about it, yes. He'd assumed too much about her purpose in coming round,' which Treasure inwardly accepted was a view he had shared with the dead man. 'Understandable, of course,' he concluded.

'You don't say? Might be to a man, I suppose.' Her

voice affected a tolerance which in no way showed on her face.

'D'you want the highly confidential story, or not?'

'Yes, please, darling,' she answered swiftly. 'And I promise not to tell another soul. There's a sticky on your chin . . . Other side.'

Treasure retrieved the offending morsel with his finger, then licked it off. 'After Rorch had spun her the tale about being against the deal, and gone over the "Wisper" campaign, pretending it justified his attitude . . .'

'About the takeover?'

'Mmm. After that she tried to get him to change his mind, and failed. Then he pressed her to share a joint of cannabis. His second, at least. Then he got wildly amorous, which she found tiresome at first, then rather . . . unpleasant.'

'He got amorous. You mean she really wasn't offering herself as part of the argument?'

'Definitely not. Not by then, anyway.'

'Curious. I remember him as a very attractive man.'

'His suggestions were also curious, apparently.'

'I see. Kinky.'

'Perhaps. Or maybe she doesn't care for attractive men. Or for men in general.' He shrugged. 'She did tell me once she might have been in love with him. It was after his death, though. Might have been said for appearances' sake.'

'I don't follow.'

'Well, if it was known she'd found him repulsive in that way, people might have thought she'd . . . er . . .'

'Done him in?' Molly suggested brightly. 'Didn't you say she'd felt rejected the night before, finding Mrs Fentley in the flat? That doesn't sound as though . . .'

'That had nothing to do with her sexual inclinations. It offended her self-esteem. Anyway, on the Tuesday she swept out, leaving him fuzzed, drunk and unrequited, standing at the top of the fire stairs. She took the lift down from the ninth floor. Then because he'd asked her to, she stepped through the fire door on the ground floor to whisper good-night. It was to humour him.'

'And that's when he fell over the banisters?'

'He was sitting on them. They're very narrow. He overbalanced. Came down head first. Nasty mess on the basement floor, and a terrible shock for Helen.'

Molly poured herself more coffee. 'But she recovered her presence of mind quite quickly.' She looked across at her husband. 'And you believe her story?'

'Yes. So did the coroner. And the police,' he put in defensively. 'She realizes she's been stupid. Showed deep remorse.'

'I've always said tragedy's easier to play than comedy. So she does get away with everything?'

'Not really.'

'The "Wisper" campaign?'

'Carter Cousins turned it down. Didn't like it. Given the business to another agency. I gather that's advertising.' He grimaced.

'I thought it quite a good name. The idea too, for the commercial.'

'So did I. Carter's consumer research panel gave both the thumbs down. Too up-market for a down-market product. Whatever that may mean.' He frowned. 'Or was it the other way round? No, I think I got it right first time. Anyway, the thing's not on for Carter Cousins. Howard Crabtree tells me "Wisper" may shortly make a comeback, though, as a Jebbit, Fowler product. They're not proud, and they like the concept. Lee Jackson got JF to register the name in as many countries as possible. The JF account is now with RTB-Crabtree, as it's now called.'

'But doesn't the campaign sort of belong to the other agency?'

'Fentley? Yes, but that's also being taken over by Crabtree.'

'More shekels for Miss Wintly?'

'Afraid not. She paid too much for her sixty per cent in the first place. Over-estimated the value of the property. She was really banking on their getting the Carter Cousins business. She's going to carry quite a loss on that one.' He pouted while roughly calculating how much.

'But she still has the money from the sale of the RTB shares. The ones Mr Rorch left her.'

He shook his head. 'Alas, she mortgaged most of that on the Fentley purchase.'

'So she just has a fat salary as Chairman. Or does she prefer Chairperson?'

'Makes no difference. She resigned yesterday.'

Molly smiled over the top of her cup which she had stopped abruptly, just short of her lips. 'You did a deal. You clever old thing.' She blinked her approval, then drank some coffee.

'Something of the sort. Actually, Howard knew too much of the whole story to feel comfortable, as he put it, about Helen running the company in London. Question of client and staff attitudes, and so on. So, yes, we came to an arrangement with her. I got a bit involved.'

'Which is why you didn't feel the coroner need be bothered with all those tiresome details.'

'Tiresome and irrelevant details.'

'So Mr Timms becomes Chairman?'

'Mmm. In a strange way, Carter Cousins turning down that campaign seems to have done something for his self-confidence.'

'Because it demonstrated Roger Rorch wasn't infallible? Miss Wintly showing she had feet of clay must have helped as well.'

'I expect so. Jackson was strongly in favour of Timms replacing Helen as Chairman. That's once he heard about her witnessing Rorch's accident.'

'The expurgated version? Like the coroner?'

'Yes. He and his wife feel Helen showed a lack of moral fibre. Mrs Jackson's a born-again something-or-other.'

'Must be painful at that age,' mused Molly, turning back to the paper.

'I think Jackson's very insecure. He certainly twigged Rorch might be promoted over him in New York. He may have had the same thought about Helen.'

'He's to be President when Howard's father retires?'

'Probably. And with Timms running their London office, it's a general triumph for mediocrity. Of course, Joe Ziebal may still find someone better for New York.'

'Do I know Joe Ziebal?'

'I told you about him. You've never met him. In a way I wish I hadn't. He's a fixer. He's placing Helen Wintly in a pretty fancy job in Sydney.'

'That'll be nice for her. Long way away, though.' She nodded approvingly, then looked up. 'Do you really believe her story?'

'More than enough to allow her the benefit of the doubt. Enough not to let the doubt increase and wreck her life.' He looked out at the pouring rain beating on the patio. 'I'd say she has a very promising career ahead of her. London's taught her a lot.'

Molly smiled wryly. 'Like thinking twice before calling my husband when he's ready for bed?'